BY THE SAME AUTHOR

A Woman Undefeated
Dreams Can Come True
Ping Pong Poms
Innocence Lost
Shattered Dreams

With Best Wishes
From
Vivienne Dockerty.

HER HEART'S DESIRE

Vivienne Dockerty

DISCLAIMER.
Although places and events exist in my story, this is a work of fiction.
All the characters, names, incidents and dialogue is from my imagination
or have been used fictitiously.

Matador
9 Priory Business Park
Kibworth Beauchamp
Leicester LE8 0RX, UK
Tel: (+44) 116 279 2299
Fax: (+44) 116 279 2277
Email: books@troubador.co.uk
Web: www.troubador.co.uk/matador

ISBN 978 1780885 605

British Library Cataloguing in Publication Data.
A catalogue record for this book is available from the British Library.

Typeset in 11pt Aldine401 BT Roman by Troubador Publishing Ltd, Leicester, UK

Printed and bound in the UK by TJ International, Padstow, Cornwall

In loving memory of my sister Barbara Mary, also an aspiring author, who would have loved to have read my books.

PROLOGUE

Set in Victorian Merseyside in 1893, eighteen year old Lily imagines herself to be in love with her cousin, Lawrence, a sea captain.

Charlie, a twenty-one year old shipyard worker, knows that he is in love with Lily. According to Lily, who is from a better class background, a romance between them will never do.

Lawrence marries Bertha, Lily's older sister; now she will never be able to have her heart's desire.

Fate takes a hand when both Lily and Charlie find themselves in loveless marriages that neither had wished to be in.

In 1903, Lily becomes a widow after Roland, her army officer husband, is killed in the Boer War. Meanwhile, Charlie is also left a widower after his wife dies in childbirth.

Will fate intervene and bring the pair together?

CHAPTER ONE

Lily Griffiths looked out at the rain that was tippling down the glass of her bedroom window. It looked as if she was going to be trapped in the house for the afternoon; her older sister, Bertha, was sure to have something to say if she suddenly donned her walking outfit and headed for the front door. Especially when Lily had promised to sit for a while with her grand-mama that day.

They all had to take a turn sitting with Grand-mama. Well, those of the sisters that still lived at home, that is. Lily was one of eight sisters; three were married with their own households and two were working, so were not obliged to do this duty. This just left Bertha, Ellen and herself to sit with the old lady for a little time each day. Grand-mama was a tartar, at least that was what Lily's mother was apt to say in private to her family. The spacious, red-brick, semi-detached house in Rock Ferry belonged to Grand-mama and the old lady could be relied on to remind you of that fact, should anyone do anything to give her cause to complain.

Lily had often wondered why her parents had never purchased their own place. Her father could afford it – he owned a large, busy coal yard for heaven's sake – but maybe they would never have found such a large and rambling house to have brought up their ever-increasing family in. Not that there would be anymore sounds of little Griffiths feet, as Mother, worn out from producing a baby every couple of years, had taken to lying on the settee in the parlour most days, leaving Bertha to run the house and Father to grow his empire.

Lily sighed and wished not for the first time that her father would allow her to go out to work. Anything would be better than hanging around the house all day, being at Bertha's beck and call.

None of the things she did for her sister were good enough. She couldn't clean a room properly, nor could she make an appetising meal; her bread never rose, her cakes were all soggy; she couldn't even make a good job of preparing the vegetables, as she never sliced things thinly enough, or so she was told by her elder sister. Bertha called her a dreamer and perhaps she was. If that was thinking that nice things would come along in her life one day, then a dreamer was a good word to call her.

She rubbed her hand on the patch of condensation that she had created with her breath on the window and stared out at the rain sodden landscape before her. Perhaps it was this view that kept her parents here. Not much of a view at the moment, because of the mist that was hanging over the river, but on a clear day it was a marvellous view if you liked watching the shipping activity on the River Mersey and looking at the ever-increasing amount of new buildings that had sprung up recently on the opposite shore. She hoped it would be a mist free day tomorrow, as Lawrence's ship was docking in Liverpool.

Lawrence was a cousin of the family – well, Lily thought he was a cousin because he was related to the Patterson's, which was the same as her grand-mama's surname. He had just completed his first voyage as a sea captain and would be calling to see Grand-mama after tying up at the Port of Liverpool. He always did that, called to see his grand-mama that is, after every trip he had made abroad. First a trainee officer in the Merchant Navy, then he had worked his way up through the ranks under Captain Faraday; now, at twenty-eight, he was the youngest sea captain working for the Allison shipping line.

"A feather in the family's cap," Grand-mama had said, looking fondly on at her handsome relative, when Lawrence had proudly made his announcement in front of her and the family one Sunday afternoon. "Took my advice and didn't follow your father into trade, as everyone expected you to."

No, Lawrence had wanted to be a mariner, just like his Uncle John Wallace, after being fed the tales of a sailor's travels by his father's elder brother before he could even walk.

Lily's heart skipped a beat as she thought of Lawrence. He had always been her hero; he was the stuff of her dreams. Tomorrow, when he came to visit Grand-mama, she was going to present him with a floral buttonhole, one that she would make herself from a red rose gleaned from the florist shop, where one of her older sisters, Mabel, worked. *That's if the rain would stop and I could make my way to the little shop on Borough Road*, she thought impatiently. He could wear the rose in his lapel when he attended St. Peter's the following Sunday and he would know then that she loved him. She couldn't make her feelings for him too obvious, of course, but her small gift might make him look upon her romantically.

She sighed as she peeked into the ornate mirror on her dressing table, playing idly as she did so with a large, cut-glass perfume bottle full of *eau-de-cologne* – a present from her father for her birthday. Would he still see her as his little cousin? She had altered quite a bit since he saw her last in June. It was November now, five months since he had sailed away on a cargo ship that visited various ports on the eastern seaboards of America, picking up goods for the merchants of Liverpool to trade.

He had missed her eighteenth birthday, the day that her mother had said she could put her hair up if she wished. Instead of the girlish shoulder-length style, her chestnut hair was now caught back into a pretty, curly bun, kept in place by numerous hair pins and tied with an ivory satin ribbon, which went well with her high-necked, cream lace blouse and brown ankle-length bustle skirt that showed off her small, heeled, black button boots. Tomorrow, when he visited, she was going to wear the string of pearls that her grand-mama had given her for her birthday and the matching pearl band from her mother, which would adorn her hair.

Lily rubbed a little bergamot oil onto her neck – a present from Eliza, one of her older sisters – then gazed again into her mirror at the pair of blue-grey eyes that were staring back at her solemnly. Was she being vain if she compared herself to Bertha? She would be the only other person in the family that Lawrence might want to marry. That is if he wanted to marry a homely kind of person, instead of a pretty girl such as she.

Bertha was plump and plain of face, though nearer his age at twenty-two and she had never had a courtship. Neither of them had, now she came to think of it. Father didn't think she was ready to be introduced into society just yet, nor did he think that his pretty princess should go out to work, seeing as she was the baby of his family. That's if you didn't count fifteen year old Frederick, the last of the Griffiths children, who could never be thought of as a prince, given that he was such a studious dormouse and lived away at boarding school. No, Father thought there was plenty to occupy his youngest daughter in the home until he decided it was her turn to marry. Given that Mother needed a companion, or so the doctor had said, that, at the moment, must be her role in life.

Grand-mama, who could be relied upon to give her opinions whether they were sought or not, was of the view that Mannion Griffiths, her son-in-law, had a guilty conscience. He had given her youngest daughter, Hannah, nine children, eight of them girls. He should have behaved with a certain level of decorum, instead of giving in to animal like desires. He was nothing like the husband of her elder daughter, Patricia, who had taken himself off to sleep in a different room now that Patricia was nearing the end of her childbearing years.

Not that Lily was told of the old lady surmises, but it had to be said that the girl liked to eavesdrop, as that kind of topic was never discussed in front of a child. Now she knew why Mother rested a lot; she was worn out from childbirth and had to recline either on her marriage bed or on the chaise in the parlour.

Lily was suddenly recalled from the study of her pale-skinned face by the voice of her sister carrying up the stairs. She rushed onto the landing, trying to think of a reason why she should be there in her bedroom, having not offered to help with the drying of the plates after luncheon. However, Bertha's face didn't look angry as she stared up at her younger sister; in fact she seemed rather serene, if the truth was told.

"Oh, there you are, Lily. Mother's gone to have her nap and

while I was clearing Grand-mama's lunch tray, she asked could you be spared for a few moments or so. So, be a dear and run along to her room. Don't worry about helping with the washing up, Ellen has it all in hand."

Ellen could always be relied on, thought Lily, as she walked along the small corridor sedately, instead of rushing along like she would have done had she been younger. Ellen was obviously in training to take over Bertha's duties, should Bertha ever find herself a beau. Ellen would probably always be a spinster, as she had no looks to speak of, unless she found herself an ugly man. She'd always looked peaky for as long as Lily could remember, being the first to fall ill with any winter coughs or chills.

"Ah, Lily, do come in and make yourself comfortable," said the formidable looking Margaret Patterson, who was dressed from top to toe in black and indicating that her granddaughter should sit on the plush maroon velvet sofa, near the marble fireplace in which a fire blazed merrily.

There was a myriad of clutter in the high-ceilinged room, with small mahogany tables covered with floor-length embroidered cloth; a writing desk, a black piano sporting a couple of large, white candles in silver holders; an ebony display cabinet showing off a highly prized porcelain tea set from China (courtesy of Lawrence) and an upright moquette-covered armchair, in which the old lady spent most of her days within the oppressively heated room. On the small mantelpiece above the fireplace, there was barely a space on top of the brown chenille tassel cover, where pot dogs vied for room with framed family pictures and blue and white statues rubbed shoulders with inscribed porcelain souvenir mugs of members of the royal family.

"What have you been up to since I last saw you, Lily?" Grand-mama peered in her direction, scorning the use of a pair of lorgnettes that were sitting on a side table, though her sight had deteriorated with age. "Have you been helping your mother, as I asked you to?"

"Yes, Grand-mama, I helped her by looking through the drawers in the bedrooms this morning, to see if anything wanted mending or darning. Sister Eliza said she would take the mending home with her after her visit at the weekend."

"Good, good. All my grandchildren seem to have been gifted with some sort of talent – with the exception of you. Do you perhaps have a talent that we are unaware of?" The elderly lady stared haughtily at her youngest granddaughter, hoping that she had applied enough severity to her words to make the child consider. Lily just seemed to drift through her life and didn't appear to devote herself to anything.

Lily gazed back, taking in the smell of lavender that always lingered around her grand-mama. She was reminded, not for the first time, that Grand-mama had a likeness to the queen. She had seen Queen Victoria; her father had taken her to Liverpool in May 1886, when Her Royal Highness had visited the city, with the Duke of Connaught and Prince and Princess Henry of Battenberg. It was principally to declare the Exhibition of Navigation, Travelling, Commerce and Manufactures open, but the exciting part was when the royal party took a river cruise. Lily and her father, from their position on the landing stage, saw them embark on the steamer, *The Claughton*, before their very eyes! Grand-mama even wore black, lacy, fingerless gloves and a similar black lace headdress, just like the queen did, though her long-sleeved, floor-length dress of black bombazine wouldn't have cost as much.

"Lily! I asked you if you have any talent that we are unaware of? Pay attention, child, you really are a dolly dreamer."

"I seem to be good at arranging flowers, don't you think, Grand-mama?" Lily directed her gaze to a small, white posy bowl sitting on a nearby table, which held the last of the few roses picked from the garden the day before. "If Father would let me, I would quite like to become a florist like Mabel and open my own shop one day."

"Pipe dreams, I think, Lily. As you know, Mabel is allowed to go out to work, for reasons I would rather not be drawn into discussing with you. Your father would prefer that you, the last of his female children, make a good marriage. Flower arranging, I am sure, will be much appreciated by a devoted wealthy husband, if a suitable one can be found. Perhaps I should have given you piano lessons; as you know, I cannot play a note with these fingers now."

Lily cast her eyes to the ground demurely. Piano lessons indeed; no one had ever been allowed to touch the ornate ebony instrument that took pride of place at the side of the mantelpiece (except to polish it, of course), only Grand-mama. Recently, though, her fingers had become so red and swollen that she hadn't the hand span she needed to play the Chopin that she loved.

As to her father finding her a wealthy husband, there was only one man on Earth that could be suitable for Lily and that was Lawrence Patterson.

"Would you excuse me, Grand-mama?" she asked a little later, after an uncomfortable silence had developed between them. She had noticed that the rain had turned to spits and spots on the windowpane, with a rainbow beginning to appear in the distant sky. "I would like to go for a walk now that the rain has stopped and I am sure Bertha will have some errands for me."

"Yes, yes, do go and have a walk, Lily. I can feel your restlessness and I am sure that you would benefit from some exercise. Do remember to wear a raincoat over your jacket and take an umbrella. I wouldn't be happy if you came home looking like drowned rat."

Lily smiled at her grand-mama's attempt at humour, glad to escape the cloying atmosphere of the room where the large sash windows were permanently shut.

"Where are you going, Lily?" Bertha had heard her sister's boot-shod feet tapping along the quarry tiles in the hallway. She poked her head out of the kitchen doorway, her round face lighting up with a smile as she looked upon her younger sibling fondly.

"I've had permission!" Lily took her navy walking coat down from the highly carved regency hall stand, which was crowded with the different jackets and outdoor apparel belonging to various members of the family. "Grand-mama said a walk would do me good and I have a mind to walk to Borough Road and have a word with Mabel."

"Then take an umbrella and make sure your hat is securely

pinned this time. I don't want to hear about another hat of yours being run over by a mail coach."

"You won't. Remember you gave me two pearl hat pins for my birthday so that it couldn't happen again."

"I did too, Lily, and I'm glad you've remembered to use them. Well, if you are going into town, would you fetch me some flour from Westaways on Huskisson Street? I thought I would make a special cake for when Lawrence comes tomorrow for afternoon tea. I have enough of the other ingredients, but I'm getting short of flour."

Lily tried to feign indifference to the mention of their cousin's visit, but it was hard to keep the excitement from her voice as she replied. "Do you think he'll bring us gifts like he did last time? I loved my fan, but this time with him going to the America's he may bring trinkets. Perhaps a beaded bracelet or necklace made by an American Indian."

"I am sure it is quite possible, my dear, though we should pray for his safe return to Liverpool, not be looking forward to any presents he may bring."

"I didn't think. Of course I hope he had a safe journey across the Atlantic. It's a lot of water to travel from New York back to Liverpool; I'm sure I'd be sea sick."

Bertha nodded in agreement before turning on her heel back into the kitchen. "Wait a moment. I must raid the housekeeping tin in order to give you a sixpence for the purchase of the flour. We don't have an account with Westaways, but it's too far for you to walk to the Cooperative Store and be back again by dark."

"Yes and it may come on to rain again, Bertha. If I don't hurry, I'll be meeting myself coming back."

"Oh, you are silly." Bertha smiled indulgently at her younger sister, then bobbed back into the kitchen.

"Where are you going, Lily?" Ellen, Lily's next sister in age, came out of the kitchen. She looked her usual untidy and ugly self, dressed as she was in an old green serge dress and an all-enveloping white pinafore. Grand-mama always joked that Ellen was a changeling. According to Grand-mama, the real and prettier Ellen had been swapped by the midwife, who was jealous that another pretty daughter belonging to Hannah Griffiths had been born.

Lily fidgeted while she waited for Bertha to appear. She never knew what to say to Ellen and tried to avoid staring at the pale face and squinty eyes. "I thought I would take a walk over to Mabel's place of employment. It will do me good to take the air. I've had to help Mother *and* sit with Grand-mama today."

"Oh," said Ellen, who had peeled the vegetables in readiness for dinner, washed the breakfast dishes, scoured the saucepans, scrubbed the scullery floor and was now thinking of heating up the flat iron on the fire, in preparation to do a little goffering after putting the crockery away. "Will you be back to take Grand-mama her afternoon tea? You know how I get nervous in her company."

"Oh, if I must. It means I will have to make great haste though, because I must make a detour to Westaways. Grand-mama won't eat you, Ellen, it's just her way."

"I'll take Grand-mama's tray up, Ellen," said Bertha, who had heard the exchange between her younger sisters as she came to give Lily the small coin. "You can get Henrietta's tea when she returns from Father's office. Lily and I'll sit with Grand-mama for a while."

Lily, free at last from any obligation, walked as fast as she could through Victoria Park, which the family home partially overlooked. Drops of rain dripped upon her from overhanging trees as she kept to the narrow stone slab path, which was lined on either side with rhododendron bushes awash with pink flowers. She felt glad that she had fastened a length of matching voile around her navy tricorn shaped hat, as well as the hat pins, in an effort to keep the damned thing on, as the long stemmed umbrella kept catching on branches as she sped along. Mother had been quite annoyed when she had returned hatless from a sojourn on a windy day a few months ago, though she was more worried about what the neighbours would say if they saw one of her daughters without a hat.

"Lily, wait for me."

A familiar voice broke into Lily's fanciful thoughts, as she imagined herself and Lawrence walking up the aisle on their wedding day at the nearby St. Peter's church. Only one more sleep and then he would be there in Grand-mama's sitting room and she could feast her eyes upon him to her heart's content.

She turned to see a slender young man, small of stature and neatly dressed, running along the muddy pathway after taking a shortcut from the esplanade. His normally pale face was aglow with the pleasure of seeing Lily, having not seen the object of his dreams for some time.

"Lily," he said breathlessly, not being a very fit young man at the best of times. "I haven't seen you for a while. How are you? I saw you coming into the park and hoped to catch up with you. May I accompany you to your destination? I have some news that I would like you to hear."

"Oh, if it's about your allotment again, Charlie, I don't want to hear your news. Beans and peas do not interest me, unless I am eating them."

"No, silly. I wanted to let you know that I have finished my apprenticeship at the shipyard. Do you remember the last time I saw you, when I said that there was a possibility they may continue to employ me, but in their new development department?"

Lily nodded. The last time she had seen Charlie, he had waylaid her on her way back from visiting a friend one Saturday afternoon.

"Well, they have done just that," Charlie beamed.

"That is very kind of them, considering you have spent the last seven years at their beck and call whilst working there. Does this mean you will get a wage now?"

"Of course it does," Charlie said happily. "It also means I can ask your father's permission to walk out with you. I will be able to support a wife and family one day." His earnest face looked into hers confidently. Surely Lily Griffiths, from one of the smart houses on Rosemount Hill, would agree to his courtship of her now.

"I don't think Father will give his permission, Charlie," Lily said, trying to bring a wistful note into her voice, in order to let her would-be beau down gently. "He wants me to marry into money and I'm sure a man employed by the shipyard wouldn't do."

"But Lily, I won't be just a labourer; I'm to have a job as an electrical fitter and perhaps I will work on one of the new submersibles that I have heard they are thinking of tendering for. Any man who works on such a dangerous assignment would be paid very handsomely, I am sure." He didn't add that according to the broadsheet that he read avidly every day, it could be years before the navy made its mind up over the use of submarines in warfare, as some top admiral had said that covert operations were not to be considered, when one should always meet the enemy eye to eye.

"It won't make any difference, I'm afraid," Lily replied. "Father wants me to live in a mansion and have servants at my beck and call. I know that your heart will be broken now that I have told you of his plans for me, so I will allow you to walk with me as far as St. Catherine's and then I will walk on my own the rest of the way."

Charlie looked so downcast that Lily, for a moment, felt sorry that she had destroyed his happiness and confidence with her cruel statement, thinking that perhaps she should have let him down more gently. After all, he used to walk her home when she had attended the Ashmore School for Young Ladies and he a nearby charity school. He had been her hero then, when he had escorted her past raggedy boys from the orphan asylum and she knew he would defend her forever from the slings and arrows of life, if he were allowed.

"Lawrence, my cousin, is coming to tea tomorrow," she said brightly, beginning to walk briskly in the direction of the park gate.

"He has just completed his first voyage as a newly appointed captain to the eastern seaboards of America and we are holding a small celebration for him. According to my grand-mama, at twenty-eight he is one of the youngest captains that the Allison Line has ever employed."

Charlie nodded in agreement. It was something that he had also wished to do, when his thoughts had turned to employment in adulthood whilst attending the charity school. A life at sea and being aboard the training ship *H.M.S Conway*, which was anchored in the River Mersey, then visiting all those far flung places that his father, before he'd died, had visited. His father had even been to Australia – a place where thousands of emigrants made their way each year, across treacherous and mighty seas in search of a better life for them and their families. It was unfortunate that his body had never been strong enough to follow in his father's footsteps, subject as he was to wheezing, but at least he was able to hold his own in the locally based shipyard.

Of course his mother would never have let her only son embark on such a foolish notion, even if he had been as fit as a flea. Having had her dearly beloved husband perish under the waters of the River Mersey, after the ferryboat *Gem* was in collision with a sailing ship during dense fog in November 1878, she was reluctant to allow Charlie even to catch the ferry to Liverpool, never mind travel the seven seas!

"It was something that I always wanted to do," he said wistfully, keeping in step with Lily, who was a few inches short of Charlie's five feet five, so that their strides had become equal.

She quickened her pace on seeing more blackening skies.

"But, of course, Mother would never have stood for me being a mariner and as you know, being the man of the house, I had to leave school when I was fourteen."

"Yes, such a great pity. I too would have liked to have gone on to attend an academy to study meaningful things, instead of spending my days waiting for a rich husband to come along. It is so boring. Did you know that, according to Lawrence, people are leaving our shores in thousands to build a new life in America? Now, *that* would be something to look forward to."

"For some maybe, Lily, but I would like to think that I could at least have sight of you, even if you did walk by me on the arm of a rich husband."

Lily patted him on the arm kindly. "You are bound to find a young woman worthy of your adoration one day, Charlie. I am most flattered that you think of me in that way."

"But not enough to allow me to ask permission to court you?"

"Of course not, dear Charlie. You and I would never do." *He has always had a way of making me feel uncomfortable*, she thought, as she waved back to him gaily, whilst he stood watching her progress down the hilly street. His eyes seemed to bore into her soul, as if he could see beyond the affectation of petted daughter to the woman she would be in her later years. "Pull yourself together, Lily," she muttered, as suddenly a chilly wind made her body shiver. "He's just a strange young man and you'd do well to steer well clear of him."

CHAPTER TWO

"Is that you, Charles?

Jane Wilson sounded a little disgruntled when she heard her son coming into the small two storey cottage, which was situated on Whetstone Lane, a main road that lead down into the town of Birkenhead. She turned from the range in the kitchen-cum-living room, where she had been stirring something in a large, black cooking pot. "I thought you might be home earlier than this. You know I must leave by half past four."

"Yes, I'm sorry Mother, something held me up. Whatever it is you've been cooking smells good. I've just realised how hungry I am."

"Well, I can't see why you want to hang around the waterfront looking at all those ships when you'd never be well enough serve in one. I could have done with your help on the allotment this afternoon."

"Mother, the sight of that battleship being floated from the shipyard will stay with me for the rest of my life. *The Royal Oak* is the largest vessel ever built by the Laird Brothers; in fact, it's the biggest ship ever to float on the Mersey. The length alone is 380 feet. You should go and look."

"Another ship for men to go to war in," sniffed Jane, disdainfully. "They never learn. No doubt some politician will be casting around, wondering who to start another war with as we speak. I've not time to serve your stew, I must away." She pulled the heavy pot onto the trivet that stood near the glowing embers of the small fire within the cast iron range. "I had mine earlier, so leave the pot to cool when you've had yours and tamp down the fire when you decide to go off to bed. It will depend on what time His Worship the mayor decides to leave with his guest and head off back to Myrtle House, as to when I'll be home again. I'll walk back from the town hall with Mary Casson, so don't worry about meeting me."

"I might walk down that way around half past nine and have a pint at The Grapes," said Charlie, jingling a few coins in his trouser pocket. He earned a little money from the errands he did for some of the older men at the shipyard.

"Well, see to it that it's just the one," said Jane primly, taking her black shawl from the back of a chair and putting it over her prematurely white hair, which was braided into a neat bun on top of her head. She checked her appearance in the round, speckled mirror that hung on the cottage wall. A sallow face with down-turned lips stared back at her as she inspected her outfit; a white, flat-collared, long-sleeved blouse; a black, ankle-length skirt that showed the tips of her shiny black boots; a black, short-waisted, long-sleeved jacket and a pristine white pinafore that she carried over her arm. "I don't want you ending up like Ernie Morris from up the road. I feel like suggesting to his wife that he joins the Temperance Society."

"None of our business, Mother," said Charlie, mildly. "Now you get off, or you'll be getting the sack for being late. Oh, what was it you wanted me to do on the allotment? I could give you a hand after church in the morning."

"Thou shalt not labour on the Sabbath Day," Jane chastised with an outstretched finger. It was said with tongue in cheek, as she didn't stick to that commandment herself when there was a little money to be made. "I wanted some cut flowers for the cemetery and I need to take the scraps for the hens."

"Oh, was that all? I'll get the buckets and load them onto the cart for you. That will give you a good start in the morning and the hens are overfed anyway, so it won't harm them to do without now and again."

"You're a good fellow, Charlie. They'll be fresher if I cut them first thing. By the time I'd waited on at Bella's, then come back to start our meal…"

"Go, Mother, or you'll be late." Charlie took off his brown twill jacket and put it on the back of one of the solid oak kitchen chairs. It was hot in the small room, as Jane kept the fire going all day. Used for both cooking and heating, the fire in the range was never allowed to go out.

He glanced into the mirror as Jane had just done, his pale blue eyes staring back at him confidently. He wasn't a handsome man, but he wasn't ugly either. His fair hair was neatly cut – not short like an army man, but allowed to touch the neck of his white and brown striped collarless shirt. His oatmeal coloured waistcoat, recently purchased for him by his mother as a present for his twenty-first birthday, held his deceased father's fob-watch in the breast pocket, as luckily his father hadn't been wearing it when he had been swept out to sea. *Any decent girl would be very happy to accept my suit with a view to marrying me*, thought Charlie proudly, especially now that he was to receive a man's wage at the shipyard. Perhaps it was time to cast his eye around the spinsters of the parish, instead of pining over someone he could never have. *Though that wasn't really true*, he thought, as Lily *would* be his one day, he was certain of it. The thought of that made his heart feel lighter.

He carried his bowl of blind scouse, a stew made from potatoes and vegetables as meat was only served on a Sunday, to the heavy oak table that was covered with a red damask tablecloth. He sliced himself a piece of bread from the homemade bloomer loaf that had been sitting in the pot bread bin. Although a slimly built man, Charlie could pack away a decent helping and if he didn't control himself he could have eaten a whole loaf on his own. Jane would only moan if there was nothing left to toast over the embers in the morning, as she liked to bake every other day with there only being the two of them.

Life had not been easy for Jane after her husband had been taken from her. She could have returned to her parents' home – a small farm deep in the Lancashire countryside, the nearest place of note being Blackpool – but knowing that the place could only support the elderly couple and would bring hardship if she landed on them with her young son, she petitioned for a piece of land on the corporation allotment near her cottage to supplement their food.

She had found those first two years there extremely hard work, clearing away the weeds and debris of the ground that had been previously allocated to a lazy man. However, after digging out a trench and filling it with waste matter and rotting vegetation gleaned from her fellow allotment holders, her wigwams of beans and peas grew profusely. Her flower beds were neat and trim, with rows of bushy carrot leaves, leafy green cabbages and stumpy looking potato plants growing in regimented drills. She had also acquired some chicks that had become good layers and her produce could be found in the casual area of the Friday market in Birkenhead, whilst the flowers, albeit seasonal, she sold outside the local cemetery. To make ends meet, she was a standby waitress at the town hall and a part time skivvy at Bella's Cafe on Bellfield Street.

Charlie had never known what it was like to go hungry. Jane had always tried her best to clothe and feed him well – not like some of the little chaps who went to the charity school that he had attended. The cost of the schools upkeep was donated from the great and the good of the area, or by money bequeathed from various 'honourables' after their deaths. No, some of Charlie's fellow pupils had their bottoms sticking out of their ragged trousers and wore hand-me-down clothes. He was eyed with envy when he'd brought out a boiled egg, with a slice of bread and a layer of best butter upon it for his midday meal. Jane had scrimped and saved for Charlie's apprenticeship indentures. She took out a loan from the tally man to pay for his first new suit and could proudly say to anyone who would take the time to listen that she had done her best by him.

It saddened Charlie, but made him proud, when sometimes his mother talked of the man whom he remembered, but never really knew. According to Jane, his parents had met on the promenade at Blackpool. His father, a sea-going man who had voyaged to most of the new world by the time he was thirty, had decided on a trip to the northwest seaside town, which was fast becoming popular with the masses. He and a mate had travelled on the railway from Liverpool to Preston, then had gone on the branch line to stay at one of the boarding houses that had sprung up along the front at Blackpool.

Jane had been walking with a friend, a woman she knew from a nearby village and had been friends with since a child. A sudden strong gust of wind had blown the diminutive Jane, who stood at just over five feet, into the path of the strolling sailors. She had been caught in the arms of James Wilson, who had been giving her admiring glances as he had walked behind. After utterances of confusion and embarrassment, the four had repaired to one of the shelters that the town's people had erected for the shielding of locals and visitors from the whooshing wind that could catch one unawares off the Irish Sea. They had spent the next few hours in each other's company. Within weeks, James, or 'Jimmy', being known as a fast worker, had taken Jane Oakes, a spinster pushing thirty, to be his lawful wedded wife and set her up in a one-up-one-down cottage near his family home in Birkenhead.

In 1878, when Charlie was seven, after his father had been discharged from the ship that had visited Australia, India, China and America during its voyage of the past two years, they heard that Jimmy had been one of those who had perished. The ferryboat he was on, when he was coming back from visiting one of the many seamans' clubs in Liverpool, had collided with a clipper ship anchored in the middle of the Mersey during thick fog. His body was never found, no doubt swept out into the Irish Sea on a fast flowing tide. All they had left was his sea chest, which was kept upstairs on the little landing, along with various papers that had been found inside. Why he was on the ferryboat that was bound for Egremont, no one ever knew, given as the family lived nearer to the Tranmere landing stage. Being as Jimmy was an honourable man, it was decided that, because of the fog, he had boarded the wrong vessel.

Feeling full from the generous helping he had taken, Charlie took his plate to the small scullery and rinsed it under the tap, which only spewed cold water. He left it in the stone sink for his mother to swill with boiling water from the kettle the next morning. Although epidemics of cholera and typhoid were few and far between now that the corporation had installed sewer pipes and built a waterworks locally, Jane was an avid washer of plates, cutlery and their persons and had petitioned for their landlord to install an outside flushing lavatory. Now that the Lake Vyrnwy Reservoir was up and running, people were a lot more confident about the quality of their water supply.

Charlie sat in his armchair and glanced at his newspaper, glad of the light from the oil lamp because messing about with candles was such a chore. It was November and still mild considering it would be Christmas in a few weeks time, though there had been a lot of rainfall that year. He thought back to the fearful storm that July, when a lifeboat on its way to helping the crew of a stricken ship capsized, with two of the crew missing. A newly built ship was also towed by a tug from Greenock and went down off Port Erin in August. No wonder people who lived in the area joked that they should have been born with webbed feet.

His newspaper was full of the generosity of a man named George Fowler, a provision merchant from nearby Rock Ferry where Charlie's beloved, Lily Griffiths, lived. He had bequeathed £20, 000 for the establishment of a hospital for incurables in Liverpool and another £4, 000 for other good causes too. *What it must be like to be rich and live the grand life,* thought Charlie, his mind quickly going to Lily again, as he imagined them married and living in a great house built in the Cheshire countryside. She'd want for nothing; he would employ servants and they would go on holidays to Paris and Rome and their children would attend the very best of boarding schools. He would buy his mother a smart detached dwelling in Bidston, with a view that would extend as far as the Irish Sea and over the Mersey to Liverpool. Poor Mother. It had been hard for her, all these years without a husband. She might have married Alf Hewitt, a mate who had gone to sea with Jimmy and who had kept coming to visit on his shore leaves to ask if there was anything he could do to lighten her heavy load. But Jane had only room for one in her heart and that was her one and only son.

Thinking of his mother spurred Charlie to his feet and out into the backyard, where the privy and the wooden lean-to lay. The cart, really a large barrow and needing all of Jane's strength to push it when loaded with her tin pails and the last of the season's dahlias and chrysanthemums, was up against the brick wall that separated their yard from next door. She had sheltered her containers under it and Charlie decided to leave them there – they'd be full of rainwater if he loaded them for her that evening. He went inside to bring out the coal scuttle and by the light from the kitchen window he filled it full of slack to tamp down the fire.

"Can I get yer another?" asked a rough looking man, who was leaning up against the bar at The Grapes downing his tankard of beer, as Charlie passed him by to go to the lavatory in the backyard.

"No, yer all right, Ernie," he replied, lapsing into the local dialect, as he didn't want to sound as if he was a cut above the chap.

"Yer mammy not like yer out too late then?" It was said to rile the young upstart, who lived a few doors away from him. Rumour had it that he had been given a cushy job in the development department at the shipping yard, while he, Ernie, was a lowly labourer.

Charlie carried on to the backyard and ignored the jibe. The man was out for a fight; he was one of those who couldn't hold his beer and could get nasty.

"I'm on me way ter meet me mam from the town hall, Ernie," Charlie said pleasantly, as he came back, having to pass the man by if he wanted to leave by the front door. "She had a job on this evening, some sort of charity do."

"Aye, they're full of their damn charitable works, them nobs who own the shipping lines and the factory owners, who've never done a hard days graft in their feckin' lives. None of it comes to me and our Betty."

Charlie could have said, "Well you have employment and it

isn't up to the great and the good to support your ever increasing brood of children." Nor could he point out that Ernie should have been home with said wife and children instead of giving most of his wages to the brewery. The man was easily angered and if it wasn't him who caught a punch in the mouth, it would be his wife, God bless her, when her husband finally made it home. "I'll say goodnight," he said, nodding also to the barman who had served him earlier on.

"Well, I'll keep me money in me pocket then," Ernie said, belying his words by holding out his tankard to the barman for a refill. "Yer'd best get off, little mammy's boy. Yer don't want yer botty slapped by yer ma."

Charlie ignored the great guffaw of laughter that followed him through the door, as other labourers from the shipyard joined in Ernie's brand of levity. 'Turn the other cheek' was Charlie's motto when others tried to rile him and up to now it had served him well.

The back streets were quiet as he sped along them towards the town hall in Hamilton Square, except when he had to pass the ale houses, which stood on nearly every corner on his way. Noisy men spilled out onto the pavements, their faces animated in the dull glow of the recently erected gas lamps, as they laughed and joked with their inebriated mates. Small ragged children played in the gutters, whilst older ill-clad boys hung around in groups. He quickly passed the market place, a building erected in 1845 that had served the people of Birkenhead with produce from the outlying farms and fisheries of the Wirral for many years. Vagrants slept under the tarpaulins purloined from the outside stallholders, who frequently used them as shelter on rainy days. A shabby looking man scavenged through abandoned containers, no doubt looking for a meal from the discarded food not fit for selling on the next trading day.

Charlie checked his watch, as he saw from the few lights in the town hall windows that the janitor had been shutting down in an effort to lock up the building for the night. He sighed, as he remembered that Jane had said she couldn't be sure of her finishing time.

"Early doors," said the night watchman, not moving from the warmth of his brazier, situated as it was in the shelter of one of the portico buildings, a mixture of sumptuous dwellings for the rich or offices for wealthy merchants. "'Is 'onourableness was away forty minutes ago."

Charlie nodded, feeling deflated that his noble act of accompaniment had been thwarted, though deep down he thought it had might have been the fact that his mother was walking back with Mary that had inspired his journey. Mary was what could be called 'a comely lass'; she had good childbearing hips according to his mother, who didn't really want her son to marry anyone, but if it had to be so, she wanted a woman who would give her lots of grandchildren. A little older than Charlie, Mary had never been on his list of eligible girls to consider as producer of the next generation of Wilsons. Top of the list had always been Lily, but just in case his senses had got it wrong and she went ahead and married into the gentry, Mary, though second best, could be his choice of bride.

"I was wondering where you'd got to," said Jane, when Charlie eventually made it home after his fool's errand. "I were that glad to have Mary for company tonight. We were just coming around the corner of Argyle Street and one of the warehouses had gone up in flames! It must have only happened in the last half hour, as the firemen had only just got there. We had to drop back to the New Ferry Road or we could have been burnt to cinders."

"Well, would you believe it, I was down that way myself looking out for you and Mary, but I wasn't near Argyle Street or I would have seen the fire too. It'll be one of them arsonists, I'll be bound. Got a grudge against something or other. Is that a brew you're making, Mother? I'm parched."

"Sit yourself down and I'll pour you a cup. I must be getting old, that walk back from work tonight fair jiggered me."

"You do too much, Mother; now I'll be earning a man's wage

you can cut down a bit. Perhaps you could give up the waiting on and concentrate on what you'd like to do instead."

"You're a good lad, Charlie. I don't know what I would have done without you when your father drowned like he did. Having you here gave me a purpose to carry on. I never understood why his family cut us dead, though, after he'd gone. I would have thought they'd have rallied round a widow and a little lad."

"Takes all sorts. They've got their own lives to lead and no doubt they thought you were capable of getting on with yours."

"I sometimes see your Aunt Emily visiting her parent's grave at the cemetery. She never buys her flowers from me, just nods my way as she passes by."

"Like I said, it takes all sorts. She's a way to come from Wallasey, so maybe she's in a bit of a rush to get back to her family."

"Yeah, you're probably right. Well, I'll be away to my bed. I'll nip to the allotment early enough, then be ready for church by eight o'clock. I assume you'll be coming with me."

Charlie nodded, then settled into his chair, sipping his drink as he let the day's events unfold before him. The excitement he felt whilst watching the busy shipping on the River Mersey had never left him. Since he was a child he would find himself drawn to his spot by the landing stage, where he scanned the sides of the nearer vessels for the name and its home port, then avidly read the *Lloyds Shipping Gazette* to see the country or countries that the ship and its crew had come from. In the small area that he called his bedroom (half of an upstairs room that he shared with Jane, divided by a heavy curtain), his collection of past copies of the gazette sat waiting for perusal in his father's old sea chest, along with Jimmy's papers of discharge and indenture and a book of romantic poetry. The latter was hidden from his mother, as she would have called him a sissy. It was a busy port, the City of Liverpool, across the river from his home. Lives were affected by the ebb and flow of decisions made by the shipping lines, the merchants with their warehouses who stored their imported goods from exotic places so far away and the economic vagaries that might force a man to take his family to one of the new colonies, to seek a better life.

He let his thoughts wander again to his beloved Lily, still in denial over the hurt he had felt when she had spurned him that day. It didn't do to let such hurts fester; he must drink from the cup of life that was always half full.

CHAPTER THREE

"Does my hair look silly with this ribbon in it, Ellen?" asked Lily, as she and her sister sat on Lily's bed staring into the dressing table mirror, waiting for Lawrence to visit.

"You always look pretty to me, Lily," said Ellen wistfully, wishing she had the beautiful chestnut tresses that her sister had, instead of thin, lank, mousy hair that looked as if it always needed washing. "Why don't you wear that cream flower comb that Bertha bought you last Christmas if you aren't happy with the ribbon? It will go very well with that blouse and skirt that you are wearing. Cream and brown go well together, don't you think?"

"I wore this the last time Lawrence came to tea," Lily pouted. "What will he think when he sees me wearing it again? He'll think that I don't get enough dress allowance, that is what he will think."

"I doubt if he'll notice. He'll be too busy looking at his bride to be."

"Oh, do you think so?" Lily's voice was shrill with excitement. *Bride to be* – did Ellen think, like she did, that Lawrence might be on the brink of a proposal? She had been *so* looking forward to this day and hadn't slept a wink the night before, imagining what might happen during her cousin's visit.

"Yes, I'm sure of it. Anyway, I'd best go back and help Bertha. It's an exciting day for her as well."

Lily couldn't see why, unless Bertha was looking forward to Lawrence's admiration of the special cake that she had baked.

"Tell her that I'll be down shortly and then I'll help her with the table in Grand-mama's sitting room."

Lily proceeded to twist her hair into different styles, placing the ornate comb this way and that, then deciding to put her crowning glory into a French pleat, with the comb firmly embedded. She dreamed again of walking down the church aisle on her father's arm, whilst Lawrence stood by the altar dressed in his very smart uniform, turning his head towards his lovely bride in frothy lace. She was still staring dreamily at her reflection when she heard the front door open, which caused her heart to beat rather quickly. She ran quickly to the landing to see if her beloved had arrived.

"Welcome." Lily heard her father's booming voice, after he had opened the door to his long awaited nephew by marriage. "How did it go then? Good, good. We'll catch up later in my study."

"Come in, my dear." Lily's mother had risen from her afternoon nap and was now standing at the side of her husband in the hallway. "I trust everything went well?"

"Indeed it did, Aunt Hannah. I am looking forward to seeing Grand-mama and the family again, so I can tell you all about my travels."

Voices continued on, albeit muffled, once Lily had returned to her bedroom and the trio had climbed the stairs to Grand-mama's quarters, where the door was closed to keep the warmth in. Lily decided to make a grand entrance, forgetting that she had promised Bertha to help. She waited until she heard her sister's heavy footsteps and Ellen's light ones come past her door, then clutching the red rose that she had begged from her sister in the florist shop, she followed them through the open door of Grand-mama's sitting room.

Her sisters, including Mabel and Henrietta, the two older ones, who still lived at home but were allowed to go out to work, were sitting on upright chairs and were suitably attired in their Sunday gowns and lacy shawls. Their heads turned expectantly in Lily's direction as she faltered in the doorway looking towards her parents, who appeared to be in serious conversation with the one that she loved. There was a strange atmosphere in the large, cluttered room and for a fleeting moment she wondered why Lawrence and her parents were standing together by the fireplace. She had presumed that the announcement of their youngest daughter's betrothal to a favourite nephew would have been the cause of much happiness, but instead they were all looking a little glum. Maybe Bertha was going to say something to spoil it all, seeing as she had just got up from her chair and was blocking Lily's way. Grand-mama, however, was looking happy, though a little smug.

"Lily, how lovely to see you," cried her handsome, smartly-dressed cousin in his sea captain's uniform when he spotted her hovering in the doorway. He held out his hand for her to go to him, addressing her as he would a child, "My, my, you do look pretty and you are just in time for our announcement."

Lily's heart began to beat very quickly; so much so, that she was in terror of falling into a faint, so she quickly rushed to be by her beloved's side. He smiled at her impulsiveness, putting out his hand in an effort to steady her, or so she had thought. However, instead it had been Bertha whom he had been beckoning to stand alongside him, not Lily, because he was about to announce that the pair of them were to be wed. The family quickly came to their assistance as the two sisters fell against each other in the rush and Lily, being the lighter, was elbowed to the ground.

"It will be the effects of a fever, brought on by walking down to Borough Road in the rain yesterday." Lily could hear her mother's muffled voice, after she came around from her few minutes of wooziness, during which time Mannion had carried his youngest daughter to her room.

"I think you will find it is the shock of being the bridesmaid and not the bride at the nuptials," Grand-mama remarked sourly, as she followed closely behind. "I think she quite fancied being Mrs Lawrence Patterson herself."

"Shall I send a boy to fetch the doctor?" Bertha's voice sounded a little peeved, because after the announcement it should have been her who was the centre of attention.

"No dear, but bring me my smelling salts," said her mother. "We'll get her to come around from her swoon first, then see what she's got to say."

Lily stayed silent, trying to keep in the pain and frustration that she was feeling, hearing that it was her plain-faced sister, Bertha, who her heart's desire had chosen. She had snatched him away from under her very nose. How was she going to live in a family whose whole topic of conversation was going to be 'The Wedding' for the next few months? How was she going to live with a sister, who by all sorts of underhandedness had managed to snare her beloved? *It wouldn't do*, she thought despairingly, but perhaps there was some way of winning dear Lawrence back again? Perhaps she could poison Bertha with deadly nightshade, or perhaps a rope stretched taut across the staircase instead? After coming down from serving Grand-mama her lunch, she would take such a tumble down those open stairs. Or perhaps she could insist that they travel together across the Mersey, to look at things for the wedding in the newly opened department stores. It would be easy enough to push against her sister, whilst the boat was tying up on choppy water and the gangway being laid. Though then she would be jailed for trying to drown her sister and hung by her neck at the gallows of Walton Jail. The thought of her own demise sobered up her mawkish thinking and she resolved to run away from the problem instead.

Strangely enough, it had been Mabel that Lily had thought might have been the one who had snatched her beloved. It had come to her in an instant; she had realised that Lawrence wasn't beckoning to her, he was beckoning to somebody else. Mabel, who had been sitting near to Bertha, with her usually healthy face as white as a sheet, had been looking over towards her animated cousin and was perhaps in love with Lawrence as well. Mystery seemed to surround her twenty-six year old sister and Lily wondered why she had been given permission to work in a local florist shop after she had returned from a finishing school a few years before, instead of making a suitable marriage. According to their mother, Mabel had attended an academy somewhere in the south of England and had excelled artistically, so surely a good marriage could have been arranged for her as well. Mabel wasn't a plain girl if you compared her looks to Bertha, but it seemed that now her talents were being used in the creation of bouquets and flower arrangements and she was in much demand for her accomplishments in the busy little shop.

"Lily, my dear." Her whiskery, round-faced father held her by the hand, his voice full of concern as she lay still with her eyes closed. "Lily, here's Bertha with Mother's smelling salts. Do inhale them, my dear."

She did as she was asked, as she always did if her father made a request that she could adhere to. A heady smell of lavender brought her slowly to a sitting position and she smiled weakly and apologetically to her audience, who stood around her bed looking concerned.

"Are you all right, Lily?" Grand-mama pushed her way to be at her side. "It must have been a bolt out of the blue hearing dear Lawrence make his announcement. We had decided to keep it a secret until he had completed his first voyage as captain of one of the largest steamships ever to leave the Port of Liverpool. We are very proud of him, aren't we Hannah? A feather in the Patterson family cap."

Lily nodded, aware that if she were to make some remark other than a congratulatory one she would be in big trouble, so she kept her mouth shut.

"I'll stay with Lily for a little while," said her father. "You all carry on with the celebration, but save me some of that cake."

He winked at Bertha, who was no doubt in a hurry to get back to her betrothed or at least to make sure he was helping himself to some of the delicious looking food that she had spent a lot of time making.

"A bit of a shock, my dear Lily," Mannion Griffiths said kindly, when her family had left her bedroom. "I've always felt that you were sweet on Lawrence, but it would never do, you marrying someone who's married to the sea like your cousin is. Bertha is at her best running a home, preparing wholesome meals and delicious desserts, creating a safe haven for Lawrence to come back to on his shore leaves. You will need a man who can give you everything your heart desires. Someone like me, but younger by thirty years."

"I don't want anyone else but Lawrence, Father. I have loved him since I was a little girl. I thought the feeling was returned, as he always made a fuss of me when he visited our home."

Lily's voice sounded tearful.

"Lawrence is kind to everyone, my dear; you have mistaken his kindness for affection, but he needs a homemaker for a wife, not a socialite as you will become one day. Bertha will fit the bill nicely, having been taught to run a home by your mother and her cooking skills are second to none, as you know. You are akin to a precious hothouse plant that would need a man to treat you with delicacy and with Lawrence away so often, he wouldn't be here to do that. I am sure that the man you will marry is just around the corner, Lily. Be patient and put on a brave face for your sister's sake."

"I was thinking that perhaps you could allow me a little time away from the situation, Father," Lily said in her little girl voice, intent on escaping imprisonment with a victorious, betrothed sister. Her wheedling usually worked on her besotted father, but this time he appeared reluctant to agree. "Perhaps I could go for a week to Aunt Patricia's in Southport? I know she would have me if you asked."

"I'll have to think about it, my princess, as I'm not really keen to have you out of my sight. I seem to be slowly losing my authority in this household of mine that is full of women. Only Frederick knows who is boss; it's a pity he's away at boarding school." It was said in a light-hearted manner, as Lily's father liked to appear jovial, but underneath he was a hard-headed businessman, something he had to be in the world of coal distribution. There was always someone waiting in the wings to undercut his prices, when the acquisition department in the town hall asked for tenders to provide the boilers with fuel for the many public buildings that belonged to the borough council.

He had fallen on his feet when he had married Hannah Patterson. Grand-mama Patterson had been left comfortably off when her husband had died of a heart attack in his forties, just when he had been riding high on his good fortune as the many pies he had his fingers in were beginning to pay him back with interest. Of course, for Mannion, marrying into the family had been a godsend, given that he was an astute minded man and was conversant with the world of commerce. He had worked as a clerk in a Liverpool financial institution, but he knew it could easily slip between his fingers if he took his eye off the ball.

"Let me think on it for a few days, Lily," he said, after kissing the top of his daughter's head and fussing with a bed cover that had fallen askew. "Christmas isn't far away and I rather think you will be called upon to help with the festivities here. Southport will be very chilly at this time of year and I've never thought your aunt's place well heated."

Lily didn't answer, just pouted instead, hoping that her father would change his mind if he didn't get the smile he expected, but he turned away. Some other thing, no doubt, had sprung to mind for him to consider. She sat up when he'd gone and began to pull the petals off the discarded rose that she had still been clutching when her father had carried her to bed. Had Lawrence even noticed her offering? She had gone to all that trouble yesterday. Braving the threat of more rain as she walked to the florist shop after completing Bertha's errand, knowing that it could have spoilt the nap on her raincoat; having to endure the attentions of that dolt, Charlie, who thought that just because he used to walk her home from school he had some claim on her affections and always seemed to be there when she turned a corner; going to great lengths earlier to make sure her appearance was suitably attractive to Lawrence's gaze. She waited for the tears to spring into her eyes as she sat on the bed wallowing in self-pity, but strangely enough they didn't come; only a childish desire for some sort of revenge upon her sister, who was the cause of this unhappiness.

A timid knock on her door heralded Ellen, no doubt bringing her some hot, sweet tea to aid the recovery from her shock. Lily sat erect and stared into her dressing table mirror to see if she looked suitably peaky, but it wasn't Ellen who came into the room bearing a cup of tea. It was Mabel.

"Oh," said Lily, in a surprised voice. "I thought you were Ellen. Is that for me?"

"Yes, I thought you might need it." Mabel, quietly pretty but meek of manner, put the teacup and saucer on the lacy doily, which lay on the dressing table. Lily leant over to sip from it gratefully.

"Tea's good for shock, isn't it?" Mabel said, sitting by Lily's side and looking into the mirror a little self-consciously. "I knew this was going to happen yesterday when you came into the shop, blithely unaware that Lawrence was going to announce his betrothal to Bertha today. I suppose I could have warned you, but I wanted you to find out about men the hard way. Not that I have had much dealings with them, you understand, but they can make you do things that can bring on terrible repercussions… or so I've heard. I think that men are cunning like foxes, deceitful and sly and if they were not necessary for the continuation of the human race, it would be better to have them flushed down the crapper at birth."

Lily looked on in horror after her sister had uttered her pronouncement. It sounded so strange coming from the mild-mannered Mabel, who never had much to say for herself and who usually went straight to her bedroom when she came in from work. She only joined her family at meal times and never entered into any of the discussions that abounded, before being given Mannion's permission to leave the room.

"But Lawrence isn't like that in any way!" Lily cried. "He's kind, well-mannered, courteous and has never asked me to do anything that could bring on terrible repercussions. I think you've been reading too many books where the heroine falls prey to a bounder, Mabel. Although, thinking about it, when I was about seven, he did leave me sitting in a tree when we were all playing hide and seek at Aunt Patricia's. He forgot all about me and if it hadn't have been for one of the gardeners hearing my plea for assistance, I suppose I could have sat there for a very long time."

"Silly goose, you are such an innocent. Hasn't Mother told you anything about… you know…? About when you become a woman?" Mabel broke off abruptly when she saw that Lily hadn't a clue about what she was talking about and began to study her nails in minute detail, looking embarrassed. "You know, when you started your bleeding?" she said softly. "It comes and goes every four weeks or so and you have to wear a napkin?"

"Oh, you mean my monthly visitor, is that when you become a woman? I thought that was when you were twenty-one. Anyway, what has caused you to be so against the male population? Father and Frederick are quite bearable in small doses. Do you know Mabel, I thought it was you before that Lawrence was holding his hand out to, not Bertha."

Mabel smiled ruefully, then answered bleakly, "I don't think so, Lily. Lawrence is looking for a homemaker, not someone like me whose only talent is floristry."

"Didn't you meet any presentable fellows when you attended the academy? Oh, you were so lucky to be able to leave this stuffy prison and travel."

"I've been told by Father not to discuss my time away," Mabel said stiffly, getting up suddenly. "I am very fortunate that he allowed me to come back and take up employment at the florist shop, when many fathers' wouldn't have. Though at my age I suppose he had to, as I am destined now to be a spinster and will need his protection." Without another word Mabel walked out of Lily's bedroom, leaving her to mull over another curious twist in her older sister's tale.

They had never been close, because of the eight years difference between them and Mabel shared a bedroom with Ellen, so if there were any confidences to be had they would have been shared with her. Lily furrowed her brow, trying to remember any small clue that could have pointed to any discord in her family around two years ago, but there was none, other than that Grand-mama had ordered a carriage to take Mabel to the station, so that she might make her way to Liverpool to catch the London train. She had thought it strange, as usually Father would accompany his daughters to Lime Street Station in person.

"'Curiouser and curiouser,'" she quoted to herself, as she picked

33

up *Alice in Wonderland*. She decided she would wait until Lawrence had left before she joined the family again. She didn't want to see him, nor have to congratulate the happy pair. She could hear muted voices, a loud laugh now and again from Father, footsteps passing her room of the female kind. Then the heavy footfalls of Lawrence and her father, as they journeyed together to the male domain of the study, where no doubt they would be sampling a tot or two of the brandy that Lawrence would have brought with him from his voyage.

She took her mind off the frustration of having to wait for his departure by reading a couple of pages from the book by Lewis Carroll. It always made her smile when she read about the white rabbit who was always looking at his fob-watch and the dormouse who was put in the Mad Hatter's teapot. She would have liked to be Alice, experiencing a different world where all the animals could speak.

Henrietta was her next visitor. Having just turned twenty-one in the summer, she had proudly introduced her beau, Matthew Tucker, during a family gathering in Grand-mama's sitting room one weekend, when he had been invited to tea one Sunday afternoon after he had asked to speak to her father. Matthew was studying at the Birkenhead Theological College with a view to being ordained in a few years time. According to Henrietta, they had been introduced at a church fundraising event, where money was being sought for housing children who were destitute. It was a bit of a *fait accompli* for this dumpling daughter who had always gone her own way: a bit of a blue stocking if truth was told and quite happy to wait for her wedding day living in the bosom of her family. She shared a room with Bertha, whilst working for her father in his coal agent office in Hamilton Square.

"I thought I'd bring you some of Bertha's betrothal cake," she said quietly, bringing in a tray with a matching cup, saucer and plate upon it. " It's quite delicious. I wish I had a light hand when it comes to baking as Bertha has." She smiled down at her younger sister sympathetically then sat beside her after depositing the tray on the bedside table. "Are you feeling better now?"

Lily nodded, feeling rather wicked in the company of someone who was going to become a curate's wife. Only a little while ago she was thinking up ways to get rid of Bertha, so that Lawrence would marry her instead. Now she was being asked if she was feeling better. Better than what? Had her name been written in God's black book?

"I think it was all the people sitting together in Grand-mama's sitting room," she improvised. "It's always warm in there and I was feeling very tired from my long walk yesterday, because Bertha asked me to walk all that way to Westaways. I couldn't sleep at all last night and that is why I didn't come to church this morning."

"Well never mind." Henrietta took Lily's hand and, ever the pragmatist, said, "Eat your cake and drink your tea then perhaps you could come and join us. Lawrence has brought us all a little gift and I'm sure you will be delighted with yours. He has gone to visit his mother now and of course Bertha has accompanied him. Naturally she wants to show off the ring he bought her and I think there will probably be a gathering at the Patterson's. I think we should help Ellen in the kitchen later, it is only fair that we share the burden on the seventh day."

"And where's Father?" Lily asked, getting up to do Henrietta's bidding, as she agreed it was only fair to lighten Ellen's load and, secretly, she was wondering what her gift could be. "I asked him earlier to consider my request to visit Aunt Patricia. I think the change would do me good."

"He is a busy man at the moment, Lily, with winter being upon us and people stocking up for the Christmas season. I personally have been rushed off my feet in the office and some of the coal men are being paid double time."

"I can't see why father has to accompany us wherever we go, Henrietta. Do you remember when we went to Llandudno and he insisted that he drove us there in the carriage? What a squash! Mother said she would have preferred taking the train there."

"It's his way, Lily. It is difficult for a man to have so many daughters and see that each one is well chaperoned. He loves us all dearly and still worries about the daughters that have married and moved away. Why, when Sister Eliza went to visit her mother-in-law in Chester whilst Robert was sailing to New York, he insisted on driving her there. But of course, that was in the summer when demand for coal is at its lowest."

"I am quite able to catch a ferryboat across the Mersey, walk to the railway station and take a train to Southport, Henrietta. Aunt Patricia would send her driver to pick me up at the station when I got there."

"Be patient, Lily. If it's God's will for you to stay at Montgomery Hall, so it will be. Now, let me see a smile on your face and we'll go downstairs to see what needs doing. Mabel, poor girl, is in particular need of cheering up; she looks as if she has lost a sixpence and found a penny instead."

CHAPTER FOUR

It was still dark that morning when Charlie awoke to the sounds of his mother moving around downstairs. He peered at his fob-watch by the light of the gas lampost directly outside the bedroom window. It was half past seven. Another half an hour in bed before he had to be up and get ready to attend the meeting at the Weslyan Church on Maybank Road.

It wasn't that he was particularly religious, but he admired the brothers John and Charles Wesley. John had travelled the length and breadth of the country, preaching his brand of evangelism, which was a lot punchier than the insipid sermons of the Anglican Church. Charlie liked to hear a good Bible story, delivered with admonishment towards the members of the congregation. Generally a good thumping on the pulpit accompanied the minister's words, emphasising his point and making Charlie's hair stand up on the back of his neck. It appeared the list of sins were endless and one you didn't even know about could be committed, unless you went to be advised of them at the chapel each Sunday.

"Are you awake, Charlie?"

Jane knew that he would be because he was such a light sleeper and would have heard her moving about.

"Just a bit of dripping on some bread this morning. I forgot to check if we had any eggs, before I went to the allotment."

Charlie groaned as he heard her; he loved a fried egg on a piece of toast at the weekend.

"I'll go up to the allotment then." He leapt out of bed, splashed some water on his face from the china ewer that was kept in a bowl on an old battered dressing table, dried his face then dragged on his trousers and shirt over the vest and long johns he wore to bed. His socks, lovingly knitted by Jane, stayed on whatever. He only took them off for his weekly scrub in the old tin bath, when he had a change of socks and underclothing.

"You can't be that hungry," his mother said, when Charlie passed her by wearing his best tweed overcoat, his hand outstretched for the bowl of scraps that his mother had ready for the hens. "You ate best part of that scouse last night and I was going to make a pie crust for it. Ah, well, I'll put that bit of beef into the oven. While you're there, get whatever is left on them sprout stalks."

Charlie saluted, smiling to himself as he left the cottage, knowing that all her moaning was tinged with love.

It was still a little off dawn, as he plodded along the quiet street towards the land where his mother had her allotment. Above the roofs of the rows of cottages, terrace houses and the occasional shop or cafe, the lighting of the sky heralded a fine day. It gave him hope that he would be able to take up his usual position by the landing stage later, to look with interest at the busy river as vessels took anchorage from around the world and crews were ferried back and forth. With it being Sunday, he could see the difference in the level of the docks and warehouse activity.

The hens clucked a wearisome response as he gently opened the coop door, hoping the birds wouldn't set off all of a clutter when they saw the scraps he had brought them. It was a day of rest for most godly people around and they wouldn't be pleased to be woken by their clucking.

"How do?" said a voice a few feet behind him, causing Charlie to nearly drop the eggs he was clutching in his hand.

"Mr Hewitt!" he said, turning quickly to see his father's old sea-going mate, standing across from Jane's cabbages that were nearing maturity. "You didn't half give me a fright, what are you doing about so early?"

"Don't seem to be able to sleep nowadays." The grey-haired, slender-looking man in his early fifties looked glum as he glanced over. "Never should have given up the sea like I did, had no trouble sleepin' then. No, I saw yer ahead when I was on me way up to the cemetery. I thought ter meself I'll find out how Janey's doin', I've not see 'er fer a while."

"In a couple of hours she'll be sitting outside the cemetery with her barrow if you want to see her. She was here cutting her flowers only a little while ago." Charlie quite liked this man, who had always tried to befriend his mother after his father had died.

"No, I've other fish ter fry today. I'm just goin' to 'ave a look at me mam's grave, make sure she's all right, then I'm off ter see the nippers over at Bootle. Me sister's got seven of the little blighters, wore out with the lot of them she is, so I likes ter go over on a Sunday and 'ave a look at 'em."

"Well, my mother's doing fine. A bit of a struggle making ends meet while I was an apprentice, but Lairds have told me they're putting me in their development department and I'll be on a man's wage then." Charlie couldn't keep the pride out of his voice as he spoke, though he didn't want to appear boastful.

"You always were a clever chap," said Alf. "I bet Janey's proud of yer. Well, tell 'er I asked about 'er and she knows where I live should she need any 'elp or anythin'." He looked a little sheepish and had trouble meeting Charlie's eyes as he was talking, but Charlie put it down to embarrassment after his mother had given him the bum's rush, friendship wise. Or had it been more? Had Mr Hewitt tried it on with his mother and being a newly bereaved widow she had told him where to go? He'd never know unless he asked her and that was something he would never do.

Charlie looked across at the few pink and white dahlia heads, left on the clumps of plants that his mother had supported with wooden stakes, situated in front of a small reed fence that she had got him to erect in an effort to give them shelter. She had cut the best and they were sitting in her pails on the barrow, ready to be put into bunches and sold outside the cemetery. The bronze and white chrysanthemums a row or two behind them would be next.

Poor Mother, what a life, Charlie thought sadly. If it hadn't been for the ferry going down in the Mersey, she could have her feet up now. It was hard to remember his father from all those years ago, though he remembered there was a lot of shouting when he was back home on his shore leaves and Charlie had wept a lot of tears when he'd heard this. Still, he wasn't going to dwell on what might have been; he'd get back and eat his breakfast, go to chapel, then take up his favourite position down near the landing stage.

"I saw Alf Hewitt when I was up on the allotment," Charlie said to his mother, more for conversation than gossip, after he had finished mopping up his egg with his bread.

"Oh aye, what did he want?" Jane said from the scullery, where she was rinsing her plate and soaking the frying pan in the stone sink, before bringing the big kettle with boiling water in.

"Wanted to know how you were doing." Charlie brought his plate through. "He was on his way to the cemetery to see his mother. I said you'd be there in an hour or two."

"Not in my grave like his mother, I hope." Jane made an attempt to joke. "He knows where I live if he's that worried about my welfare, but I haven't seen hide nor hair of him for a long time."

"Perhaps he doesn't feel welcome here." Charlie didn't want to pry, but now he'd got this far he may as well continue.

"Or perhaps it was something to do with shooting the messenger." His mother sounded bitter as she passed her son by on her way to the kitchen. "Anyway, I've said enough on the subject, let sleeping dogs lie."

"Oh." Charlie felt intrigued, but he knew his mother would only clam up if he started ferreting and his father had gone for all these years, so what was the point?

"Right then, if we get a move on we'll get a front seat. I've heard tell the minister's attempting a bit of healing this Sunday." His mother wiped her hands on a piece of toweling, which she kept on a nail at the back of the scullery door. "I'll just get my best coat on and we'll be off."

It had begun to drizzle as the congregation – renewed, refreshed and ready for whatever the new week had to throw at them – shook the hand of the minister at the door of the chapel and sped off to their homes. As usual Mr Bryson hadn't held back as he brought each of the Ten Commandments to their attention, especially the one about working on the Sabbath day, knowing that he would probably see Jane Wilson sitting at the side of her barrow as he passed the cemetery gates later. Of course, the commandment could also apply to him, as Sunday was his busiest working day, but he was sure he had divine absolution. He was working on behalf of Him upstairs, so that would make it right.

Poor Mrs Wilson; she was a hardworking soul with three jobs to make ends meet. Charles, her son, was a polite young man who must make his mother proud and he was seemingly quite sweet on Mary Casson, who had sat with them in the chapel that day.

"Let's hope he doesn't attempt that healing stuff too often," Jane said, as she stood under her umbrella in the churchyard with Charlie and Mary. "I felt really embarrassed for him, there's no way Bessie Johnson will ever throw away that walking stick."

"At least he tried and something must have given him cause to think he was channeling the good Lord's healing powers." Charlie had felt quite intrigued when he was watching the minister using all his concentration to channel healing through his hands, in an effort to bring relief to the elderly woman's painful knee. It was something he hadn't seen the minister attempt before.

"Anyway, I'll leave you two young ones whilst I nip off home and get changed into my working clothes," Jane said, hoping that pushing the pair together might result in a courtship. "I don't think the rain will set in all day, there's enough blue in the sky to make Molly Mac a pair of bloomers. See you on Tuesday, Mary love; it hasn't half come around quick."

"Another "do" for an honourable?" Charlie began to walk in step with Mary, who intended to cut across the park to her home. "Would you like me to walk along with you? I'm in no hurry."

"Yeah, that 'ud be nice, Charlie. No, me and 'er 'ave been asked to wait on at Mrs Phillips' 'ouse on Temple Road. She's 'avin' one of them sworrys. Yer know, we'll wander around with bits of things on a salver and make sure 'er guests 'ave their glasses full."

"Oh, yes, I read about her husband being made a stipendiary magistrate, it'll probably be some sort of celebration for him."

"I don't know about that, Charlie." Mary looked a bit flummoxed at his answer, as she didn't know anything about a stipendiary magistrate, unless it was the fellow that threatened to put one of her brothers away in Walton Jail for setting a haystack alight. "I go where yer mam gets me a job, me and 'er are great muckers."

Charlie sighed inwardly, as he continued to walk along with the comely Mary. Now, Lily would have known exactly what he had been talking about; she probably even knew the Phillips family. Her father, although a coal agent, could often be seen rubbing shoulders at charity events with the great and the good. Poor Mary was the eldest of ten, lived in a rundown dwelling near the river and her education had been non-existent, given that she was needed to help with the Casson babies that kept appearing each year. He had wondered aloud once to his mother why Mary hadn't married, given that she must be good with children what with having so many back at home. Jane had said that was probably why she hadn't married, as there was enough of them in the family without adding more.

"So, 'ave yer got a sweetheart, Charlie?" Mary's question was direct, given that she had no social graces to fall back on. "Only yer mam was sayin' that you liked a girl from up on Rosemount Terrace. I said she must be kiddin' – Rosemount folk are not fer you!"

"Can't see why not, we're all God's creatures." Charlie suddenly felt irritated with his mother for egging Mary on. Mary was pretty, but in a blowsy kind of way. With her round face, plumpish body and light brown hair she would surely go the same way as her mother, and *she* was a hefty lump. He felt disinclined to ask for a courtship, as until Lily Griffiths got her wealthy man he was still in with a chance.

"We could go fer a ride on the ferry boat, if yer like Charlie?

Like yer mam says, it won't be rainin' all day."

"I'll leave you here, if you don't mind, Mary." Charlie stopped short of the park gate and arranged his face into sorrowful one. "I've just remembered, I promised my mam that I'd help her with the buckets. I'll have to hurry to catch her up."

The cottage was quiet but for the occasional click of a piece of slack as it settled amongst the other embers in the bottom of the grate. Charlie lifted the latch on the front door and decided to have some time alone, before heading out to sit on the riverbank. His mother had been happy to see him when he had caught her up and offered his help in pushing the handcart, though she was puzzled as to why he had left Mary to walk home alone.

"She's a lovely girl, son. Hardworking, loyal and would make a good mother for my grandchildren. You'll have to marry one day and it may as well be her. You're setting your sights too high with that Lily Griffiths. Her sort's not for you, son."

Her well-meaning words rankled Charlie. He was as good as any man who walked the Earth and he'd show his beloved Lily that some day. In the meantime, was it fair to let Mary think that she was in with a chance with him? And what if Lily came to hear that he was stepping out with Mary – that *would* blow his chances. Ah well, what would be, would be; Charlie was a great believer in his destiny.

He climbed the narrow stairs of the cottage, intent on finding his father's oilskin, which he liked to wear if he thought it might rain. There was something comforting about donning the smelly old garment that had been worn by his father whilst sailing the seven seas. He sat upon the sea chest trying to imagine the scene. A clipper ship, white sails billowing, tossed on the waves of the Atlantic, steered by a capable captain to the shores of America. The crewmen, sailors drawn from the teeming streets of Liverpool, fleet footed, venturesome, intrepid, married to whichever vessel they happened to be serving on at the time. They'd have tales of dusky maidens, exotic palm tree covered islands, faraway places with names that no one had heard of. He could see it all in every detail, his imagination bright with mind's eye pictures. It was strange how he could see those visions flickering when he sat upon the battered sea trunk, but he could never conjure up his father's watery grave. He shivered, pulled himself together and carefully trod the steps down the stairs.

The chains holding up the landing stage clunked loudly, as the ferocious wind that blew along the river caught in the securely bound wooden platform, causing it to rock alarmingly. People who waited for the two smoke stacked ferry looked across nervously as the vessel neared its destination, its captain fighting with the swelling currents to moor alongside. A crashing wave nearby, held back by the strength of the esplanade wall, sprayed its spume across the footpath, sending people running for shelter – including Charlie, who had been anxiously watching the scene.

It isn't a day for observing the current movements of the shipping, he thought, looking across the river where vessels lay at anchor. The smaller ones jerked with the turbulence, the larger ones rode out the roughening waves. Across the river and along the docksides of Brunswick and Coburg, sailing ships and steamers waited to discharge their cargo, whilst increased trade at the busy port had shaped the city skyline, with newly built structures everywhere.

Charlie retraced his steps along the footpaths, heading for the cemetery where he knew his mother would be. If *he* felt chilly and he was wearing the heavy oilskin over his Sunday clothes, how must she be feeling? He would try to persuade her to go back home. She was sat on a raised paving slab just outside the iron gates of the cemetery, with only her shawl covering her bodice-clad shoulders. Her black bonnet, which she had placed a piece of newspaper over, caught the rain drips from an overhanging tree and her sodden black skirt was tucked around her legs and boots. She looked miserable, forlorn and very lonely; Charlie's heart felt heavy to see that his mother had to earn her living in such a way. It was half past three; dusk was fast arriving and no one was going to visit the dead at that time of the day.

"Got that wrong, didn't you Mother?" he said, as cheerfully as he could manage, noticing that she had one last bunch of dahlias in the old tin bucket. "Enough blue in the sky to make Molly Mac a pair of bloomers, you said, and it's been raining on and off since then."

"Aye, Charlie, got that wrong didn't I? Not many folk been out and about neither, but the flowers are nearly gone. One more bunch and I'll be away."

Charlie felt in his trouser pocket for a few small coins. "Thruppence did you say, missus? Cheap at the price; a nice bunch of flowers for my dearly beloved." He dropped the money into her lap.

"Oh Charlie, you haven't got a dearly beloved. No, take the money back, you'll be wanting a pint between now and your wages." Jane tried to rise, but sitting as she had on the stone cold pavement had stiffened her muscles and she fell back in agony. "Help me up, there's a love," she gasped. Her face filled with pain and her head was full of worrying thoughts about how they would live if she couldn't manage to get about to earn some money. "I'll have to make a cushion, something to put my bottom on now there's wintry days."

"You say that every time you come up here, Mother," Charlie said, shaking a finger at her as if she was a child, before using all the strength in his small body to lift her. "Anyway, I *have* got a beloved and I'll see she gets these flowers before the end of the day."

CHAPTER FIVE

"Who was that at the door, Ellen?" asked Grand-mama, after summoning any one of her grandchildren that were in the vicinity by ringing the small brass bell she had on a table nearby.

"A man with a bunch of flowers for Lily," the young woman answered, as she put her head around her grand-mama's door. Her voice was filled with admiration for her pretty sister, who could get a man to bring her nice things.

"I wonder who that was?" Grand-mama's face wore a serious expression. "Was it a bouquet delivered from a florist shop, or just a bunch of flowers picked from somebody's garden? No, it wouldn't be a delivery, the shops are shut today."

"It was a bunch of pink and white dahlias wrapped in newspaper. I have seen the man who brought them before."

"Oh, does he have a name, this man whom you have seen before?"

"I don't know it, but he used to walk Lily back home from school."

"Did he now? Then tell Lily that I wish to see her. She may be sleeping and I know that she must have had rather a shock earlier, but lying in bed moping doesn't do anyone any good."

"Yes, Grand-mama, would you like me to bring the flowers so that you can show them to her?"

"Of course, Ellen and ask your parents to come along too. Then I can find out exactly who this young man is."

Lily had been lying on her bed reading her book. Now that she had made her mind up that Lawrence was making a big mistake by marrying Bertha instead of her, she had put the matter from her mind and was concentrating on the fascinating story. How anyone could believe that a human being could be reduced to the size of a little finger was beyond her, but the author had made it quite believable in *Alice in Wonderland*.

She heard someone's tread on the stairs and groaned inwardly; another member of her family coming to pat her on the head. It was dark now, so much so that she couldn't see who was at the front door when she had looked out of the window when she had heard the knocking earlier. Whoever it was, someone had dealt with them and the household had settled down to its usual sounds.

"Lily, you're wanted." Ellen poked her head around the door, lacking the social nicety of knocking first in case her sister was asleep. Lily hastily pushed her book under her counterpane; it wouldn't do for Ellen to see that she had been reading.

"Who wants me?" she asked in a plaintive voice, wondering childishly if Lawrence had realised his mistake and had come back to tell her so.

"Grand-mama – and be quick, she wants to retire early, says all the excitement of the day has been too much."

A summons from Grand-mama – everyone had to obey *her* command, it didn't do to not. Sighing, Lily slid her indoor shoes on, a type of ballet shoe with a black satin ribbon tied around the ankle. She pushed her cream blouse into the waist of her skirt, hoping that her elderly relative wouldn't notice how rumpled her outfit had become. She quickly glanced into the cheval mirror as she passed by it, noting that she looked as of she had been dragged backward through a hedge.

"Hurry, Lily," Ellen frowned as she saw her sister tweaking at her hair and smoothing her skirt down. "You'll get me into trouble if you continue to dawdle. Why didn't you put on your wrapper before you got into bed?"

Lily shrugged. Had she cared about donning a wrapper, when all she could think of was Lawrence and Bertha and their underhandedness? She should be the one who was showing off her ring to the Patterson family, taking the congratulations from all and sundry and listening to her cousin's endearments and professions of love. Why did it have to be Bertha, who would get more pleasure from seeing her cakes rise, or polishing the satinwood tables until they had a mirror-like shine? How was it that she had not seen it coming? She was always listening at her Grand-mama's door.

"Ah Lily, there you are." Grand-mama's tone was brisk, as she beckoned her granddaughter into her sitting room and motioned her to sit on the sofa by her father, whilst her mother sat in an upright chair by the fire. Lily felt troubled. What was so important that her parents had been summoned as well, while the rest of the family wasn't? Had she done something very wrong by making such a fuss before?

Grand-mama held up a very bedraggled bunch of flowers, wrapped in a piece of jaggedly ripped newspaper. Her expression was one of distaste as she stared across the room.

"A person of the male variety handed these in at the door earlier. What have you got to say for yourself, Lily?"

"Why should a bunch of flowers have anything to do with me, Grand-mama?" Lily was at a loss as she stared at the wilting dahlias, pink petals beginning to drop on Grand-mama's lacy shawl that she wore across her knees.

"Ellen informed me that the young man who left them for you was a follower, Lily. It appears he used to walk you back from Ashmore School – something we were quite unaware of."

"Oh." Lily's brow cleared from the frowning she had been doing. "That will be Charlie Wilson, he's always hanging around me."

"Then he will have to be stopped," her father broke in, sounding angry. "You can give me his address and I will go and see this young fellow-me-lad. I will make him see the error of his ways so that he won't continue to pester one of my family."

"He was only protecting me from some of the orphan boys, who I had to pass on my way home." Lily felt quite surprised to hear herself defending him. "I think his mother sells flowers outside the cemetery. Anyway, that was years ago. I can't be blamed for his attention nowadays."

"That's enough, Lily." Grand-mama looked askance at her granddaughter. "Consorting with a young man whose mother sells flowers for a living isn't what your father wants to hear. Isn't that so, Mannion?"

"That is so, Mother-in-law." Lily's father nodded in agreement, somehow missing the fact that Mabel, another daughter, was also a purveyor of the blooms. "I have decided that your request for some time away from home will be granted, Lily. However, you will not be sent to stay at your Aunt Patricia's in Southport. There is a possibility that you will be going to stay with an acquaintance of your grand-mama's, who lives near a small village called Greasby. Let me finish, Lily…" Mannion could see that Lily was about to argue. "No, I think your grand-mama should let you know of the rest of my decision."

"As you know, Lily, your father has always wished for you to be married into a wealthy family." Grand-mama was feeling gracious towards her son-in-law, although she had only made her suggestion to Mannion once she had seen her granddaughter's distress at Lawrence's announcement. *What a silly innocent,* she thought. "It has been brought to my attention by a member of my bridge club that Mrs De Crosland, someone that I met in my younger years when I was a guest at Arrowe Hall, is hoping to find a good wife for her son, Roland. He is an army officer. He is at present overseas with his battalion in Burma, but according to Millicent Broster, my partner at bridge, he will be returning very soon.

"Under the circumstances, Lily, I feel sure that a stay for a week or so with Mrs De Crosland might be just the making of you."

Mannion, taking up the thread of his mother-in-law's suggestion, looked on with pride at his daughter, who he knew could charm the squirrels out of the trees if she put her mind to it. "You will get to know her very well and as you are from a good family, I am sure she will agree to present you to her son, as the perfect future wife on his return."

Up to now Lily had been silent, speechless because she would not have been allowed to speak while her elders were talking anyway. However, she was more astonished that her family were already making plans for her future happiness, even though she had behaved so badly that afternoon. The more she began to think about living in Greasby – a place she had only heard about at school when shown a map – the more the idea of marrying an officer appealed to her. She would be able to cock a snoot at Bertha, show Lawrence that he wasn't the only pencil in her drawing box and imagine their envy on seeing her abode, when she invited the couple there for afternoon tea.

"Grand-mama, do you know anything about the family's residence?" That was the most important requirement in Lily's eyes, as she had to have somewhere grand to show off to her family.

"I think the place is called Brookvale." Grand-mama looked thoughtful as she cast her mind back to when she had stayed in the area, when her best friend from a ladies college invited her to stay one Christmas. "I seem to remember it was on the road down to Frankby, near the crossroads. I met Lydia at Penelope's, before she married into the De Crosland family."

Three pairs of eyes looked at Lily expectantly after the elderly lady had finished speaking and her mother was smiling encouragingly.

"The village of Greasby happens to be mentioned in the Domesday Book."

Charlie walked back quickly along the road from Rosemount Terrace. He was trembling, either with the cold or excitement, which one he didn't know. He pulled his oilskin closer to him and wondered at the onset of the shaking that had hit him, as soon as the young woman had taken the flowers from his outstretched hand and had closed the front door. She had obviously been the live-in maid, unused to polite society; she would have at least expressed some kind of appreciation if she had been a member of the family.

He hoped that Lily was at that moment enjoying the smell of his mother's last precious flowers and would be effusive with her thanks next time they met. Pity it was at the expense of a pint at The Grapes at some point, but to have Lily's affection would be worth it in the end. For now, a plate of his mother's Sunday roast, the meat having been cooking slowly since she had put it in the oven before trundling off to the cemetery, was fast approaching and his stomach rumbled at the agreeable thought.

The room was dim as Charlie walked through the door of the cottage; the oil lamp shed a feeble light and the fire was reduced to a faint glow. It was obvious that Jane had taken herself off to bed, probably worn out with all the work she'd had to do. He opened the warming compartment of the cooking range and found that his mother had left a plate of beef and vegetables. Ravenously hungry, after taking off his oilskin and laying it at the foot of the stairs to be carried up later, he carved himself a hunk of bread then took a seat at the kitchen table.

His mind floated to his beloved. What would she be doing at this time of day? He imagined she would be sitting amongst her family in the parlour. He knew she had many sisters, because she had told him so one day. They would be busily engaged in all manner of ladylike pursuits; perhaps Lily liked to crochet, draw or write in her diary. She could even be writing at that moment about the flowers she had received that day. He felt happy, warm and comfortable and with a full stomach to content him, he supposed he had better take himself off to bed.

A tapping somewhere in the house, or maybe from the next cottage, brought Charlie wide-awake the next morning. It was Monday, the first day of the rest of his life as a fully-fledged worker. Today he would be walking through those shipyard gates not as an apprentice, but as a person who had been taught all there was to know about the installation and maintenance of electric equipment. Well, perhaps not everything, only what Lairds had taught him before assigning him to the development department. He had been told they were to work on something very secret there.

He could hear his mother breaking wind beyond the curtain

and courteously tiptoed out of the room, rather than bring her attention to the fact that he had heard her. It was strange that she wasn't up and moving about, but when he glanced at his fob-watch that he had left on the kitchen table the night before, he found it was only half past five. He didn't start work until eight; there was no point trying to go back to sleep again, instead he would use this quiet time wisely – light the lamp, bring the fire to a glow once more with a few choice coal bits and boil an egg for breakfast.

He put on his black trousers, part of a very smart three-piece suit that his mother had collected from the 'off the peg' tailors on Borough Road, precisely for that day when Charlie would be out of his time as an apprentice. It was another call on her purse, as she could only afford to buy it through a voucher system, paying a bit off weekly to the visiting tally-man. Checking his appearance in the mirror after a quick wash in the scullery sink, he decided he didn't need to shave as he found it hard to grow whiskers. He put on his long sleeved white shirt, with the turned back cuffs and ivory buttons, fastened the black buttons on the waistcoat that were made from the same material as his suit, then shrugged into the matching jacket. Next he donned his black leather lace-up shoes that he had polished to a mirror-like shine. Finally he slicked his fair hair down with pomade that he had purchased himself at the market. Thus suited and booted, Charlie felt ready to face the world.

Of course there was still his breakfast. Perhaps he'd been foolish to wear his suit, when it was quite possible that he could get some egg upon his waistcoat and coal dust would be a devil to brush off should the wind outside be in the wrong direction when he brought in a fresh scuttle. He glanced above, hoping that he could hear his mother moving about. When her footsteps could be heard at the top of the stairwell, it was much to Charlie's delight.

"There you are Charlie," said his mother, glancing over to where her son was attending to the oil lamp. "My, you do look smart. You certainly pay for dressing; Mary Casson would be pleased to see you in that get up."

Charlie groaned inwardly at the reference to Jane's would-be daughter-in-law, wishing she would give the subject a rest.

Jane looked tired as she shuffled around in her voluptuous, white nightie and down-at-heel shoes that she wore for slippers, before checking the water level in the kettle. "Take that nice jacket off will you, Charlie, and fill this up, then when you're done get me a scuttle full." She sat down quickly on one of the kitchen chairs, looking pale and drawn. "I don't know what's wrong with me lately. I'm just as tired when I wake up, as when I go to bed."

"You're doing too much." Charlie took the kettle to the scullery and filled it to the brim. "Now that I'll be getting a man's wage, you can start getting your feet up."

"That will be the day, son." Jane sounded bitter. "One day you'll marry and have a wife and family to keep, so I'll have to keep going to put something by for a rainy day."

"I'll probably not get married, Mam, so I'll be living here with you and taking care of you like you've looked after me since I were a nipper. There's only one girl I want to marry and if she won't have me nobody else will do."

"Get on with you, Charlie, I've told you before that Lily Griffiths isn't for the likes of you. Mary Casson is much more suitable."

"I'll have a boiled egg this morning, Mother." Charlie changed the subject, heartily sick of his mother pushing Mary in his direction. She was a nice enough young woman, but certainly not for him.

"Talking of Mary, do you think you could write a note and push it under her doorway? I might not be up to the Temple Road soiree, so could you ask her to drop in?"

"Mam," Charlie groaned. "Do I have to? It means walking all the way down to the river and it's much quicker for me to cut along by Mersey Park."

"Well, I suppose I could add it to my list of things to do this morning. Feed the hens, dig the cabbage patch over, pick the last of the sprouts, do the washing, black lead the grate and nip into the grocers to get some flour."

"Oh, all right then you win. I'll get some paper and you can tell me what to say."

Mary's dwelling could only be described as a 'hovel', certainly ready for demolition according to the town hall planners who had been asked to consider a tanker berth there. Until a place could be found to house the Casson family, they lived in squalor. It was up to a newly formed committee attached to the Birkenhead Council to find accommodation for families that were removed from the area compulsorily. Having always lived in rat-infested surroundings, where the winds from the Mersey air-conditioned the dwelling summer or winter, whether they liked it or not, the ten offspring of the union lived cheek by jowl. Mr Casson had decided he was going to be choosy about the area they were sent to. He quite fancied living in one of the larger terraced houses at the back of Hamilton Square, close to the warehouse, where he earned a pittance unloading the dray wagons that had come over from the docks at Liverpool. Until someone forcibly removed them from the place where his ancestors had lived since before William Laird created the new town of Birkenhead, he was staying put.

So when Charlie turned up that morning with the note from his mother tucked into the pocket of his new suit, Mr Casson, who was lighting a cigarette on the muddy pathway and just about to set off for work, saw red when he spotted the official looking young man about to come sneaking around his property. He was stopped in his tracks when he heard his elder daughter shrieking from the doorway. Charlie, by that time, was suspended in the air choking, whilst Mr Casson clutched at a handful of the poor lad's shirt.

"Leave 'im Father, that's my beau, me and Charlie's bin walkin' out and I won't 'ave yer treatin' 'im that way!"

"Ahh, sorry mate, I thought yer were from the council. 'Ere I'll just brush yer down, yer'll soon be right as ninepence."

Whilst Charlie fought for his breath, the man apathetically smoothed down his suit and Mary patted him hard on the back, calling her father nasty names that Charlie thought a decent young woman shouldn't even know. He was surprised that the church going Mary would speak to her father in such a way and felt distaste once he'd got his breath back and could speak again.

"I was bringing you a note from my mother, Mary. She's not very well and wondered if you would call in on her." He noticed that Mary's father was still standing there, finishing off his cigarette whilst he listened to his daughter assuring Charlie that she would go to his mother's just as soon as the pavements were aired. If Jane needed a hand with the allotment then she would help her there as well.

"So, how long 'ave yer bin walkin' out with our Mary?" Mr Casson asked in a wheedling voice, trying to make amends; this young whippersnapper looked as if he might have a bob or two.

Charlie looked nonplussed. He didn't know he was walking out with Mary Casson, in fact he had left her at the gates of Victoria Park last time he looked. "Well err…" He looked at the size of the man standing five feet ten to his five foot five and panicked – he needed to get to the shipyard in one piece that morning. It was the first day of his job for life and the manager in charge of prototypes wouldn't take it kindly if he was late. It was quite a walk to the buildings just off Princess Dock; dawn was still an hour away and the gas lampposts to light his route were few and far between in that area. Trapped, he acknowledged that he was indeed his daughter's beau, but had only just begun their courtship and regretfully he was in a bit of a hurry and must be on his way.

CHAPTER SIX

Grand-mama's letter to Lydia De Crosland was sent in the next morning's post. Not that Lily had any indication of what had been put in the correspondence, but a few days later she was summoned back to Grand-mama's sitting room again. This time there was only Mother and the elderly lady in the room, as Father had business to attend to and, really, the minor details of his daughter's sojourn to the country was women's work.

"Lydia De Crosland has invited you to stay next weekend," Grand-mama informed Lily, reading from the sheet of cream vellum writing paper that she held in her hand. "In fact, she has invited me to stay as well and on this occasion I will accept. We will be able to catch up on mutual friends we knew from our girlhood. Your mother and I have discussed the clothes that we will be taking and as it is quite short notice, we won't involve the dressmaker this time. Suffice to say a travelling outfit, your gabardine mackintosh, galoshes, something for the daytime and a change for the evening will be enough. Personal items can be packed into your reticule."

"Are you happy with these arrangements, Lily?" asked her mother gently. "You don't have to go if you prefer not to. Grand-mama can send a letter of cancellation, rather than of acceptance, should you change your mind in the next few days."

"Hurrumph." Grand-mama didn't seem to agree with her daughter's sentiments and her face took on a sour look. "If Lily wishes to marry into a better class of family than you did, Hannah, then this is her chance to do so. Opportunities such as this don't come along very often. It is her chance to better herself and move in the best of circles."

"If you say so, Mother, but she *is* only eighteen."

"Fiddlesticks, I was only eighteen when I married your father and a better marriage there has never been."

"Yes, Mother." Hannah Griffiths didn't continue to argue, as her mother already had experience of marriage arrangements; she had introduced Patricia to her wealthy husband, whose seat was the rambling Montgomery Hall. Her mother's circle of friends was extensive and she had to admit that she had never heard a cross word between her parents at all.

"I am very happy that you have taken the trouble to do this for me, Grand-mama. I am pleased that you will be coming with me too, as I would feel a little nervous if I had to meet Mrs De Crosland on my own. I will look forward to it, Grand-mama. Do not worry Mother, I am sure that once into the New Year, I will be announcing *my* betrothal too."

She couldn't wait to announce her trip to the rest of her family; Bertha was in the kitchen as usual preparing their evening meal and Ellen was brushing down the yard outside, where an overhanging tree from the small garden next door had shed its leaves. Both sisters were generous with their good wishes once they had appraised the situation, but there was just a hint of envy in Ellen's eyes. Henrietta, when she came back with Father from the office mourned the fact that three of the Griffiths girls were getting wed and the family was dispersing even more.

Mabel, however, was inclined to recommend caution as she sat on Lily's bed that evening, listening to her excited sister outlining her future plans from the minute she was to set her eyes on Roland, until the day she walked down the aisle. "You might not even like him, Lily. He could be coarse and vulgar. Spending time with other men in his regiment, he won't know much about female things."

"Then I'll teach him and I don't know much about men things either. I only know Father and Frederick, so we'll both have to learn together, won't we?"

"What if he decides that you are not suitable? Perhaps he has his eye on somebody else and hasn't told his mother."

"Then I will have had a very nice weekend staying with Grand-mama in pleasant surroundings and someone else will have to be found for me. Anyway, he won't be there. According to Grand-mama, he is still bound for Liverpool on a troopship."

"I marvel at your pragmatic outlook on this situation, Lily. I knew that you were sweet on Lawrence, so it must hurt that you may well be settling for second best."

"Lawrence will always be my heart's desire, Mabel, even if he is to marry Bertha. But as I can't have him, I will have to force myself to consider someone else."

And lucky she is to have the choice, thought Mabel miserably, as she walked along the landing to her bedroom, to lie on her bed and brood on what might have been if she hadn't been consigned by the actions of her uncle to spinsterhood. Even now she could remember in detail that terrible day when she had walked along the first floor corridor at Montgomery Hall to her bedroom, feeling weary from the furious game of tennis she had just been playing with her cousins and looking forward to a long soak in the bath. She had been at the peak of womanhood; her breasts straining against the bodice of her white pleated tennis dress, her shapely calves and ankles peeping becomingly below the daring hemline and her pretty face glowing with exertion from the game.

Her heart had skipped a startled beat when her uncle, dressed in a navy padded dressing gown and matching leather slippers, came out of one of the bedrooms as she began to pass the door.

"Ah, Mabel," he had said in a silken voice, his rat-like face peering out from a profusion of greying whiskers, his breath reeking of brandy or some other spirit, which caused her to recoil. "I wonder if you could do your old uncle a big favour? I have a problem that perhaps you can help me with. Come in here, dear, and I'll explain."

Looking back, even then she'd had her misgivings, thinking it wasn't right to enter a bedroom on her own with a man, even if he was related. However, being an obedient girl and not liking to upset her uncle by her refusal to help in any way she could, she had meekly followed him.

What had happened next had become locked away in a mind full of mortification. She had never seen a man's appendage, never mind being told to grip the thing and give it a good pumping. Her uncle had sat on the edge of the bed with a very queer look on his face, flopping back a few minutes into the deed, after clutching at the sweaty thing whilst it erupted with some sort of evil smelling liquid. This had given Mabel her chance, mesmerised by the whole distasteful situation, to run from the room and sit shaking in her quarters until Aunt Patricia had come knocking on her door.

Fearing that her niece had suffered from some sort of brain fever, as Mabel could only tremble and quake and make no sense in her ramblings, her aunt, on the advice of her now serene looking husband, had called for their driver to take her back home. Grand-mama was bound to get to the bottom of whatever was ailing the girl and could arrange for the family doctor to call. It was all a blur, after a scandalised Grand-mama realised that if she took the side of the gibbering girl there would be a rift in the family. Poor Patricia had enough being married to the boar without having this to add to his list of indiscretions, so she had arranged for Mabel to stay for a while at a place which took in distressed females, though the family was told she was attending an academy. There Mabel had met a kindly lady, who after listening sympathetically to the awful tale and encouraging her to reveal what the horrid uncle had got her to do, was told to try to banish all her troubling thoughts. Mulling over those feelings of disgust and shame would be like picking at a horrible sore, but it had left Mabel with a strong loathing of all things male.

Wearing her best blue travelling outfit and a matching saucer-shaped hat, Lily was helped into the hire carriage by her father on the following Saturday. Grand-mama was already sitting in the black barouche, looking even more like Queen Victoria in her black widow's weeds, with a small veil hiding her face from any onlooker.

"I've given the address to the driver and negotiated a fair price,"

Mannion explained through the open window to his mother-in-law. "He will collect you on Monday morning at half past nine. Bring your bill to the office, Tommy, and get one of the clerks to pay you."

The driver saluted his assent, flicked the whip lightly across the bay in the harness and with Lily blowing kisses to her parents, sisters and anyone else who may be watching on the pavement, the carriage set off.

"Do sit down properly, Lily." Grand-mama glared in her direction, as Lily wobbled against the black, leather upholstered seat after the carriage began to sway. "Concentrate on the reason we are undertaking this journey and act with a little decorum."

"Is Greasby far away?"

"I imagine it is about six miles away, considering that when I stayed at Arrowe Hall, Greasby was a short walk through the grounds and along a country lane. Not that I ever visited the place myself, as we attended the Holy Cross at Woodchurch."

"I can't wait to get there. I do hope that Mrs De Crosland likes me and I can live there forever."

"I'm sure you and Lydia will get on very well, Lily. According to Millicent Broster, there was a daughter, probably a similar age to you when she died."

"Oh." Lily wasn't sure she wanted to hear this information. The thought of death always made her feel shivery, as if someone had just walked on her grave. She lapsed into silence, noticing that the narrow streets of Birkenhead were giving way to the occasional row of whitewashed cottages. There was a tavern standing at a crossroads; gates leading up a track to a red brick-built farmhouse and acres of stubble-bound fields, the stalks left over from the oats or hay crop still visible.

"Is it far away now?" Lily was getting rather bored looking at the vast farmlands and the small copses of woodland that appeared over the hedge-lined roadway.

"If my memory serves me correctly, we should see the gates of Arrowe Park in a few minutes after we have climbed this hill. The hall there is owned by the Shaw family and in my day John Ralph Shaw was the lord of the manor, but of course nowadays it is the county council that holds the balance of power."

"Oh", said Lily, watching a man shoving the last of a herd of cows down a narrow lane, their destination no doubt a milking shed. "Do you think we will be there for luncheon? My stomach is rumbling."

Brookvale was in a hollow, halfway along the Arrowe Brook Lane. High wooden gates and bushes of rhododendron hid the dwelling from view. Across the lane was a low, whitewashed farmhouse and the approach of the horse and carriage had set the geese in the yard cackling. A dog barked, adding to the cacophony and an irate man dressed in a stained white smock, gaiters over his brown corduroy trousers and heavy boots came ambling across to speak to their driver.

"Bin up since afore dawn, can't a fella catch up a bit on his snoozin' without interruptions from your sort?"

'Your sort' must have applied to Lily and her Grand-mama and, seeing that the man had come out of a nearby barn, he was perhaps having a bit of a nap without the knowledge of the farmer.

"Yer've come the wrong way if yer after Greasby Hall. Turn round and take the next turning on the left and it'll tek yer through Greasby village."

"It's this place, pal, Brookvale. The fella drew me a map. Can I take the carriage in or will it be too bumpy?"

"I'd put 'em down 'ere, no sense in gettin' yer axle broken. It'll tek 'em five minutes up the track to get ter the front door."

"I say, my man," said Grand-mama, putting her head out of the window and shouting to the driver. "My son-in-law has directed you to deliver us to Brookvale. You will not be paid if you leave us at its entrance, so open the gates and get a move on."

There was a bit of muttering going on between Tommy and the farmhand, which resulted in a jolting of the carriage as the driver turned the horse and vehicle around.

"He says to leave it 'ere and 'e'll keep an eye to it." Tommy had jumped down and was talking through the window to the outraged elderly lady, whilst Lily clutched at her reticule ready for their escape.

"Are you expecting me to walk along a track with two valises and my granddaughter's portmanteau? I think not! No, you can go ahead and inquire of the lady of the house if she has some sort of conveyance to put me in. A bath chair, perhaps."

"I could get a barrow," said the farmhand, who had been hovering about listening to the exchanges with glee. "It's a bit smelly, seein' as I carry the horse muck in it, but I could put a newspaper on top."

Grand-mama ignored him and glared at the driver instead. "In the next few minutes please."

Lydia De Crosland herself came back with the driver, pushing an old battered wicker lying-chair on wheels ahead of her. Meanwhile, Grand-mama had worked herself into a frothing state, as the farmhand stood near to the carriage window chuckling to himself. Exhorting Grand-mama to take no notice of the little weasel, Lydia watched as Tommy first of all helped Lily down, then the grand-looking matriarch in her widow's weeds. The farmhand looked at her in horror then. Had he just been taking the mick out of their stately queen?

"Be off with you, Samuel, or I'll come across and see Farmer Thornton. He won't be very happy to hear you've been wasting precious daylight hours. Margaret! How many years has it been? And this must be Lily. What a beautiful name, taken from the Bible?" The lady herself was pleasant faced, with white hair that she wore in a type of a cottage loaf on top of her head. She was dressed in a dark blue tweed skirt that came down to her ankles, a pale blue knitted garment that had long, loose sleeves and a brown plaid shawl around her shoulders that had seen better days. On her feet she wore a pair of men's heavy boots with the laces tied in a knot.

She shook Lily's hand and briefly patted Grand-mama on the

shoulder, then motioned that her elderly visitor should climb into the chair, whilst the driver followed with their luggage behind. Lily found it difficult to keep her face straight, as she tiptoed behind her reclining grand-mama. How the family would smile if they could see their rather grand relative being pushed along a muddy track by a woman of a similar age!

The rutted track, which was lined with what appeared to be an endless dark forest of oak, ash and birch trees on either sides, with the sounds of twittering birds above and the scurrying of little animals in the undergrowth, caused Lily to reflect on her possible move to the countryside. There would be no more walks to the park, or to the shops on Borough Road, or even a bracing sojourn along the esplanade, if she were accepted in marriage into the De Crosland family. Here in the gloom, where trees still dripped from the last shower of rain, she would be trapped forever. Perhaps her only relief would be a trip to church on a Sunday, or a visit now and again to the bosom of her family. She would have to be very much in love with the man she may marry; waiting for his return from his forays in foreign lands may cause a lot of heartache in the end.

Then she thought of the glory, the acclaim from her doting parents, the envy from her sisters, because she, Lily Griffiths, a dreamer with no obvious talents, had managed to snare a man from a well-to-do family. A De Crosland, whose ancestors were around at the same time as the Magna Carta had been signed – that was if grand-mama was to be believed. Her spirits were high until the party rounded the corner and Brookvale Hall came into their view.

When Brookvale Hall had been built in the previous century, an earlier De Crosland (a gentleman farmer) had lavished great amounts of money on it; the seven bedroomed, red stone, ivy covered manor house. It boasted a turreted entrance porch, with the family coat of arms carved into the archway above; square, leaded windows in the gabled wings, which stood either side of the portico and two wicked looking griffins, standing guard by the thick oak doorway.

However, years of neglect from the family descendants, who

used their birthright to capitalise on the name of De Crosland, had left the place heavily mortgaged to a wealthy man in Liverpool, who had let the house fall into disrepair. The army pension from Lydia's now deceased lieutenant general husband's estate, along with a little inherited income from rented property in West Kirby (courtesy of Lydia's deceased parents), could only cover living expenses and the occasional urgent repair. The land that had been rented, part of the Arrowe Estate that had been sold in 1867 and its seasonal income from oats and wheat, along with the sale of many valuable paintings and artifacts, had soon disappeared from the family purse.

"Welcome to *chez nous*," Lydia said cheerfully, as she came to an abrupt stop by the portico, nearly causing Grand-mama to be pitched headlong. "Put the baggage over there, Driver, and then you can be off to find another fare."

Tommy, nervous now as he looked at his surroundings, was quick to do her bid, then sped off with promise of his return on Monday morning. Lily was left to wonder if she would see their driver again.

"I thought an early luncheon after such a long journey," Lydia said, as the three women walked into a large entrance hall, stone-floored and bare except for a fox head mounted on a wooden baton and staring balefully down from the whitewashed wall.

The house felt chilly, even more so when they stepped into a large, oak-floored room, sparsely furnished with a heavy oak table, its legs carved with figures carrying baskets of fruit or flowers and under which were plain oak chairs, upholstered in faded red velvet. The stone chimney piece with its ornate over-mantel lay ready for the mistress of the house to set a match to the slow burning kindling, though it looked as if the well swept black marble interior hadn't been used overmuch.

"We tend to live in the kitchen," Lydia remarked to her guests, as she lead the way through to another door that was set into light oak paneling, which lined the robust looking walls. "To tell the truth, since I had to let my live-in maid go I like to be where it is warm and comfortable, so I only light a fire in here when it's of necessity. Of course, I still have a daily woman who comes in to help me, so do come through the both of you as she has made us a light lunch."

Grand-mama looked dismayed. Mannion wouldn't be at all pleased when he heard that they had been on a wild goose chase that weekend. According to Millicent Broster, the De Crosland family were well heeled and from a very good background. Grand-mama made her mind up to never speak to Millicent again. *Good gracious*, she thought, as she stared at the stone flagged floor, the wooden bench seat that lined one of the whitewashed walls in the kitchen, the old fashioned rectangular table in front of it and the fire grate. From the large black kettle and the blackened stone pot beside it on the hearth, it looked as if the cooking was still done as if they were in an earlier century. At Rosemount Terrace, the cooking was done on a modern range with compartments for plate warming and the proofing of bread.

"Do sit down, Margaret, Lily," Lydia said, not attempting to take their outer garments, although there were glowing embers in the grate, keeping the room quite cosy. "I'll just bring the kettle back to the boil. I take it that you would both enjoy a warming cup of tea? Then we can settle down to our luncheon. The ham and cheese is from Thornton Farm across the way."

On platters – not china plates as they had at Rosemount – lay thin slices of bread, portions of yellow, crumbly cheese and slivers carved from a small leg of ham on a silver salver, which was still on display at a nearby oak buffet. A small stone jar, that on investigation held brown chutney of unidentifiable ingredients, was the only relish on offer.

"A bit last century, compared to a Victorian built house in the Rock Ferry area, which you have I hear?" Lydia said ruefully, once they had all helped themselves to food that was really quite delicious. "I can see from your face, Margaret, that you were expecting something more lavish, considering that the house was built by a wealthy family. Unfortunately, Brookvale has been let down by a few descendants whose only concern was spending their inheritance on frivolity. Inept management and the repeal of the Corn Laws, which has allowed foreign wheat to come in, has also added to the family's misfortunes."

Grand-mama had the grace to look a little sheepish at Lydia's words and Lily reddened slightly, as she suddenly worried that instead of perhaps a privy in the yard, she might have to go searching for a midden when she needed to pass water. Was this really what she wanted, to be buried in the countryside in a residence which was poor and in need of much repair and restoration?

"Of course, with a little money spent on restoring the place to its former glory," Lydia went on to explain, "many more generations could enjoy its position and history." Hadn't she been saying just that to Roland, before he had sailed off with his battalion to some heathen land many miles away called Burma? He was there to keep the peace and keep the trade routes open, as the French were threatening the British monopoly on teak.

Roland had been adamant for many years that he wasn't going to supply an heir for the continuation of the De Crosland family, but with his mother's pleading ringing in his ears every time he came home from another foreign foray, he had weakened. Now that his father had died at the hands of a vengeful Zulu some twelve years before (although he hadn't actually been fighting, he had been sitting directing operations in the officers tent), his mother was alone for many months on end. This time it had been for two long years and she wasn't getting younger, though it had to be said she was a tough old bird. He had written in his last letter from Yangon that, as he would be boarding a ship early that September, perhaps she could find a willing candidate from an exemplary background.

Lily Griffiths would not be chosen for her exemplary background, Lydia thought, as she watched the girl delicately dabbing her mouth with one of the monogrammed De Crosland napkins that Lydia had been able to keep a hold of. No, it was the thought of her wealthy background that made a marriage to her son so attractive. Margaret Patterson's husband had left his wife an inheritance that was not to be sniffed at, according to the gossipmongers. Some land, a couple of houses, a thriving business in coal provision and it was rumoured that she had a son-in-law who had his fingers in lots of pies. This could only improve Lily's attractiveness.

Not that she was a plain girl; she was sure that Roland would be proud to walk such a pretty bride down the church aisle. The question was how to tempt this girl to live a life of loneliness, deprived of all the luxurious things she was used to and her only companion a mother-in-law. Outings would be a trip to Birkenhead market if they could persuade William Thornton to give them a lift in his cart, or a long walk through the lanes to the villages of Irby or Greasby.

"I've some cake that you might like to try," she said, seeing that her guests had drunk the tea that she had provided from an earthenware teapot, which she had purchased recently from the market. "It is freshly made and I can spread some delicious damson jam upon it. The damsons are from our local trees, then perhaps when we have finished you would like to be shown to your bed chambers. We've closed the ones in the far wing, but the one's in use are nice and dry."

The two rooms that had been allocated to Lily and her grandmother were small, but perhaps just as well that they each only held a light oak wardrobe, a wooden bed consisting of a carved bed head and foot panel and a matching oak chest. There was nothing to be gained by their choice of room, as they were both identical. Lily, however, saw that one of the rooms overlooked an orchard and a small vegetable patch, though beyond stood a thicket that looked dark and gloomy.

Grand-mama asked if Lydia would find it impolite if she was to rest for a while; the journey had been quite long and she wasn't used to rising as she'd had to do so early that morning. So Lily and her prospective mother-in-law sat back in the kitchen and drank another cup of tea.

"I had a daughter who would be much the same age as you are," Lydia confided sadly. "We were the best of friends, although not at the end when she took it into her head to run off with the local school teacher…"

"I had heard from Grand-mama that your daughter was dead?" Lily couldn't stop herself from saying, although she knew that she might be causing her hostess some pain with her outburst.

"A rumour put out by my husband, Lily, and a confidence that I hope you won't share with anyone else if you are to become a member of the De Crosland family."

"Oh, does that mean you have decided that I am suitable?" Lily's voice rose with excitement at the thought, although later there would be a few misgivings.

"I think so Lily, and I am certain that Roland will think so too."

CHAPTER SEVEN

It was around lunchtime when a tapping on the office window caused Charlie to look up from his desk in surprise. It was Mary and how she had got past the man who sat by the shipyard gate, employed to ensure that the secrets of the drawing office didn't get into the hands of the public, was beyond him. *It was lucky that the building was single storey*, thought Charlie inconsequentially, as he asked his supervisor if he was allowed to speak to the woman who seemed a bit distraught. Perhaps his mother needed him to run an errand for her later, or perhaps she had sent him a little lunch; a sandwich or a piece of cake. He had forgotten to bring his carryout and had left it on the kitchen table.

"Your mother needs yer," Mary said breathlessly, her long hair all over the place and her face all ruddy, as once the outer door had been opened carefully it tended to blow of its hinges if there was a ferocious wind. "I found 'er face down in 'er vegetable patch when I went to see why she wanted ter speak with me. I ran as fast as I could down ter that St. Caths place and they sent somebody up ter see ter 'er."

Mr Hammond, the office supervisor, nodded, as he had stood at the back of Charlie listening to the woman's business. "Couldn't have happened at a worse time, Charles, but listening to the circumstances, I'll make an exception."

By this time Charlie couldn't have cared less if he had been sacked on the spot for not continuing with studying the drawings of the proposed underwater submersible, a project beginning to take shape in a large shed nearby. His mother's health was much more important in the scheme of things. Automatically tidying his desk and covering over the plans he had been looking at, he shrugged into his overcoat and promised that he would be back to his employment as soon as he could.

"Get your girl to make you a strong cup of tea at the next opportunity," said the affable manager, full of sympathy when he saw the sudden pallor on his staff member's face. Charlie just nodded, then fell in step with Mary, who was in a great hurry to be somewhere else it seemed.

"She's been working too hard," Charlie said, feeling short winded as there was a bit of an incline, but making an effort to keep up with Mary, who was pounding along the street as if her life depended on it. "I feel bad that it's come to this, when I could have given her a bit more of a hand."

"She wouldn't 'ave took it, yer know 'ow independent she were. The man at the 'ospital said it were 'er 'eart."

Charlie stopped in his tracks at Mary's words. "What do you mean it 'was' her heart? Are you telling me she's a goner? I thought you'd come to tell me that they had taken her to the hospital at St. Caths?"

"Yeah, the mortuary at St. Caths! Oh, Charlie…" Mary grabbed him around his shoulders and drew his slight body to her, her voice trembling with emotion. "Oh, come 'ere, love. I'll stop with yer, I'll 'elp yer through it, if yer'll let me."

For a moment he was touched that she cared so much and responded to her like a child wanting to be held in the warm embrace of its mother. Then he pushed her from him and ran.

It was a chilly day when Jane Elizabeth Wilson, née Oakes, was buried at the very cemetery that she had sat outside the gates of whilst selling her bunches of flowers. Charlie had been inconsolable when he arrived at St. Catherines, blaming himself for her early demise and sad that when at last he was able to give her his proper wages, she wasn't there to enjoy a few little luxuries. Mary had been constantly at his side, guiding him through the bureaucracy concerned with laying a loved one to rest, making sure he was eating and listening to his tearful tales of Janey's love for her son.

Mary was a practical girl but she could also see an opportunity when one came along. Knowing that she was no beauty, but could cook and care for children, which most men of that time would think were attributes in a wife, she tried to make herself indispensable to her friend's bereft son. Although she knew that the gossipmongers would have a field day, she installed herself on the sofa at night time, telling Charlie that he only had to call and she would be there for him. Not that Charlie ever took her literally, but in the grief filled world he found himself in he didn't question her presence, relying on her for food and more. It was Mary who had contacted the Co-operative Undertakers, although once done there was little more she had to do. Now was the time when friends from Jane's various employments, a few neighbours and Mr Bryson, the minister who had conducted her funeral, all crammed into the tiny cottage room, ready to partake of the post funeral spread.

A late edition to the invited guests was Mary's mother, a large woman with a body of strange proportions. Her notably pendulous breasts seemed to overflow under the waist of the voluminous skirt, which she wore with a cream blouse and a long sleeved navy jacket. As she handed around the sandwiches that she had helped Mary make earlier along with the slices of currant cake that Mary had purchased from the bakers, it was noted that it wouldn't be long before Mrs Casson was in need of a pair of false teeth.

A surprise visitor, who had made an appearance at the side of Jane's graveside, was Alf Hewitt. Word had got around quickly in the small community and later, after he had shaken Charlie's hand and whispered words of condolence, he had taken a plate and a couple of sandwiches from Mrs Casson and had situated himself by the front door. The minister, who was taking his fill of the funeral spread and had just accepted a cup of tea from the teapot that Mary was holding, spotted a possible candidate for the future attendance of his chapel and wandered over to speak to him.

Charlie listened dully to the muted conversation between the two men from where he sat on the nearby sofa, nodding in agreement to himself when the minister mouthed words of commiseration to the family friend. It was only when the name of James Wilson, husband of the deceased came floating passed his ears, that he paid attention. James Wilson, the father who had drowned whilst crossing the Mersey River in a ferry boat called *Gem*, according to Alf Hewitt, was still very much alive!

"Going to confession is a great cleanser of the soul," Alf was saying to the minister. "I was able to square my part in the whole chicanery, that's why I don't bother with you lot anymore."

Charlie looked aghast, as the minister, taking Alf's words as a monumental insult and no doubt secretly thinking that this sinner should be in hell, moved away. Charlie shot up from the sofa and, to the surprise of the other mourners, grabbed Alf by the arm and asked if he could speak to him outside. Alf was just as surprised, as he put down his plate on the windowsill and the two men walked out onto the pavement.

"Do you think that there's something the matter with my hearing?" Charlie asked in a voice full of sarcasm, because he didn't want to believe that whatever he was going to be told next wasn't going to be to his liking.

"Ah, about your father." Alf looked guilty and endeavored to move away a little, in case Charlie got handy with a couple of punches. "She meant to tell yer. Many a time I asked if she had got round to doin' it, but she said what yer didn't know wouldn't hurt yer."

"So tell me now," Charlie said through clenched teeth, wondering why the hell his mother would pretend she was a widow, struggling to get by on what little she could earn, when all the time there was still a husband in the background.

"She thought it was best that you were in the dark. You didn't really remember 'im as 'e was away at sea a lot and it was easy to make up a story when the *Gem* 'ad just collided mid-river and men were swept out to sea. It was yer parents' way of throwing the towel in, without resorting to divorce or a church annulment."

"Yes, I remember the shouting and the bickering and I even

72

heard my mother throwing a pan against a wall one day." Strangely enough this revelation wasn't such a shock as Charlie thought it would have been.

"That would be 'is dinner." Alf tried to make light of the situation. "They were chalk and cheese, your parents. If they 'adn't of done summat about it, one of them would have ended up swingin' on a rope at Walton Jail."

"That bad?" Charlie found it hard to imagine his mother getting in such a temper that she would have gone so far.

"Fraid so. Anyway, if yer ever want ter see yer dad, I 'ave 'is address and you could look 'im up. 'E lives in Wallasey now."

"I don't think I would want to be in touch with him now, Alf. I've done without him all these years and he's never put himself out to see me. Even Aunt Emily used to walk past my mother with her nose in the air."

"Ah well, that's up ter you, Charlie. I've kept him up ter snuff on what yer were up to, but 'e 'as another family now and 'e gave up the sea after 'is supposed drownin'."

"Bully for him. Anyway, I think we should get back to the reason we're all gathered together; Poor Mother, God rest her soul. Perhaps we'll raise a glass to the eccentricities of life and to the living."

They were all there, the mourners of a fine woman's passing and Charlie noticed, as he walked back into the dwelling with shoulders hunched and a solemn look on his face, that each person was holding a glass in their hand. They were his mother's gold-rimmed sherry glasses, a wedding present from someone or other all those years ago. It hit him just at that moment that he hadn't even considered informing the Lancashire side of Jane's family, then corrected that thought, as he didn't even know where she had lived. It seemed that his mother was adept at keeping secrets. Now, having been given the knowledge that his father hadn't been assigned to a watery grave, he wondered if her family were really buried somewhere in the countryside near Blackpool. Charlie hoped that there weren't any more skeletons to be revealed to him that day, besides wondering who had provided the bottle of sherry.

When Mr Bryson, the minister of the Weslyan Church that he and Mary attended, asked for everyone to raise their glass to the life of an exemplary woman, a wonderful mother who would have been very happy had she heard the news of her son's intended marriage to Miss Casson, Charlie shrugged his shoulders mentally and helped himself to a glass. Who was he to change the course of his destiny? His mother was gone, his beloved had turned her nose up at him and Mary seemed very eager to become his wife!

To say that the problems in Charlie and Mary's marriage could be laid squarely on the trouble they had in the bedroom department would be an understatement. Perhaps they could have eventually worked on them, at least to one person's satisfaction; however, it was Mary's lack of education and her tendency to fill the small cottage with her mother and as many of her small noisy siblings as she could find a place for that caused Charlie to wish that he had the gumption to sail the seven seas and eventually jump ship! He began to stay longer at work each day, his admiring office manager praising his dedication to the other staff, causing them to steer clear of the little upstart and sending him to Coventry. The Grapes welcomed a regular evening visitor, as the bar became supporter of another inebriated soul. Weekends saw Charlie with his notebook down by the landing stage, avidly recording the comings and goings of the world's shipping trade.

It was Mr Bryson who brought Charlie's attention to the state of his marriage, having noticed after five weeks of non-attendance at his church services that neither of the couple had put in an appearance. Charlie had been one of the most dedicated people in his flock and he had thought when he was marrying them that it was the starkest wedding he had ever officiated at, given that Charlie didn't even have a groomsman and the bride wasn't wearing a pretty long dress and veil.

He decided, in his capacity of being God's instrument, to call upon the cottage. Perhaps the couple felt there was no need for an hour's uplifting in the house of God on a Sunday morning, when they were happy to have a lie in bed instead!

Charlie had his notebook in readiness at the kitchen table, a sharpened pencil residing in the inner pocket of his jacket and was making himself an egg sandwich to eat before setting off down to the river. Mary had withdrawn all aspects of wifely servitude including feeding him, until he began to show her some affection in their bed. It was a lovely day, warm for April and she had taken some of her siblings to the park. Charlie was wary when he saw who was standing on the doorstep. It wasn't as if he was a Catholic, when the priest would automatically come calling to round up his missing few. "Why, Mr Bryson! What a surprise to see you. Do come in, is there anything I can do for you?" He decided on politeness. After all, the man was only doing his job by checking up on the welfare of one of the members of his flock.

"We've missed you Charlie and I wondered if there was a problem I could help you with? Not that I could help you with anything... erm... you know... to do with matrimony... as you know I have never had the pleasure of having a wife, but something else perhaps?"

"I will make you a cup of tea then, Minister, seeing as you've taken the trouble to call. I was about to eat a sandwich and Mary has gone to the park with some of her younger sisters and brothers." Charlie walked on ahead to the kitchen, his face set in grim resignation that he might be missing out on some vital moment in the river's history.

"Ah Mary," the minister said quietly, whilst settling himself on a dirty blanket that Charlie had thrown over the sofa, in an effort to stop the children wrecking it whilst using it as a jumping board. "How are you and Mary? If you don't mind me saying so, I was surprised when Mrs Casson announced that you and Mary were to wed, especially as you had only just buried your poor mother. But besides that, it didn't seem to me that your marriage had been made in heaven. Chalk and cheese, the both of you."

Charlie's answer sounded muffled, given that he was over by the kettle bringing it back to boil for the minister.

Encouraged, the man carried on. "Yes, I was very surprised, you being employed by Lairds in their offices and Mary waiting on for a living; you being an only child and Mary one of a big family; you living in this very nice cottage and Mary living in what I can only describe as a slum. Such differences, Charlie; marriage is for the rest of your life!"

Charlie felt like crying as he passed over the man's cup of tea, trying to stop his hand from shaking and slopping the hot liquid into the saucer. It was the last of Jane's saucers from a tea set that she had managed to buy through a voucher system, as the children had smashed most of the others. How could he tell this well-meaning man, innocent of the ways of women, how much he regretted not standing firm and telling him on that fateful day of his mother's funeral that the announcement of his betrothal was incorrect and he wouldn't touch Mary with a barge pole?

She was ignorant, loudmouthed, cruel when the drink was upon her and a slut in the bedroom. He could show the man the bruises around his stomach and genitals, where she had lashed out in frustration at his inability to get 'his end up'. He could tell him of the time she had ripped up his notebooks when she had gone through his father's sea chest, laughing as she watched the flames of the fire licking around those dedicated hours of noting down the shipping activity on the Mersey. Later, she had mockingly stumbled over the words of one of his love poems, calling him a weakling.

It was true, he had conceded at the time; he didn't have the gumption, or was it the inclination, to stand up to her. Though if truth was told, wouldn't that make him as bad as Ernie Morris? So he had put up with the pain from the Chinese burn she'd inflicted when he was slow in tipping up his wages one payday, turning a deaf ear to the ribald remarks about his sexual ability made by his wife's 'know it all' mother. Where was this God that the man before him had extolled on a weekly basis, he wondered? Had he been such a sinner that the omnipotent being seriously had it in for him? The thought of being wed for life caused his bowels to turn to water. He'd only been wed for a mere five weeks, so how was going to cope with a lifetime?

But he said none of this to the man sipping at his cup of tea, no doubt thinking that Charlie hadn't made a good job of it, considering he hadn't used the tea strainer, nor had asked if his guest took sugar. What was the point? Talking about his problems wasn't going to make them disappear and admitting that he was a henpecked husband wasn't going to help his self-esteem.

On reflection, it was probably his fault when he thought back to that first night spent together after they'd been married. Mary had taken down the curtain that separated his and his mother's sleeping area, putting the two narrow beds together, as there was no money to spare on buying a bigger bed. She had spent the last of the insurance money from Jane's death policy on a fancy bed cover, no doubt wanting the bedroom to look nice for their first married night, but he hadn't cottoned on to that. She had made them a simple meal of toast and some fried bacon then gone upstairs to dress herself in a faded calico nightdress, whilst he had his head in one of his books on the sofa.

He wasn't tired and innocently told her so, then wondered why she had tamped down the fire with a shovel of slack and flounced back up the stairs to bed? Perhaps she thought she was going to be lonely, given that she was used to her siblings hanging from picture rails all over the place and wanted his presence in the bedroom. He had followed her reluctantly, taking his book, having the intention of reading by the light of the oil lamp as he usually did. But after he had got into bed, still wearing his socks and his undergarments, he was very surprised to have his book snatched away.

He had thought that she was probably tired and the light from the oil lamp was going to prevent her from going to sleep. It had been a long day, starting with the very simple ceremony at the chapel, after which she and her mother had been busy cutting sandwiches in Charlie's house. Then they had what his new father-in-law had called 'a piss up', when most of the regulars, including Ernie Morris, from the taproom of The Grapes had filled the small cottage and helped to demolish a barrel of ale. So it came as a bit of a surprise to Charlie when he was forcibly made to lie down in his bed, as his new wife was now astride him. He felt the buttons of his long johns being opened by impatient fingers, at the same time as enduring her sherry ridden breath as she clamped her mouth onto his, making him gag at the sickly smell. He hadn't realised that this was the kind of thing that went on between a woman and her husband.

In his dreams, which were usually full of marrying Lily, they had lay together holding hands, whilst shafts of moonlight showed through a crack in the bedroom curtains and they would talk of the pretty babies that would be the result of their union. Lily would drift off to sleep after accepting his affectionate kisses, then somehow, because of something, he wasn't sure what, a baby would start to grow in his beloved's tummy.

This woman, this wild woman who seemed to have abandoned any sort of decorum by trying to make him behave as if they were animals in the jungle, hadn't been wearing any underwear! Charlie had found that quite distasteful, after he had managed to push her off him and saw that she had hauled her calico bed gown to the top of her ample thighs. To cap it all, his senses told him that he was about to have a nose bleed and so, trying not to listen to the obscenities that began to flow from the mouth of this harpy who was supposedly his wife, he had jumped from the bed and fled from the room.

When he had dashed down the stairs to the scullery and found that he was indeed dripping with blood, he had felt too scared to go back to the marital bed in case of repercussions. Instead he had spent the night on the sofa, trembling with emotion at first, whilst trying to understand why his wife had turned from gentle Mary to some sort of voracious lion. She appeared to have been versed in some kind of carnal knowledge, when she should have been as inexperienced in bed as he. While his clothing dried and he took slight comfort from the warmth of his overcoat, still wary of her descent down the stairs and finding it difficult to sleep, Charlie came to the conclusion that he didn't know very much about women. He knew that they didn't have a willy like he did, because he had once seen his mother without any clothes on, when he had thoughtlessly gone into her side of the bedroom one cold morning hoping for a maternal cuddle. He had also listened to smutty comments made by ignorant boys in the classroom, when a teacher, at the end of his tether with a backward child, had put them together in the hope that some of Charlie's intelligence would rub off on the little soul. Together with various sightings of local mongrels on the backs of hapless bitches in the park and Ernie's crude conversations in the pub, Charlie was persuaded that – unlike his dreams of romantic aspirations and the purity of his love for Lily Griffiths – the disagreeable reality of his union with Mary was something he was going to have to overcome.

CHAPTER EIGHT

The wedding of Lily Griffiths and Roland De Crosland was the most talked about subject in every refined drawing room for weeks after the event. How had a coal agent's daughter, though a well educated one it had to be said, managed to ensnare a man of Second Lieutenant De Crosland's standing? The reception, after the ceremony at St. Peters, had been held at the banqueting room in the newly built town hall. Not many well-to-do families could boast of that, though a lot of the town hall dignitaries *had* been on the guest list.

It had been a fine day in June 1894 when Lily, dressed in a cream satin, floor length gown with an overlay of cream flower lace, a small puddle train and a short veil pinned down in her shoulder length hair by an ivory tiara, came down the church aisle on the arm of her proud father, followed by two little nieces dressed as flower girls. Roland, a handsome man, tall and standing erect in his dress uniform with a face bronzed by the hot sun of the tropics and, underneath his helmet, sporting fair hair cut in a soldierly fashion, waited almost nonchalantly, as if this kind of occurrence happened every day. No nerves it seemed for the bridegroom, but Lily's hand trembled as she carried her long trailing bouquet of Madonna lilies.

That fateful weekend in December had sealed her future in a way that she could never have expected. She got on very well with Lydia and, after her initial concerns regarding being buried deep into the countryside, she had been agreeably surprised with her rural surroundings, after she and her prospective mother-in-law had gone out for a walk next day. Grand-mama, scorning the offer of being pushed along the lane in the bath chair, was left behind as the two women walked towards the crossroads.

"Not a lot has changed around here since I came to Brookvale as a bride," Lydia remarked, as they wandered along the narrow lane with its neatly trimmed hedges. "The farmhouse and buildings over there are on land which extends to the border of Greasby and Irby, both places being country villages with the usual tavern and manorial halls. The Thorntons', who have the farm opposite to Brookvale, are a nice family, consisting of four daughters and two sons. Martha, the second eldest, was especially close to Roland when they were children."

But not a rival for Roland's affections, I hope, thought Lily, skirting a large muddy puddle that lay in the rutted lane.

"They're doing some repairs at the moment – replacing a few roofing slates, putting in a drain that will run into the brook and building a new privy. Farmer Thornton must be getting a good price for his crops if he can afford all that."

Lily nodded, not liking to remark on the fact that the exterior water closet at Brookvale needed some modernisation too, given that she'd had to come to grips with the sensitive tippler system, which was liable to drown one's bottom if water came surging from the scullery at the same time as one was doing what came naturally. At Rosemount, Mannion had installed a ceramic flushing toilet, commonly known as 'Grand-mama's throne'.

"And if you look over there, see? Stand on that hummock you'll see better – in the distance you can see the Irish Sea."

It was definitely the walk with Lydia that day that influenced the decision on her future. She and her prospective mother-in-law had got on well too, especially when Lydia had said that Lily would perhaps become a replacement in her affections for the daughter, who had brought shame on the De Crosland family by falling in love with a man who was socially beneath her. She hadn't gone into detail, though her voice had sounded thick with emotion and Lily was left to think that it wouldn't have been of Lydia's choosing to have an estranged daughter, rather her husband's. Being high up in the army, he would have stringent views on what his daughter had done.

The surrounding area was beautiful with extensive farmland,

deep forests, babbling brooks and tidy-looking farmhouses. If Brookvale was falling into disrepair, what of it? Her father had been tardy in finding her a wealthy man, Lawrence had betrayed her and although the De Croslands may not live up to Mannion's expectations financially, he would be overwhelmed by their position in life. She could sense his pride, as he slowly walked her up the aisle, nodding to the many guests who were looking over.

She had only met the man she was to marry twice; the first time was on the Monday morning as they were about to leave. Whilst thanking Lydia for her hospitality and wishing her a pleasant Christmas with her homecoming son, the man himself had arrived. Dressed in mufti, a perfectly tailored suit and hat, as befitted a Victorian gentleman, having changed out of his uniform at headquarters earlier, he had arrived in a hired hansom cab, travelling from the Thurstaston railway station a few miles away.

Lily had been overwhelmed in his presence. Suffice to say, Lawrence had become a mere shadow in the background when she had first set her eyes on this prepossessing man. The hand that was outstretched to Lily, after he had solemnly told her grand-mama that he was very pleased to make her acquaintance, was firm and his voice was perfectly modulated, given that he had attended a prestigious Cheshire school, courtesy of his maternal grandparents.

His clean-shaven, flawless face, save for a dark blemish on his left cheekbone, had looked with interest on his mother's guests as they were being introduced, no doubt noting the leather valises and portmanteau as a sign that these women were not penniless. The younger female must have been a candidate for his hand in marriage, whom his mother had hoped would impress.

"So very pleased to meet you, Lily," he had said charmingly, looking into her eyes as if she was the only person in the vicinity. "I trust you enjoyed your weekend here at Brookvale with Mama and agree that it is in a beautiful place?"

"Oh, yes, sir," Lily fluttered nervously. "Your mama has been very kind and showed me some of the area yesterday. We also went to worship at the local parish church."

"And thus said, we must be away," said Grand-mama, the jury still out on whether she was going to allow her granddaughter to live in such a depressing place. She had spotted Tommy, their driver, hurrying up the driveway. "Thank you for your hospitality, Lydia. It was good to catch up on all those precious years and the people who have gone on to great and good things."

"Yes, amen to that," Lydia replied, looking upon her son as if she could eat him. "Here is my soldier returned safely from foreign shores. Are you sure you can manage without the bath chair, Margaret?"

Grand-mama nodded, passing over the luggage to a breathless Tommy. He'd overslept that morning and had had to use the horsewhip on his poor old nag.

"Don't worry about me, Lydia. The rest has done me good and, if I may say so, the track doesn't look as muddy. You go in and see to Roland, you'll have a lot to talk about, I dare say."

That was the one thing that was going to spoil Lily's happy day: Grand-mama was unable to attend her nuptials. She was at that moment confined to her bed, having lost the use of her legs completely and Ellen had been chosen to keep her company. Grand-mama had been there for the betrothal meeting, though, when Roland, having pre-arranged an appointment by post with Lily's father, to discuss the possibility of an arranged marriage with his youngest daughter, had been invited on a Sunday afternoon early in the New Year for an informal discussion. Roland was to return to his army headquarters the following day, but with gentle insistence on his mother's part he had agreed that marriage to Miss Lily Griffiths was a sensible move, given that the name of De Crosland must be continued.

It was as easy as that, Lily thought, though Grand-mama had advised caution on jumping in too early with an acceptance of the proposal, because it might look as if Lily was being too eager. She drew level with her espoused and smiled a timid smile, given that she didn't know the man that she was going to spend the rest of her life with. The last few months had been a flurry of arrangements and with Roland being away on a secret mission, he hadn't got around to presenting her with an engagement ring. But apart from not having a ring to show off to her family, it had to be said that she felt extremely satisfied, as she had beaten sister Bertha up the aisle!

Mannion had paid for two nights' accommodation at the Grosvenor Hotel in Chester and so, after the lavish six course dinner for 150 guests served by scurrying waiters and waitresses, listening to repetitious toasts by well-meaning relatives and having waltzed demurely to the music of the hired five-piece band, the newly wed couple bid farewell to friends and family.

Lily had gone to the ladies room and, with the help of Harriet and Mabel, had changed into her going away outfit of a pale blue slub satin material, which had been made into a high necked, floor length bustled dress with a row of Cossack-type fastenings down the bodice. With it she wore a pair of darker blue high-heeled kid boots and a short cream cape, in case the weather turned chilly that evening.

Roland, helped by his groomsman in the gentleman's room, had also changed. He wore a grey herringbone suit with a rather swish dark blue waistcoat. His fair hair, which was inclined to be springy, was kept down with sweet smelling pomade. Their overnight valises were placed into the hansom cab, which would convey the happy couple to the nearby railway station.

It was quite eerie standing on the platform beside a man whom she didn't know, joyous wishes from the wedding guests still ringing in her ears and wearing the most splendid outfit (apart from her wedding gown) that she had ever owned. Her father had been very generous, both in the provision of a lavish day for the happy couple, a financial settlement for her husband (the details of which Lily wasn't privy) the continuation of her dress allowance and of course this sumptuous weekend at the Grosvenor Hotel.

It had been all too much, really. Lily, having spent the last few days in high-pitched excitement, plaguing any member of her family who would listen with a series of 'what ifs' and lording it over her sisters as if she was already ensconced in her manorial home, felt tears begin to prick. The man beside her had been politely respectful, showing his good manners at every twist and turn, but there hadn't been any warmth in his conduct towards her. *Did he really care?* she wondered.

According to Harriet, the sister who was to marry the clergyman, there had to be friendship and a little humour in a marriage that had to stand the test of time. Bertha had said there had to be trust, knowing that a husband loved you only and there wasn't a dusky maiden hidden on an exotic shore. Her mother had remarked on duty, especially in the marriage bed. Though her mother hadn't gone into any dutiful detail, Lily was willing to be obedient at anytime.

It was Mabel's allusion to something rather distasteful that happened between a man and woman that had Lily feeling nervous now that she was actually on her way to lying in the marriage bed. There had been hints, subtle comments and innuendoes from the sister who had a secret that she had been told not to tell. It appeared that a man had a dangly thing, which was lodged between his legs. Lily knew that because she had seen something that might have dangled between Frederick's legs once, when she had spied on him as he lay on top of his bed when they were younger, though she had been horrified to see that the dangly thing was standing to attention at the time. If Mabel was to be believed, this thing was the instrument used to create a little baby in a woman's stomach and the process that occurred in the marriage bed. When pushed by Lily to elaborate, Mabel had clammed up like a shell and rushed out of the bedroom instead.

Mother must have been very dutiful, Lily thought anxiously, *given that she has produced nine children for the Griffiths family.* She gazed up at her new husband, nervously twisting the thin, gold wedding ring around on her finger and listening to him tutting irritably, because according to his fob-watch the train that was steaming into the station was going to be two minutes late.

CHAPTER NINE

"So, guess who's wedding I attended today?" Mary said, as she arrived back from the town hall where she had been employed as a waitress for a special function.

"That girl who, according to yer mother, yer were sweet on." It was announced in a slightly aggrieved voice, as Charlie still had his head in a book when she had walked through the cottage door and hadn't even bothered to acknowledge her arrival.

"Oh." Charlie's reply was a shrug of the shoulders. It didn't do to show his wife a scrap of interest, or she'd harp upon the subject until he felt his ears were going to drop off.

"I suppose you've sat there all day doing nothing, while I've bin out workin' me fingers to the bone?"

Still Charlie said nothing. His silence was meant to irritate, but actually he had been up to the allotment, weeded between a few rows of vegetables, fed the hens after mucking out their hen house and brought back half a dozen eggs. The allotment had been kept on by Charlie, even though there were now no cut flowers being sold outside the cemetery, nor produce sold from a market stall. Even Mary, who liked to earn her own money apart from the wage of Charlie's she insisted he handed over, was loath to continue in Jane's footsteps. She liked to work at Bella's, where men from the shipyard bought their pies, lapping up the ribaldry that made her life more fun.

"I suppose yer want me to fry these up fer yer?" she said, noting the eggs that had been placed in an earthenware bowl on the kitchen table. "Yer lucky, I pinched a bit of ham. There was enough food there to feed an army. It's all right fer some, ain't it?"

"One of these days you'll get caught, Mary," Charlie said grimly, as he watched his wife bring out a heel of ham from the pocket in her apron. "It's not as if I keep you short of money that you're forced to steal from these places you work in."

He noticed her shrug of indifference, then turned back to his book while she set about cooking their supper. He had known that Lily Griffiths was to marry that day, he had seen her betrothal announced in his newspaper, but it didn't do to dwell upon it. What was the point? He had lost any chance of marriage to his beloved when he had taken Mary Casson down the aisle.

He must have asked himself a million times why he had been so stupid and let himself be persuaded into marrying her, though in hindsight he *had* been feeling numb with shock at his mother's demise. He didn't love Mary and that feeling hadn't improved as the months had gone so slowly by. She was ignorant, illiterate, crude and could be cruel in both word and deed. He had learnt to give her total deference, not wanting to stir up a hornets' nest and become the focus of her malicious tongue, but he dreamed of his escape all the while.

"Yer should 'ave seen her, Charlie. She was like Lady Muck, looking down her nose at the likes of us lot. Her shit still stinks like anyone else, so she ain't no better in my book."

Charlie nodded and moved to sit at the kitchen table as she brought his plate over. If he hadn't, he'd have been for it.

"Anyway, what about you and me 'avin' another go at this baby making? We can pretend we've just got married like that Lily has."

He flinched when Mary trapped his hand in hers as she placed his meal in front of him. "I thought you said you didn't want any children?" he stuttered. "I thought you said your mother has had enough for both of you?" His heart began to sink fast at the thought of all the shenanigans he would have to put himself through later and there would still be no satisfying her.

"I can change me mind, can't I? A little baby might just be the makings of our marriage and anyway, we've bin married six months now and me pals are thinkin' there's somethink up with yer."

"Which there is, according to you." There, it was said. He waited for an angry reaction.

"Please Charlie," she said in a wheedling voice. "Take me to bed later and give me a baby."

I'd rather walk on hot coals, he thought, remembering back to that first night when he'd had a nosebleed. He'd been flaccid and unprepared for what was to come, and for some strange reason had thought that gentle Mary would have been as innocent as him in the marriage bed and that nine months later the midwife would have brought their baby along in her medical bag. He had spent the rest of that night trembling beneath his overcoat on the sofa, after she had turned on him savagely. Still, he was having problems with his manhood, according to her.

"I could always find another man who would give me satisfaction," she said, her voice becoming full of anger at his reluctance. She rattled the dirty crockery in the scullery sink, before walking through to the kitchen to get the steaming kettle.

I wish, thought Charlie, moving back to his chair in the window quickly, in case she had any notion of scalding him out of frustration. He wouldn't put it past her, but next time she went for him, he'd pack his bags and run! In his wild imaginings, Charlie could see himself walking up the gangplank of a clipper ship at anchor over in Liverpool, then setting sail for a new life in one of the British colonies. Australia, perhaps, or maybe Canada – anywhere a million miles away from Mary.

"I'm off out later," she said, breaking into his thoughts. By this time he had got as far as imagining himself with Lily in a little cottage in the country. "Mam wants me for somethin', so see yer in bed when I get back."

Like one of your sisters or brothers, he thought bitterly, but glad of the opportunity for some time alone so that he could mull over an opportunity that had come his way that morning, via Mr Hammond, the office supervisor. The company was looking for some gallant young men to sea trial a new type of vessel up in Scotland. It would be just up his street, though he had been warned that the journey may be hazardous and the vessel could be highly dangerous, but what a chance to do something with his life! A pioneer, or an adventurer, not just plain old Charlie Wilson with a heart that beat like lead each waking moment. The prospect of being away from Mary for at least three months and becoming his own man again was very tempting.

He wouldn't tell her, he resolved, as she checked her appearance in the mirror, smoothing her hair down quickly before placing a large, navy, feather trimmed hat upon it. He would go to the shipyard, board the ship that would carry him and the other workers who had volunteered for the secret mission, jump ship in the Scottish Highlands and never be seen again. He could rent a croft from a farmer – he had a little money tucked away in his office desk that Mary wasn't aware of – then disappear like his father did, away from this soulless marriage.

Lily, who had only been married for a just a few days, was already beginning to rue her hasty decision. Roland had been a perfect gentleman, both on their honeymoon in Chester and for the few days he shared with her and his mother at Brookvale, before leaving to join his unit in the Cheshire countryside. They had enjoyed walking around the walls of Chester together and Roland had been a fountain of knowledge regarding the historical events of Roman times. The afternoon was spent sitting lazily on the banks of the River Dee, where he regaled her with tales of life in the tropics, and she'd had her first ever taste of ice cream, which they shared with two spoons from an earthenware pot. The Grosvenor Hotel, the bill footed by an indulgent Mannion, had been a place of splendor, where richly-clad ladies sauntered through the marble pillared rooms and bowing waiters served their every need.

It was the nights that were causing Lily problems. Advised by her mother to be dutiful in the marriage bed, Lily waited that first night for whatever it was she was to be dutiful about. She had worn the most beautiful white, bridal nightdress, which was cut to outline her slender body, made from satin and worn with a matching peignoir. She had brushed her hair until it shone, put a little bergamot oil on her neck and wrists, then waited in the huge canopied bed for her bridegroom.

Her heart was beating madly, as she listened to the noises of a man at his ablutions in the well-appointed adjoining bathroom. Tonight she might even make a baby, which she assumed would be the dutiful outcome of their nuptials.

How wrong was she, Lily had pondered, as she had sat with her mother-in-law in the kitchen one morning, after saying goodbye to Roland, who had set off down the driveway to meet the hire carriage that had been arranged to convey him to the train station. She had waited for the magical event that first night in the Grosvenor Hotel until her eyelids had closed, whilst lying beside a nightshirt-attired husband, who seemed to be in a state of mediation, before he said goodnight and turned away.

It had been the same when they had arrived at Brookvale. Lydia had shown Lily to the room that was to be the couple's bedroom; cosy, this time, with a warming fire, a big bed covered with a heavy white counterpane and a large cupboard taking up three quarters of the wall, in which hung her trousseau of clothes that her father had sent over by carrier. *Perhaps he was considering holy orders*, she had wondered, when each night Roland lay beside her, after saying goodnight and kissing her cheek in a friendly fashion. Or perhaps he was as ignorant as she was on how to make a child.

Lydia, brought up by parents who owned substantial property in the West Kirby area, was an earthy type of woman, more suited to being a farmer's wife than army personnel. She had met her now-deceased husband at one of the weekend parties held by members of the gentry, whose parents liked to keep an eye on their offspring under the same palatial roof. Concerned for her new daughter-in-law, as the girl was looking a little peaky and she hoped that Roland hadn't been overdoing the nuptial thing too much, she asked if the newly become Mrs De Crosland was resting enough.

"Marriage can be a great strain on a gal, initially," Lydia began, hoping she was correct in her assumptions, or this discussion that she was about to embark on would be an embarrassment to them both. "I remember when *I* first came to live at Brookvale. I wasn't sure what was expected of me; Roland's father, God rest him, was a pleasant enough man, but he was a bit of a bear in the bedroom." There, she had said it and had tried to make a joke of it. "Shall we have another cup of tea Lily, and then you can tell me what's troubling you?"

"I am sure it is nothing really, Mrs De Crosland." Lily's face was a fiery picture. "But if it isn't too much trouble and you do not mind me asking, could you explain to me how a baby is made?"

So, that was how it was done, thought Lily, as, feeling quite nauseous, she digested Lydia's detailed explanation and asked to take a walk outside, as she felt a headache coming on. Brushing aside Lydia's offer of accompanying her and quickly donning her light summer coat, she rushed down the drive as if Old Nick had been after her, intent on running all the way back to Rock Ferry if needs be. How could anyone behave in such a beastly fashion? Had her mother really had to do that nasty deed nine horrid times?

She sat on a hummock, the same one she had stood on when she and Lydia had taken their first walk together, trying to come to terms with her dilemma. If all that had been said by her mother-in-law was true, how was it that Roland hadn't tried to be a bear in the bedroom, like his father had been?

Lydia, left in the kitchen with her thoughts after Lily had pleaded a headache and had disappeared down the driveway, was in a state of confusion over her son's wedded bliss. She hadn't expected that look of horror on her daughter-in-law's face, as she had gently explained the intricacies of what went on in the marriage bed in order to make a baby. Why was it that it had been left to her to give the girl an explanation, when surely that was the role of Lily's mother or her grand-mama?

However, knowing a little of the family's history, having gleaned a bit of gossip from Millicent Broster, it was highly probable that Victorian straitlaced values had been fully embraced in Margaret Patterson's household. Her heart went out to the poor, unworldly girl faced with her son, who, being part of a battalion of voracious young men, would have most definitely known what to do with his baby maker. Though somewhere in the back of her mind there lurked a few misgivings, given that Lily hadn't an inkling of anything she had said. Was it possible that the bridal pair were innocents and even her son hadn't a clue what to do?

Lily, having wrestled with the worrying images given to her by Lydia in the hope of enlightenment, had left the grassy hummock and was determined now to face the realities of her hasty marriage, striking out for a bracing walk in the sunshine. She had decided that she really had no option other than to stick to the vows she had made in St. Peter's; how would she be looked upon by her family if she arrived on their doorstep without a good enough tale? How foolish she would feel, given that most of the last few months had been one long flurry of selfish indulgence and boasting, if the only reason she could find to leave her husband was because of non-communication in their bed.

She could imagine the look of surprise on her mother's face if she imparted that information, albeit with a great deal of embarrassment on both their parts. Then Bertha, smug in the knowledge that their cousin Lawrence had preferred her above all others, would look down her nose at her returning sister, no doubt thinking that she couldn't stay the course. Mabel would shrug and tell her that she had told her so, Harriet would throw up her hands in despair and Grand-mama, no, she couldn't face her grand-mama. It was she who had arranged this blessed marriage in the first place and probably would turn her around and send her back to Brookvale.

CHAPTER TEN

The man who walked along the shortcut from the landing stage was unrecognisable as the callow youth who had left the shores of the River Mersey nine years before. Charlie Wilson, who had always had trouble growing even a whisper of fluff on his upper lip or chin, had over the years grown full ginger sideburns, a moustache and a beard upon his face. Life as a crofter (or market gardener, as he liked to think of himself) on the four acres of land, which he rented from a farmer near Tobermory on the Isle of Mull, had filled out his small frame, leaving him stocky, fit as a flea and more assured of himself than he had ever been.

He wasn't quite sure what had driven him to leave his Scottish haven. The fact that the ground he worked was solid with the frosts of winter was perhaps one reason; he had spent the previous winter snowed up in his croft and this was something he was anxious not to repeat. A diet of carrots and neeps – the only things he had left in his vegetable pit the previous winter – had soon begun to play havoc with his guts. Nostalgia was also playing a part; a yearning to see his home again, to watch the shipping on the river, to check out their names from the *Lloyds Shipping Gazette*, or perhaps to hear of news of his beloved Lily, even if she was betrothed to another. There was also the need to ease his conscience; he had been a scoundrel by abandoning Mary and he hoped she had managed to survive without him.

Looking back to that night all those years ago, when he had suddenly made his dash for freedom, still caused him certain shame at his cowardice. Once Mary had put on her jacket and had checked her appearance in front of the mirror, she had warned Charlie again that he should be in bed on her return. After waiting for the sound of her footsteps to disappear along the pavement, he had packed a small portmanteau with a change of clothing, put in as many past copies of the shipping gazettes as he had room for, checked he had his fob-watch, hair brush, notebook and his good pair of shoes, then spent the night wrapped in his overcoat on a bench in one of the wooden shelters on Victoria Park. As luck would have it, the air was balmy from a day of June sunshine and once daylight had spread its tentacles on Charlie's slumbering face, he ambled along to the shipyard to volunteer his services.

He stopped for a moment to catch his breath, as he had forgotten how steep the incline was from the esplanade. Leaning against a stone wall at the side of a whitewashed cottage, he recalled his spirits plummeting when Mr Hammond had declined his offer. The men had already been chosen and had set off at the light of day. Charlie's face had said it all. Concerned with his sudden pallor, the slump of his shoulders and the trace of tears beginning to form in his eyes, Mr Hammond, a compassionate man, drew his employee into the office and asked if he would like a cup of tea. Perhaps he would like a confidante, he was known to have a sympathetic ear.

Five hours later, Charlie had stood on the docks at Liverpool, waiting to board a cargo ship that would take him up along the coast to Glasgow. With a reference and good wishes from a fellow henpecked husband, Charlie was free to start a new life at the Govan Shipyard. He had stayed in the employment of J&G Thomson, the shipbuilders, until one day, having spent some of his leisure time exploring along the coast of Argylle, he had fallen in love with the wild beauty of the Isle of Mull, where otters splashed in the gurgling rivers and eagles nested in the shadowy mountains. It was just a short hop on a boat from Oban, where he had sometimes stayed overnight in a large three-storey house run as a bed and breakfast by a doughty Scots woman. Being enticed to return often by her delicious tasting haggis and the promise of a comfortable chest to lay his head on should he ever need to, he had made inquiries at the Tobermory Hotel, a 200 year old hostelry formed from a row of fishermen's cottages, on the likelihood of being able to rent a bit of land in the area to start a market garden. He had done rather well from his leap of faith into the future. He had managed to put a little aside under his mattress and had a small bank account on the mainland as well.

Charlie stood outside his mother's cottage. It looked shabby, the walls needing a coat of whitewash, but surprisingly the nets in the window had benefited from a good soaking in the dolly tub. He hesitated, as a tremor of fear clutched at him, suddenly giving him a taste of bile as his thoughts went to Mary. Perhaps he had been foolish returning after all these years. She would probably give him a thumping and, if he was fair, she was entitled to. He had left her without his weekly wage; she didn't always get casual work and she would have been a figure of derision with her husband disappearing as he had. Though she had her family, he reasoned, who would have rallied around to help her. Who was to say he had hopped off and left her anyway? He could have lost his footing as he walked along the riverbank and disappeared under the waters of the Mersey, just as his father was supposed to have done. He took a breath, hoping that his chest, which had benefited greatly from the Scottish air up to now, wouldn't start wheezing in his anxiety, then pushed the latch on the wooden door and stepped inside.

The woman, dressed in black, with sparse white hair, had been standing at the foot of the stairs with a look of surprise on her face at the stranger who had walked through the door unannounced and made a beeline for the poker. No one was going to trifle with Jessica Parsons, even if she was seventy-three. Brandishing the poker menacingly, she approached Charlie, who had put his arms up in a surrender position.

"What's yer business? Coming in 'ere as if yer owned the place, I'll give yer a flat head with me poker, yer'll see."

"Don't you recognise me, Mrs Parsons?" Charlie said in a calm voice, trying to reassure the old lady that she knew him well, if she could just see beyond the facial hair.

"I remember the voice," she said, hesitant now, but still

clutching her poker, thinking her life was dependent on it.

"It's Charlie, Janey Wilson's son. I used to go to school with your Albert. Don't you remember that we lived in this house up until near on ten years ago?"

"Charlie." Mrs Parsons sat down heavily upon the sofa, still clutching the poker. "They said yer were dead. That wife of yours told everyone yer'd gone off on a secret mission to the Orkney's, wherever that is, and the ship sank just off Scotland on the way. She said that man from the shipyard told her, when she went to see why yer 'adn't come 'ome."

Good old Mr Hammond, thought Charlie, grateful that his supervisor had come up with a convincing tale of derring-do on Charlie's part. "So where is Mary now and what are you doing here?"

"I'll answer yer second question first, Charlie. Albert got me the tenancy when me old 'ouse was pulled down by the council, flippin' beggars. All ter do with the road widening fer the new oil terminal, and yer won't like me other answer about Mary. She died giving birth to yer babby, nine months after yer ship 'ad gone down. Yer were lucky, they said there weren't no survivors, but I've heard tell of folk bein' pulled from the waters and lost their memories."

"Aye, it was something like that." Charlie sat beside her on the sofa. Suddenly his legs had buckled, when he heard what had happened to Mary. How come she was having a baby when they hadn't properly done the deed? He knew now from listening to the confidences of his Oban landlady that babies weren't brought in a bag by the midwife.

"Did the baby live?" Charlie couldn't help but ask her, though what he would do if the answer was yes, he didn't know.

"No, both of them perished, so I heard. That mother of hers sold all yer furniture so that they could 'ave a big send off fer Mary at The Grapes Hotel, though there's an old sea chest still sittin' on the landin'. They don't live round 'ere now, they got a place up the North End. Our Albert got me most of this lot on the provident, as my stuff was only fit fer firewood. Can I get yer a cup of tea, Charlie? Yer lookin' right peaky. Whatever yer've bin doin' though 'as put a bit of weight on yer."

"I've a market garden up in Scotland," he replied, trying to make his voice sound even, though in truth he was in shock over Mary's behaviour. *She must have been seeing someone else on the sly, the dirty mare.* "It's doing well, though at this time of year the ground is solid, so there's not much to do until the spring."

"Aye, that'll be right, yer mother had what they called the green fingers, God rest her. I'm sure she'd be glad to 'ear yer've followed in 'er footsteps. So how long are yer stoppin' for? Cause if yer've got nothing fixed yer can stop 'ere and keep me company?"

"That would be good, Mrs Parsons. I never even gave it a thought really; I just got on the train at Glasgow and here I am."

"You always were a dreamer, Charlie. You can sleep on the sofa down 'ere, our Albert says it's very comfortable."

"I'd like that Mrs Parsons. It'll only be for a couple of days."

"Is that you Lily?" Hannah Griffiths lay on her bed and had heard the door to her room open.

"Yes, Mother. I thought you might like me to make you a cup of tea. The kettle has boiled and I was just going to make myself a cup."

"That would be nice. I must get up and help you in the kitchen. Fortunately, your father is going to his club in Oxton this evening, so there will be just the three of us for dinner."

In the nine years since Lily had left her home to live at Brookvale, there had been many changes in the Griffith household. Grand-mama had gone to her rest seven years before; Ellen, surprisingly for such a mouse of a girl, had married the postman (no wealthy man to be found for her); Bertha, of course, had married Lawrence, not with such a fanfare as Lily's wedding had been, but she waited for his leaves in the Patterson family house on Temple Road, where she was happily raising their three children and caring for two elderly maiden aunts; Henrietta married her curate, who was now a rector in a living in Yorkshire, had four plump offspring and was expecting another. That left Mabel, poor Mabel, who still had that skeleton in the cupboard; Frederick, who was now an Oxford graduate and was about to enter the world of commerce, based in London, coming home to visit occasionally; and Lily, made a widow in 1903.

It was two years since Queen Victoria had died and the ascension to the throne of Edward, the deceased monarch's son. To say that Lily was a sorrowing widow would be a fabrication. When the letter had arrived at Brookvale to say that her husband, Major De Crosland, had died serving his country fighting the Boers in Africa, there had been something of a relief. She had been all alone after Lydia had died, the poor soul having succumbed to a fatal injury whilst chopping up logs in readiness for winter, so Lily had been wanting to leave the old place anyway.

Whatever had happened to the money that Roland had been given by Lily's father on her marriage must have slipped through her husband's fingers, as no repairs or renovations had been made to the house. The roof at the back of the house leaked down the walls of the master bedroom and the chimney sweep had refused to come, as his last bill was still outstanding. It could be a bleak place at any time of the year, but the winters were the worst, when snow would drift to the hedge tops along the country lanes and they could be cut off for days.

Things had come to a head when the family solicitor, a man who had been associated with the De Croslands for many years and had been involved in selling off much of the 'family jewels' on their behalf, visited the house after Lydia's funeral to say that it was a distant relative of the De Croslands who was to inherit Brookvale. The place had been willed via the male issue of the family, so even Roland's sister, wherever she was on God's Earth, wouldn't have been entitled to the mouldering pile.

The news hadn't affected Lily too much; she could still hold her head up in the family, play the grieving widow, throw away the sham of a wedding ring that had caused her finger to turn green and return to live in Rosemount Terrace, perhaps being allowed a career in time. Her only regret, and it could have been because both Bertha and Harriet had produced a brood of children and she hadn't even given birth to one, was that she and Roland had never quite got it together in the ensuing years in the marriage bed. She, with great distaste for such an act after listening to the graphic details from her mother-in-law, had distanced herself from her husband as much as she could and Roland, obedient to his mother's wish for him to settle down and marry well to enhance the De Crosland fortunes, found it difficult to perform with a woman when he was attracted to men instead.

They had settled for polite acceptance of each other's frailties, after one attempt to make a baby early on in their marriage had caused a lot of frustration to both concerned. Lily, sickened by the whole rigmarole of having to stroke the limp member that Roland had thrust into her hand, then his insistence that she turn to face the window while he mounted her from behind, was quite determined there would not be a repeat performance. For Lydia's sake they had put on an affectionate front, being far too well bred and civilized to talk through their problems together, which had left the would-be grandma to wonder why no child had been produced.

"It is a great shame that Henrietta lives so far away in Yorkshire," Hannah said, getting to her feet slowly, as having lain for many years on her bed recovering from all the births she had been put through she had put on a vast amount of weight. "Now that her fifth child is nearly imminent, perhaps we could have helped her with the other four."

"I am sure that Henrietta will cope very well without us, Mother. She is very capable and I am sure their maid would give a hand with the children if it was necessary."

"Yes, I was always grateful for any help I could get in the early years. Grand-mama used to lend a hand occasionally and your father paid for a succession of young women to help me, just as he has made an allowance for Henrietta's maid."

Lily hid a smile at the news that Grand-mama had lent a hand occasionally; somehow she couldn't visualise the matriarch of the family changing the soiled cloths of her daughter's children.

"I have prepared a light dinner for the three of us," Lily continued, feeling a sense of pride that now she was virtually in charge of the kitchen she could make decisions regarding their meals, whereas before it was always Bertha's domain. "I thought a slice of steak and kidney pie left over from last night's meal, with a steamed plum pudding for dessert."

"That will be perfect, dear. Who would have thought you could have turned your hand to cooking, when according to Grand-mama you had no talents at all?"

"They were hidden under my bushel, Mother." Lily was well aware that it was only because of Lydia's tutelage that she was proficient in any culinary aspect, as those months, even years, between leaves whilst Roland was away policing most of the British Empire, could have been very boring if it hadn't of been for her mother-in-law. Not only had Lily become adept at cooking, preserving and bottling, she knew how to nurture a vegetable patch, skin a rabbit, pluck a chicken, make a patchwork quilt, crochet a shawl and repair the soles of her shoes. She had learnt to clean the kitchen with emery powder, used methylated spirit and a leather cloth to polish glass, clean silver with a solution of chalk, ammonia, alcohol and water and wash clothes with a blue bag. All this knowledge was needed to maintain the precarious living that she and Lydia had to endure.

There had been no social life other than if Lydia and she were invited to Griffiths or Patterson family occasions, such as weddings or christenings, or occasionally they walked on a Sunday to Greasby Parish Church. Once they had got invited to Redstone House at the bottom of Mill Hill Lane, when the Dockerty's had held a fundraising event in their garden.

Life had become one long round of make-do and mend. The allowance that Lily still very kindly received from her father went towards keeping the two women above the poverty level.

There were no new clothes and a lot of Lily's fashionable clothes that she had brought with her were adapted or left to rot in the wardrobe. If there was such a thing as a regimental dinner, which happened to coincide with one of her husband's leaves, when Lily could have worn her finery, she had no knowledge of them, nor was she invited to be friends with any of the other army wives. Sometimes she and Lydia would have a rare day out and travel with the farmer's wife, Mrs Thornton, who now had the ownership of a horse and trap to take her wares to Birkenhead Market. This enabled them to purchase a roll of durable cloth to replace their worn out skirts and jackets, or a length of cotton material suitable for making under garments. Food could have been in short supply, if it had not been for the generosity of the kindly farmer's wife. In the winter they had to live off the hens that pecked in their backyard, the fruit from the orchard and the abundant rows of brassicas in their vegetable patch.

There were many times when Lily had despaired of the luxurious life she had given up at Rosemount, replacing the frivolity of her youth with the day-to-day hardship she had endured. Stubborn pride made her reluctant to return to the bosom of the family, where she would be reminded that Lawrence had chosen Bertha to be his wife instead of her, though maturity now made her realise she shouldn't be clinging to such a foolish infatuation. Also the great affection she had developed for Lydia was enough to keep her from abandoning Brookvale, though once the good woman had passed away, there didn't seem much point to it at all.

"Pass the salt, dear," Hannah said, as she, Lily and Mabel sat together later at the well-scrubbed kitchen table. The dining room was only used when Mannion was home, as he still liked to be seen as the head of the family. "Have you been busy today, Mabel?" she asked, once Lily had passed down the condiment.

"Yes, Mother. Now that Advent is almost upon us, we are busily making Christmas wreaths, floral displays and sheaths of holly and ivy for decorating hearth and home."

"You must remember to bring me a holly wreath, dear. I do like the new fashion of hanging a wreath from a nail on the door. It is very welcoming."

Mabel nodded obediently. Still affected by what had happened to her at Montgomery Hall, she was a typical spinster of her time. Thin, gaunt even, she wore an all-encompassing floor length green serge dress, high necked, with wrist length buttoned sleeves and not a glimpse of a well turned ankle in her black comfortable shoes. Mother, on the other hand, had taken to wearing a type of kaftan, made by a local seamstress who was clever at hiding rolls of fat. Lily, of the three, looked far more fashionable in a dark brown ankle length skirt and a matching cream peplum jacket over a white chemise, having changed from her shabby overall earlier. Mannion had been more than generous on his daughter's return, treating Lily to a whole new wardrobe of fashionable clothes. The evening dress of guipure lace over a lining of dark blue linen was her favourite.

One time, in a moment of confidence, when the two sisters had found themselves alone after Mother had retired to bed, Mabel seemed to be about to spill the beans to her younger sister. It had happened when Lily had remarked that in all the time she had been away at Brookvale, and at all the family occasions she had attended, there had never been a glimpse of Uncle Bunkum. That was the name the children had christened Aunt Patricia's husband, when they had stayed at Montgomery Hall during the holidays. He had been a loathsome chap as far as they were concerned, full of swagger and bluster.

Mabel had been rather guarded as she started to make her usual derogatory remarks about the male of the species, but this time their uncle was included and as Lily had still not lost her nosiness, she pressed her sister to tell her more. It appeared there had been an incident when Mabel had gone to stay at Montgomery Hall. It had happened when her sister had returned from the tennis court after a lively match against one of her cousins.

"I was feeling rather hot, perspiring a lot and had decided to put my racquet into the bedroom, then go to have a nice, cool bath. I thought I was alone… but… No, I can't talk about it, Lily. Some things are better left in the past and for the sake of the family I should let things lie."

She had clammed up and wouldn't be drawn into what had happened next, though Lily was sure now it had been something distasteful in the bedroom department and had to do with Aunt Patricia's husband. Of course Lily could also have had a tale to tell of a man's imperfection, but there was no one that she would have confided in and probably never would.

CHAPTER ELEVEN

"So if yer want ter stay 'ere over Christmas as well, yer very welcome, Charlie. I 'ear it can get bitter up there." Jessie Parsons was a good God fearing woman and wouldn't let an opportunity to help her fellow man like this escape her.

Charlie considered. The sofa he had spent the night on in his old house had been quite comfortable and although he'd had no plans for staying longer than a day or so before he'd got here, would it do any harm to take up her offer? It would be lonely and cold in his two-roomed croft that overlooked the Atlantic Ocean, where he could watch whales and dolphins frolicking in the summer months. His only respite at this time of the year was to take a walk into the windswept town and have a seasonal drink at the tavern with some of his neighbours. He had brought his notebook and an up to date copy of the *Lloyds Shipping Gazette* in his now battered looking portmanteau, so that, weather permitting, he could take up his favourite spot near the landing stage.

He had a change of clothing, although now he was dressed in his best, as befitted a man of substance. A white, high-necked collar shirt, with a thin black tie peeping through the opening, his oatmeal waistcoat that his mother had bought him, a brown, single breasted jacket that he wore with matching narrow legged trousers, under a three quarter length herringbone overcoat. His shoes were a pair of black, highly polished lace ups with a small heel, worn to enhance his stature and his hat was a bell shaped bowler with a tightly rolled brim.

"Well, that is very kind of you," he said in an appreciative tone, glancing at the fob-watch he had taken out from beneath his buttoned up jacket, thinking that he probably wouldn't find somewhere to stay around there anyway. It would mean a trip across the Mersey to find a decent hotel. "Of course I'll pay you for your trouble, I'm not short of a bob or two."

"You certainly will not, Charlie Wilson, and I'll thank you to take that jacket off and join me for a bacon buttie."

It was the day before Christmas Eve and Lily, up to her neck in preparing food for the Christmas Day high tea that her mother had elected to provide, saying that a Christmas dinner was beyond the talents of herself and Lily for such large numbers, suddenly found that she hadn't enough eggs to make a marmalade cake. The other cakes, such as the Christmas fruitcake, plum pudding and Dundee had been made weeks before, but her father enjoyed a slice of marmalade cake, using the conserve that Hannah had made.

It was a blowy afternoon as Lily set forth to visit the allotments that were kept by local men to supplement their family's food. Many kept chickens and, to make a little money on the side, sold a few eggs to a passing trade. She put her hands into the pockets of her dark blue coat and hugged the heavy material closer to her body, glad that she had worn her warm ankle length boots as the chill in the air was bitter.

"Lily, wait for me!"

She heard a familiar voice cry out her name, as she paused to look both ways before she crossed the road. Open topped motor vehicles, omnibuses and the odd hire carriage, all used this once quiet highway and it was wise to be a little cautious nowadays. A moment of déjà vu crept into her subconscious and she turned to scan the path behind to see who had hailed her – surely that wasn't Charlie Wilson? This dapper man, dressed in the manner of a middle class merchant, a gentleman by the cut of the clothes he was wearing and carrying a walking cane.

"My, my, who got you dressed?" she joked, as Charlie caught up with her, having hurried up the slight incline. "I would not have recognised you had I passed you in the street."

"Oh, the years have been very kind to me," he replied airily, drinking in the sight of her like a drowning man. "If I may be so bold, the passing years have not altered you one whit."

Lily giggled, much as she would have done had he paid her a compliment ten years before. Back then he was a gauche and strange young man, who liked to sit near the landing stage overlooking the river, had attended the Wesleyan church and had no lightness in his soul.

"Oh Charlie, I've been married, widowed and returned to my family in all those years. I am sure I have aged considerably and *you* have developed a smooth tongue."

His heart leapt when he heard that his beloved was now a widow. Was this is a chance to press his suit and ask for her hand in marriage? Play out those many dreams of a life with Lily that had invaded his thoughts during his years away from her? *Too early*, the voice of caution was saying, but would it do them any harm to be just friends?

"Well I must continue on my errand," she said, stepping towards the kerb in an effort to show him that she couldn't stand about all day chatting. "Do you still live in the cottage on Whetstone Lane? If so I will probably see you again in the vicinity."

She was interested in seeing him again, alleluia! "Actually Lily, I have removed to Scotland where I run a thriving business, but I decided as the season of goodwill is almost upon us, to reacquaint myself with friends and relations here."

"Ah." Lily stepped back, suddenly curious as to why Charlie Wilson had found it necessary to move to Scotland to start a business. Last time they had spoken, he had just come out of his apprenticeship at the shipyard. "Have you had to leave your business in the hands of your employees, Charlie, as this is usually a very busy time of the year?"

"Maybe so in your father's line of business; everyone will be wanting fires in their hearths, but my business is seasonal. But I shouldn't keep you standing here, Lily. It is just as cold today as I would expect it is where I am now living. Perhaps you would do me the honour of taking a cup of tea or hot chocolate with me at Cavanagh's Cafe across the way?"

"I would like to say yes, Charlie, but I only slipped out to purchase some eggs from the allotments. I am in charge of the Christmas spread and my father is quite partial to a slice of marmalade cake."

Me too, thought Charlie, feeling downcast that she had refused to accompany him to the local cafe. All his prayers would have been answered had she agreed to his request.

"Are you staying long? I ask because I will be free to accompany you to the cafe on Monday, when all our social duties for the season have been discharged."

Had she said she couldn't have seen him until the following Easter, an elated Charlie Wilson would have made the trip down from Scotland just to have been near her side! He took her hand and shook it rather formally, resisting the urge to place a kiss upon it, wishing her the compliments of the season and to her family too.

He couldn't wait for the Christmas festivities to be over, although he did enjoy celebrating Christ's birth with the astonished members of the Wesleyan congregation. The Parsons' treated him as if he was part of the family and had even clubbed together to buy him a pair of woolly gloves. Life in the wilds of Scotland must be tough, they had decided, and Charlie should cover up those calluses and protect his once smooth hands. Albert had taken him to The Grapes for a couple of festive pints, where he had joined incredulous regulars who joked that he must be a ghost. Even Ernie Morris seemed glad to see him and brought him a drink for old times sake.

Lily wanted the festive season over for lots of reasons, but not one of them because she was looking forward to meeting Charlie Wilson. Christmas Eve and Day had been one long round of visiting, eating, entertaining and exchanging gifts with her extended family, waiting hand and foot on her now portly father and Frederick, who had arrived from London in one of the new fangled motor cars that had lots of smoke and made put-put noises. He was the hero of their terrace, with males of the neighbourhood hanging around the contraption at all times of the day. Lawrence was away on the other side of the Atlantic and Bertha, glad to have a multitude of willing sisters ready to share the supervision of any small kin that needed overseeing, saw the opportunity for some sisterly sniping, whilst helping Lily in the kitchen.

Since her marriage nine years before, it had to be said that the Bertha, who Lily had once known and dutifully loved, was a bit of a bore when it came to conversation of the female kind. Children, housework, a little unkind griping about her lot in life and the usual moaning about Lawrence hardly knowing his offspring, with him away at sea so much. "You would know what I mean had *you* been the one who had married Lawrence." There, it was out; Bertha had waited all this time to declare her true feelings, whilst watching her sister make, what she thought, was sheep's eyes at her husband over the years. "Let me tell you, being married to a mariner isn't as romantic as it may appear to be, especially when it is left to the wife to administer his children's discipline. My three boys are in need of a heavy handed father, but unfortunately they run rings around me instead."

Lily was speechless for a moment when she heard her sister's words. Had it been so obvious that it had been she who had wanted to marry her cousin all those years ago?

"Oh yes, Lily, I know how you resented me and thought that Lawrence only had eyes for you. We used to smile about it, 'cause he never would have married such a dreamer, a flibbertigibbet, Father's little princess. He wanted a homemaker, a mother for his children and someone he could rely on to keep an eye on his old aunties while he's away."

"And you don't think I could have done all those things for Lawrence?" Lily tried to control the trembling that had suddenly taken over her hands, after her sister had shaken her head and calmly started to wipe the dishes that she had put aside to drain.

"It didn't appear to be so when you were married to Roland. Grand-mama said, 'Had there ever been a mismatch in a married couple, it was you two'."

"And she would know, although she only ever saw us at

108

weddings and christenings? None of you had an inkling of what went on between Roland and I and I'll thank you, Bertha, not to speak ill of the dead."

Her sister had shrugged after Lily had stalked away huffily to her bedroom, to spend some time revisiting her hurts. Nobody knew what had gone on between her and Roland. They had agreed to put on a stoical front that told the world that even if theirs was not a happy marriage, because how could you be happy if you hadn't produced at least one addition to the family, it worked for them and they were content with that. She knew now that the feelings she'd had for Lawrence had been just a childish crush and she didn't like the man he had become, always barking orders at his wife and children and drinking far too much.

The sky was overcast as Lily made her way to Cavanagh's Cafe on the corner of Whetstone Lane. She had dressed accordingly, wearing a light navy mackintosh over her heavy woolen coat, black leather ankle boots and a plain saucer shaped hat upon her head, with no ornament upon it. She was known to take a walk alone, so no one questioned her destination. Sometimes she would walk as far as Storeton Woods, quite a long way away from her home. There had been nothing better than tramping along the country lanes when she had lived at Brookvale, or passing the old windmill on her way through the sandy lane to the village of Irby, when the air had been most bracing, coming as it did across the fields from the Irish Sea.

She had thought long and hard about this meeting with Charlie Wilson. He was an anathema to her really; not someone she wanted to be bothered with, given that he didn't have her background or her breeding. In fact the only reason she was there that afternoon, she told herself, was because there wasn't very much else to do. Her intention had been, after making the hastily made proposition, to forget about their meeting. He'd be in the warmth, not hanging around waiting for her on a street corner, and after a few cups of whatever they were given to drink in such an establishment, he would get the message and go.

The spat with Bertha though had caused a major overhaul in Lily's thinking, as she had tossed and turned in her bed that night. Was she to live the rest of her life like sister Mabel, a thin unhappy woman who seemed to hate all men? She could be classed as a spinster too, having never really known what it was like to feel true penetration. She was still pure and virginal, as Roland on his rare visits to the manor house, had always kept to his side of the bed. That's if you didn't count that one embarrassing time that didn't bear thinking about.

Not quite as pure as you would like to think, said her inner conscience, as she thought of the times when her body yearned for release from the terrible frustration that she felt in the warmth of her bed at night. She could make herself soar to hidden heights of the purest pleasure, if she used her index finger on her special place. Though perhaps marriage to another man *could* be the answer, especially to Charlie, whom she knew had adored her all his life. That would show Bertha, especially if she was to produce one or two children herself. This time Father would have no say in whom she married; it appeared he had no interest in his pretty princess now that he had grandchildren to pet.

CHAPTER TWELVE

"Ah Lily." Charlie sped to the door of the cafe when he saw his beloved hovering there and looking around nervously. Perhaps it had been a mistake for them to meet in such poor surroundings, but there was nowhere else to go, unless they shivered together on a bench in the one of the park shelters. "Thank you for coming, what can I order for you?" He drew her to a seat at a table near the window, which was steamy from the food and hot drinks that were being served at the counter nearby.

"A rose-hip tea would be very nice, thank you." She settled herself on a battered wooden chair, looking around at the down at heel persons sipping drinks from chipped white mugs, or eating fish and chips. Some were even smoking cigarettes!

"A rose-hip tea? I don't think they would have such a thing at this establishment." Charlie's heart began to sink when he realised what he had done. "I'm sorry, Lily." He bent down to speak in a whisper, as he didn't want anyone to hear his words or they'd think he was a snob. "I didn't give much thought to the circumstances of our meeting. I should have suggested a much more pleasant place to meet."

"A glass of hot chocolate then. I would be partial to a glass of hot chocolate on such a cold day."

"I think I will join you and we'll have a couple of butterfly cakes."

Charlie brought their drinks, not in a glass as Lily had expected, as the owner of the cafe had laughed when Charlie had requested their chocolate drinks in a glass and suggested he should visit The Adelphi Hotel instead, but in thick white mugs that Lily rather hoped had been washed thoroughly. She noticed that the wings on the cakes looked a little droopy, too, when the owner put a plate of them in front of her.

"Sorry." Charlie felt remorseful. This was his beloved, the person who inhabited his dreams and here he was subjecting her to the most awful conditions.

"That's all right, Charlie. I suppose one should feel incredibly sorry that places like this have to exist. I mean, the poor have to eat somewhere and the prices in here are really quite cheap."

Charlie nodded, he was glad that his beloved sounded sympathetic to the poor. "So, nine years. Nine years, a lot of water has gone under the bridge. Tell me, have those years been kind to you, Lily?" Charlie sat back nursing his mug of hot chocolate and hoped that he wasn't being indelicate in his inquiry.

Lily's face took on a guarded look, as she wasn't sure how much or what she wanted to tell Charlie Wilson – the truth or fiction? She decided on the latter, it wasn't any of his business anyway.

"I married a man named Roland De Crosland, who was a military man from an old Cheshire family who could trace their ancestors back many generations. I moved to their country seat just on the border of Greasby and Irby and I had a maid called Lydia, who tended to my every need. I was heartbroken, of course, when my husband died in the Boer War. He fought gallantly against the Afrikaans of Dutch descent, who didn't want to give up their mining rights to the British Empire. And now I live back home with my parents in Rosemount Terrace, taking care of my mother who is rather elderly." There, her description of her former life seemed to be very well received.

Charlie's spirits plummeted. Here he was, sitting opposite the most beautiful girl he had ever set eyes on, listening to her description of how she had spent her past nine years. She had probably rubbed shoulders with most of the local gentry and he was expecting that one day in the future she might agree to marry him – him, a market gardener.

"I have had similar tragedy in my own nine years," he nodded sadly. "My mother died and then, unfortunately, my marriage ended very early on when my wife died in childbirth. To cope with my sorrow I decided to leave the area, too many memories you'll understand, and the shipyard transferred me to Scotland, where I worked for a time on the River Clyde." *Nobody was going to tell her any different*, he told himself. "One day, I took a boat trip around the small islands in the vicinity of Oban and I chanced upon a little place called Iona, where a saint named Columba had built a monastery. Perhaps you can imagine it, Lily. A tortured soul, happening upon a place of great beauty, where monks had lived in peaceful silence, tilling the soil and making a living from land and sea. I was allowed to worship at that magnificent place and stayed for a while in contemplation, until it finally hit me on what I should do. I had a sort of epiphany, a sense of wanting to be as one with the land, as the monks had done for centuries."

"Phew, Charlie," said Lily, having listened attentively to this man, who she had always thought of as a little vulgar. "You always were good at growing beans and peas, as I remember. So what did you do next? Did you find a pot of gold at the bottom of a rainbow, which enabled you to begin your enterprise?"

"Something like that." Charlie didn't say that he had to draw all his precious savings from the bank account he had in Glasgow, as the landlord of those acres he worked near Tobermory was a canny man and wanted his tenant to pay upfront. "Finding gold at the bottom of a rainbow is all a bit of a fantasy, if you don't mind me saying so, Lily. No, I believe my fortune to be sent from heaven. At least everything I turned my hand to became reality."

"So, how many people do you have in your employ, Charlie?"

It would be something that she might mention later at their family dinner: 'Local man made good'. "Well, it's seasonal. Most of my vegetable harvesting occurs in the autumn, so that is when I need to find people to labour for me." He didn't say that most of them were itinerant, the Irish, the Romany's or holidaymakers down on their luck. "I get by with the aid of a few local men most of the year to harvest my other crops of oats or barley, as my role in the business is to market my products to the people of Mull, the town of Oban and sometimes to the smaller islands such as Barra and Uist."

"It all sounds fascinating." Lily surreptitiously wiped her tongue with a handkerchief that she carried in her reticule; the cream in the butterfly cake had left a sour taste in her mouth. "However, much as I would like to stay a little longer, I notice that the street lamps are beginning to glow and I must be away to prepare dinner for the family." She stood up, noticing as she did so that crumbs fell to the floor from her coat, as the establishment had not provided a table napkin.

"Thank you so much for inviting me to listen to your account of very fascinating travels. I would have loved to hear more, but I must away."

"May I escort you back to Rosemount Terrace?" Charlie leapt at the chance of being in her company a little longer, as this might be his only shot at asking if she would allow him to see her again. He was sure that Jessie would allow him a few more days upon her sofa and what a start to 1904, if Lily agreed to meet him again. "That footpath to your home will be quite treacherous after darkness, especially from the mud after the recent rainfall."

"Of course you may." Lily was quite relieved that he had made his offer. A solid man to cling to along the unlit path was just the ticket at this time of year. "I would imagine you are used to darker climes if you are living in the wilds of Scotland. I have heard it goes dusk a lot earlier than here." She linked his arm as they trod carefully around the puddles that lay in the potholed track.

It felt good and natural, her closeness like balm to his soul. It spurred him on. "Would there be a possibility of you and I walking out together, Lily, now that we have lost our respective partners and are alone again in life?" His words sounded trite, but he felt all of a jumble in his mind and was grasping the opportunity like a drowning man. "I could come and speak to your father if it would help."

Lily considered. Charlie Wilson; Lily Wilson. Not as grand as

Lily De Crosland, but what had she got from that sham of a marriage? A name that might have opened doors for her gentrified husband, but nothing for a commoner with only her looks. No wedded warmth, no adoration, no look of love like the look of love that she had seen today in Charlie's eyes and it wasn't as if he was penniless; he had a thriving business in the Hebridean Isles. "I'd like to walk out with you Charlie," she said softly, suddenly remembering that look of hurt on his face when she had sent him packing all those years ago. "And I'm sure that my father will agree with me that you and I will do."

If truth was told, Mannion Griffith felt quite relieved when Lily announced after dinner that evening that there was a possibility that she would be seeing a young gentleman, a business man who had a thriving enterprise on the Isle of Mull, an island that was part of the Inner Hebrides. Not that Mannion knew where the island was, but it was somewhere up there in bonny Scotland. He had seen his profits fall quite dramatically since the use of gas had been introduced for fuelling the new free standing cookers that were beginning to take up residence in many of the mid to upper class kitchens. Combined with the falling off of lucrative contracts from the town hall now that various legislations at government level had brought new rules in, he was seriously thinking of cutting his losses and retiring from his stressed out life.

The queen had died, God bless her, and with her death came sweeping changes, as the Victorian values of self help and parish care were being replaced with a raft of social services. Children, part of the workforce on farms in outlying districts, were forced under the education act to attend a school. In the pipeline was the pensions act and the national insurance act, in readiness to alleviate the unemployed and poor. When Grand-mama had died, the instructions in her will were that her two daughters should sell the house on Rosemount Terrace and split the proceeds equally. Patricia, the eldest, who lived in grandeur out at Montgomery Hall, had no need of a monetary legacy given that her husband had pots of the stuff and was persuaded by Mannion to relinquish her claim upon the property.

There had been a collusion all those years ago, when Mabel had been sent back from her summer holiday at Patricia's house, under some sort of a cloud that he hadn't been privy to. It was a woman problem, according to Grand-mama, and she should be allowed to deal with it, sending the poor girl off to heaven's knew where, down in the south of the country. Of course, Mannion had his suspicions that something was seriously amiss, finding it rather strange that Bertie, his brother-in-law, had never made an appearance at Rosemount Terrace again, but in time Mabel had come back, rather subdued it had to be said and the matter was closed, whatever it was. To say that Patricia was easily persuaded to give up any claim was an understatement and the large, rambling, Victorian house was soon put in Mannion's name, with him as head of the household, and put up for sale as Grand-mama had wished.

"You'd like Mull," said Charlie, when, on he and Lily's first real trip out together in celebration of the turn of the century, they had decided to ride on the top deck of the ferry boat to Liverpool. They were warmly dressed, given that the temperature had plummeted to below zero and Charlie was glad that he had visited a gents' outfitter on Borough Road in order to buy an extra warm coat. "Mull and the island of Iona are steeped in history dating back to Saint Columba and there are signs that the Celts and the Norse people lived there long ago. I've been there for many years now and there are still a lot of places where I haven't set foot."

"I should imagine that it would be a very nice place for a holiday, Charlie, but the countryside is not for me. Having lived at Brookvale for so many years, miles away from any civilization, I would prefer to spend the rest of my life within striking distance of a town or city."

"I see." Charlie hadn't thought of that. The dream of settling down in his neat little croft with their baby tucked up in a handmade wooden cradle, Lily in a homespun dress filling willow baskets to the brim in his potato field and him catching salmon from the gurgling river that ran through the length of his property, suddenly disappeared into thin air.

"Besides, Father is being very fair when you consider that he has sanctioned our walking out together. I don't think he would be very pleased if I suddenly disappeared to the wilds of Scotland."

"Yes, I can see that, but it is how I make my living, Lily. If I came back here to be with you, I would have nothing to support you with."

"Then it's up to you. I cannot tell you what to do, Charlie, but if your destiny is to be with me and you want me to be your heart's desire, you'll have to be the one to make the changes."

He was saved from answering her and was glad of it, when the boat hit the side of the bulwark and they were thrown together whilst trying to gain their footing. Her body trembled in his arms, whether it was from the cold or a passionate desire for them to be together, but it felt so natural standing there and Charlie knew then that they should never be parted.

CHAPTER THIRTEEN

It took ten long weeks for Charlie to settle his affairs in Scotland and once a week he would take his letter of love to Lily along to the quayside, where a kindly fisherman took it for posting on the mainland. He had struggled with his feelings on that day when he had returned to his bit of the world, where he had tilled his soil, grown his crops, felt times of despair when a hailstorm or lashing rain had knocked his precious plants over, felt satisfaction at the size of his turnips or the sprouts that he had grown in a makeshift shelter and had sighed with relief when his winter brassicas had survived destructive squalls.

It would break his heart to leave it all, this green grassy island of sparkling lochs and he knew he never would if it hadn't have been for meeting his beloved Lily again. His feelings for her were a far greater emotion, though he'd miss the sandy beach where he took his daily walks. For a time he tried to forget about the fog that could sweep in from the Mersey on a damp November morning, the shoddily built back to back houses of Birkenhead, the poor and the needy of the smut ridden town, the diseases that were rife in an ill fed community. On that fair Isle of Mull, children thrived on a diet of freshly picked greens, fish from the ocean and beef from the cattle that grazed on lush fields.

It was meant to be, he thought, when a local farmer, having recently surveyed the rows of shoots that were beginning to show themselves in an early spring and had been assured by the landlord that Charlie had paid his rent for the next six months, decided to take over Charlie's small enterprise. It ensured the man had the rest of the crop that Charlie had planted, with access to a ready market too. However, he baulked at the price that Charlie was asking and knocked him down as only a canny Scotsman could. It wasn't a lot, it had to be said, but enough money to set Charlie up with another small enterprise back in Birkenhead. It was all he could do if he wanted to be with his beloved, that and rent a stall in the market to sell his produce from. It didn't go down very well.

"A market stall!" Lily had squeaked, when one afternoon in the middle of March, after his return, she and Charlie sat in a small pavilion in the park, reunited in a bubble of love.

Well, that was how Charlie saw it, as he had been waiting for this moment since the beginning of the year. He had bought a ring; a small diamond set in a claw of nine carat gold, nestled in a jeweler's box and tucked away from sight in his overcoat pocket. Today, he was going to pop the question to his love.

"What happened to that thriving business you owned back in Scotland?"

"I sold it, dearest, but when word gets around that you are to leave the area, people are inclined to pay as little as they can."

"But you made some money?"

"Of course, but that will be needed for me to pay the rent on a desirable property. I can't stay with Jessica Parsons indefinitely."

"And you want to rent a market stall."

"Well yes, I have no other option but to ask the council for permission to work an allotment. What else is there for me to do?"

"You could go back to the shipyard, seeing that really you're not cut out to be a businessman. I mean, after building up your thriving enterprise, you're settling for a market stall."

Lily's face hardened and Charlie glimpsed a side of her that he hadn't seen before. "I have heard that Lairds are desperate for workers, I heard my father saying so. Seeing as you served your apprenticeship there, they'll take you back with open arms."

"Mmm." It was something he hadn't thought of; he wouldn't want to work there if he didn't have to. "I suppose I could inquire…" *If you don't it will be the finish of your courtship*, a small voice inside his head jibed.

"Yes do inquire Charlie, then you will be able to propose to me and settle a date for us to be wed."

It turned out that there was a need for skilled electrical fitters, preferably with experience in submersibles. Of course it was right up Charlie's street and he had an even deeper feeling that all that had been happening was meant to be. Was it his mother directing him from the spiritual world, or was there a divine presence hovering that kept him from falling from a righteous path? He didn't know, but returning to worship in the Wesleyan church, had given him a certain peace in his bewildered soul.

Mr Hammond had retired from his role as office manager, but Mr O'Neill, who had worked his way up from apprentice to draftsman in a similar way that Charlie had, was pleased to welcome back an ex-employee who was conversant with the job. It appeared that the British government had ordered five submarines a few years earlier for use by the navy and each one needed checking over before they took delivery. It was a piece of cake for Charlie, who only needed a little on the job training and the wages paid were excellent, allowing him to rent a three bedroom villa overlooking Mersey Park. Though it had to be said, he wasn't looking forward to the future sea trials, as having spent so many years in the fresh air of Scotland, burial beneath the muddy waters of the Mersey wasn't that appealing.

Arrangements were well ahead for their marriage, according to Lily. Not at St. Peters, as unfortunately her father thought a second wedding there would be inappropriate, seeing as she'd had lavish nuptials all those years before to a man of note, and local people had long memories. This time it was to be in Charlie's Wesleyan church and she was to wear her dress of guipure lace. It was more suitable for a simple ceremony, as only members of the family were to be invited and the reception would be held in the adjoining church hall.

It had to be said that this time, Lily felt like a poor relation. She knew that her father was facing some financial difficulties, it was the only topic of conversation whilst the sale of the house on Rosemount Terrace was going through, but this time her marriage was a love match, wasn't it? She loved Charlie – well, she thought she did – and he was much more attentive towards her than Roland ever was, but there was nothing romantic about being married in a tin roofed building, which was Charlie's church. St. Peters was built in 1842 and with its steeple, mellowed stone, and stained glass windows it was every girl's ideal venue, but Mannion stuck to his guns. She had done all that before and it wasn't as if she was a blushing bride this time.

Her mind had gone fleetingly to Lawrence, as her father went on about romantic notions that soon disappeared once the nuptials were over. Lawrence had put on weight now, grown a heavy beard and was known to tongue lash his family now that he wielded power on a ship; he wasn't the dashing, clean-shaven, young sea captain that he used to be. Roland, then; no she must not think of Roland. He could have been her heart's desire if he had been the man she had wanted him to be. Charlie, dear Charlie, who loved her right down to her fingertips, but who would never make her heart beat madly or turn her legs to jelly at the sight of him. But he was kind, considerate, tried to get along with his fellowman, brought her flowers and would make an excellent husband when all was said and done.

Mabel was to be her only bridesmaid. Still she was reluctant to tell her secret to Lily who, with her nosy nature, had tried on several occasions over the years to get to the bottom of whatever troubled her sister. She had managed to find out on that occasion, when she was asking if Mabel would stand for her, that it hadn't been an academy that Mabel had gone to when she had been sent away, but to a sanatorium! An establishment where distressed gentlewomen could find peace amongst the nuns that ran the place and where she had learnt that she had a skill in floral design. Anything more than that she wouldn't reveal, but had said she thought that from what Lily had told her about her prospective husband, she was making the right decision by marrying someone like Charlie.

He had only been to Rosemount Terrace on one occasion – two, if you counted the time when he took the flowers all those years ago. Mannion, a little more relaxed with life now he had given up the reins of his company and passed it on to another male member of the Patterson family, was more than willing to meet the man that Lily had chosen. This man, it seemed, had a bit more stuffing in him, given that he'd had a thriving business he understood in Scotland, and could take some of the financial burden of a daughter from him.

The air was warm considering it was an April afternoon and Charlie had left his heavy overcoat behind at his new abode on Mersey Mount. He was dressed in a three-piece suit of striped navy twill, a black bowler hat and patent leather shoes, looking every inch a business man invited for afternoon tea. In fact, when Mannion answered the front door to his knock, he was rather taken aback by Charlie's appearance: he certainly looked the part.

He was shown into the drawing room, which was what the Griffith's liked to call their high ceiling front room, decorated with white turtle doves on a green background wallpaper and tastefully furnished with only a few good pieces of furniture from Grandmama's sitting room. Charlie soon found he was the subject of his prospective father-in-law's scrutiny. Had he the means to support his daughter, now that he had returned from owning a seemingly lucrative business in Scotland, in the pursuit of love? Personally, Mannion thought that the man must be an idiot to have thrown it all away just for the love of a woman, even if that woman was his daughter. It was a bit of a come down to work at Cammel Lairds as an employee, like before.

Charlie, ever the peacemaker and not wanting to cause estrangement, stayed unabashed by Mannion's questioning, though he thought at the time that it was undeserved, given that he was thirty one, a widower and his finances should not be up for discussion. He was grateful when Lily appeared, carrying a tray of scones and sandwiches, followed by Hannah with a tray laden with cups and saucers and a pot of tea, or he might have felt inclined to tell his inquisitor where to go.

Lily had appeared satisfied with the rented villa on Mersey Mount that Charlie had decided would be their marital home. He took her to see it, after persuading the landlord to employ a man to give the white, distempered plastered walls another coat. It was a sunny day and she was much taken with the way the front room lit up with bright sunshine, though complained that their rugs and furnishing may fade if they forgot to draw the drapes. She exclaimed at the unglazed tiles on the hallway floor, far more suitable than the red quarry tiles at Rosemount, which were apt to crack with their rigidity. She seemed satisfied with the cast iron kitchen range, which had a boiler at the back to heat the water and a Belfast sink in the scullery. There was a pantry fitted with marble shelves that would enable their food to stay chilled on warm summer days and upstairs, where three bedrooms of a good size and a separate lavatory from the bathroom resided, she was happy with the view of the garden, as a previous tenant had made a pretty rose trailing bower where she could sit.

It was as they walked along the esplanade later that Charlie realised his beloved was already making plans for their future. Renting a small villa for the rest of their life was not what Lily had in mind; they must strive to own their own place, even if she had to go and earn a wage herself. Alarm bells had sounded at her pronouncement, though a sentimental Charlie told himself that once Lily was settled and holding their little baby, she would soon change her mind.

Conveniently for the young couple, Mannion succeeded later in selling the house on Rosemount Terrace and had found one just down the road from where Bertha lived. It meant he was anxious to be rid of all Grand-mama's old furniture from the sitting room, as most of it wouldn't fit in their smaller place. He could take his time and choose the modern, light, Edwardian furniture that was fast appearing in the Grange Road shops, as there would be only three of them in the household.

Lily was fast despairing of her intended, who seemed to be a bit stingy when it came to how much they could spend on their home, chose the best that was on offer from the sitting room, including a Chinese reproduction cabinet, complete with the eggshell china that Lawrence had once brought back from his 'China run' as a present for his great aunt, and a black German piano. None of this had gone down well with Hannah, who was loath to see any of it go. In all of this Charlie kept his counsel; it was wiser to be that way.

CHAPTER FOURTEEN

With the nuptials over, Lily and Charlie found themselves in the same position that both of them had been in nearly ten years before. Mannion, flush with funds from the sale of his mother-in-law's rambling house, had paid for an overnight stop for the happy couple in the Scarisbrick Hotel, an elegant building built in 1881 and situated on Lord Street in Southport.

It had been a slow trundling train ride from Liverpool after the wedding ceremony, though quite exciting for Lily, as she usually travelled in a horse and carriage to Southport. They alighted at the seaside town's station, dressed in their best and feeling rather nervous as they walked arm in arm across the road to the hotel. It was getting dark on their arrival, only time to eat a light supper in the elegant dining room, then turn in. To say that the pair were nervous was perhaps an understatement; both were remembering with not a little aversion, what they had both been through.

Lily, the first to use the bathroom at the bottom of the corridor, sat in her white bridal nightdress and dressing gown, on the edge of the maroon, satin covered bed. She was full of trepidation and couldn't meet Charlie's eyes, when ready with his soap, towel and flannel he brushed passed her to the bathroom. She felt even more dismay after he returned, now dressed in a pair of blue striped pyjamas, with a white cord tied at the waist and a pair of leather slippers. She fell into a fit of giggles; he looked like a little child, who was coming to his mother to have his hair brushed. All he needed was a teddy bear.

To scowl at her flippancy could have put a grave dampener on their honeymoon. After all, Charlie had just given himself a talking to in the bathroom, reminding himself of the repercussions that could occur if he had a nosebleed and she was probably feeling as nervous as he. He drew her gently under the bed covers and began to caress her throat and neck with tiny kisses, taking his time and wondering as he did so why he was being so gentle, when already his member had enlarged in response to her proximity.

Lily lay passive, making no attempt to help him disrobe her, with no answering sighs or movement in response to his. Then he wondered, as he noticed by the light of the outside street lamp that had found its way through a crack in the curtains, why she had her eyes closed and a distasteful looking grimace on her face? He drew back startled by what he saw, but not before he had an untimely ejaculation, which had left her lovely nightgown splattered in a nasty smelling goo.

Horrified by what had happened and seeing Charlie lying back on the bed, clutching at his now naked manhood and moaning gently, too embarrassed to open his eyes and look at his beloved, Lily leapt from the bed shrieking that she must get a doctor to come and tend to him.

"Won't someone come and see to my husband!" she cried, once she had managed to turn the lock on their bedroom door and had run into the corridor, where concerned fellow guests who had heard the noise in consternation were gathered in readiness to help in any way. It took all his strength and a dogged insistence, after covering his naked parts with his dressing gown, to drag her back into the bedroom again.

It had taken a while to calm poor Lily down, but with loving assurance that there was no need for him to see a doctor, as it was all a natural process in an effort to aid procreation, they slept together fully dressed in their night attire until morning arrived, when nothing more was said on the subject. Lily refused to get changed in front of him, dashing off to the bathroom in an effort to conserve her modesty and after breakfast, before catching the train back home again, they wandered along the bustling Lord Street, before watching people enjoying their holidays on the Southport sands.

Back in Mersey Mount, Lily fluttered about trying to make her nest with the aid of a few more rugs on top of the red and black linoleum downstairs, carpet runners at each side of their metal framed bed and trying to find places for the many vases, crockery, cookery books, canteens of cutlery and household linen received as wedding presents from friends and family. Charlie went back to the development office, a married man and well satisfied.

Lily was the stuff of his dreams and, judging by the little gasps of pleasure he heard whilst straddling her smooth, pert body in their marital bed, she had relaxed and become a willing marital partner. He also found that she could cook well, was adept in household management and always had a tasty dish on his return from work. Life was good and perhaps it would have stayed like that, but in August 1906 Charlie was asked to be part of the crew that was taking a submarine to Scapa Flow to see how it performed under the deep waters of the natural harbour, situated as it was between sheltered islands in the Orkneys.

At first he was reluctant, knowing that he would have to face up to his demons by enduring prolonged periods in an underwater craft, which would probably set off his breathing problems. Suffice to say that since his exposure to the bracing air of Scotland, his chest and lungs, or whatever it had been that had caused his wheeziness, had not been a subject of concern.

The remuneration if he were to go on the sea trial was excellent, no doubt because of the secret nature of the exercise, the dangers that it could possibly involve and the fact that they would be away from Liverpool for more than a few days. Besides that, it was rumoured that there was a distinct possibility the vessel might be moored at Longhope, a place that Charlie had always wished to visit and the crew would be allowed ashore.

He was away for four days, long enough for Lily to miss him and wait up in her nightie in case he returned. She had grown used to his presence in the still of the night, listening to his even breathing and feeling his warm body next to hers. What a revelation her wedding night had been! How was it that she and Roland had experienced such difficulties, when now she found the whole coupling thing with Charlie as easy as falling off a log? During the time that he was away she visited her mother, who had become bedridden because of her excessive weight. She also helped with the cooking and cleaning in her parents' Carlton Road household, in order to give her sister Mabel a bit of a break.

Charlie, full of trepidation as the vessel submerged into the narrow isthmus of water off the mainland of Orkney, with it's conning tower disappearing from view, suppressed his terror as the lights went dim. He counted the minutes, as the captain barked his orders, after viewing through his periscope for hazards out of sight, then heartfelt relief when the craft floated to the surface. He was rewarded for his sufferance with a bracing walk along the anchorage wall at Longhope, where two Martello towers and a gun battery had been used in earlier years for protection from foreign privateers.

During this time, Lily had an inkling that she and Charlie might have made a baby. She felt sick most mornings, disliked the smell of the coffee that her mother liked to drink, hadn't seen her monthly visitor for a while and looked a little pale and wan when she surveyed herself in her dressing table mirror. She desperately wanted it to be so, if only to be able to hold her head up high amongst her sisters, who had probably viewed her with pity over the years. The person to talk to then was Bertha. No use asking her mother on all things birds and bees, as her mother still had her feet planted firmly in the moral strictures of Victorian times, but Bertha, having given birth to three of Lawrence's children, could be relied upon to give her sister chapter and verse.

Once again, Lily was struck by the gruesome details involved in producing a baby for the next generation. Though she wondered if Bertha was exaggerating in an effort to scare her as perhaps she was still feeling slightly antagonistic, but to say that the seed that Charlie had planted would make its way through the place where she passed water in at least eight months time, seemed to be a bit of a fabrication. Didn't a doctor cut you down the middle and take the baby out? She was sure that she had heard that story whilst eavesdropping outside her Grand-mama's sitting room door.

Charlie was delighted to hear of the possibility of him becoming a father, when he returned from his baptism of fire around the islands of Orkney. A baby, the ultimate act of a couple in love and would celebrate their union. It would be worth all the fear that he had felt when the submarine had first dived under the waters, just to know that he was doing it for his beloved and their child.

A baby girl, delivered the following April, confirmed what Bertha had told her when Lily gave birth the natural way, not via a cut to her belly. They decided to call their offspring Isabel, who turned out to be a colicky child who could cry for hours on end.

Lily, tired from the disturbed nights, anxious days and a wish that she could have her slight figure back again, was more than a little grumpy and not in a receptive mood when Charlie told her one evening after work that he couldn't cope with the sea trials and must look for something new. His fear of being trapped inside a 'cigar tube' had come to the fore and his nightmares during his sleeping time were causing bouts of nerves.

"Your nerves, what about my nerves?" Lily had exploded, handing the wailing child to Charlie and storming into the kitchen, where she had been about to warm a bottle of milk for Isabel. "I don't think you know what you're talking about. Try looking after that one all day and all night. We've got the christening next Sunday, I'll be mortified if she shows me up in front of the family."

"I'm sure I would rather look after Isabel than stare death in the face every time I step aboard a floating coffin. I've made my mind up Lily, I'm going to pack it in."

The serious tone in his voice as he followed her into the kitchen made her realise that Charlie wasn't joking. Not known for discussing his feelings, as it wasn't a manly thing to do, he must have been bottling it up for ages, as he had carried out four sea trials since the transfer from his office job.

"But it's such good money, Charlie. How are we going to manage if you give up such well paid job?" Lily took Isabel from him, pushing the bottle teat into the child's mouth and sitting down suddenly on a kitchen chair.

"We'll never be able to afford one of those new houses that they are building in Tranmere, if you decide not to continue with the job."

"So being able to buy a house is more important than my health, Lily?" His spirits plummeted as he searched her inscrutable face for an answer. It would seem it was so.

"We can't live here for the rest of our lives, paying rent to a landlord that can't even be bothered to fix that slate on the roof when you asked him too. No, we have a good amount in our bank account and it won't be long before can afford to put down a deposit."

"My bank account, Lily." Charlie, unusually for him, played the head of the household, he was so worked up with agitation. "Let's not forget that it is me who has his name on the savings book, not you and I'll decide what we'll do with it."

"Please yourself." Lily went upstairs with the baby, her body taut with anger at his attitude. So this was how it was to be in her marriage to Charlie; she'd be the little woman without a say. She felt relief when the exasperating child had stopped her crying. She'd withdraw his privileges when they went to bed, that would teach him.

Charlie, left alone with his thoughts in the kitchen, poured himself a slug of whisky that he kept out of sight in his shoe-shine box. It calmed his nerves before reporting for duty at the shipyard wharf.

It was a moonlit night in September 1908, two years after Isabel was born and Charlie stood at the dockside with his colleagues, technical observers, navy personnel and a couple of apprentices, who were anxious to sail in this wondrous vessel called *HMS Bravery*. The submersible was about to do its sea trials out in Liverpool Bay and they were waiting for a tugboat to pull alongside the wharf, which would escort it on its voyage out to Liverpool Bay.

Charlie was dressed in denim overalls over his navy blue guernsey, as it was likely he would be called upon to check the wiring if there was a problem. He shivered in the cool air and smiled encouragingly at Jimmy Baines, his apprentice. At nineteen, Jimmy was full of bravado on the outside, but inside was a quivering wreck.

"It's a piece of cake, Jimmy," he said quietly, as the lieutenant commander, who was in charge of the mission and was standing only a couple of feet away, complained loudly that someone's head would be on the block if the tug didn't turn up in the next few minutes. "This is my tenth time and, except for feeling a bit strange when you find yourself under the sea, you get used to it." A bit of an understatement really, because Charlie had never 'got used to it' and could already feel tightness in his chest as he waited to board the thing. *This was going to be the last time*, he promised himself, as the tug drew closer and the order went out to climb down the metal ladder attached to the side of the deck. *The very last time, even if my beloved never speaks to me again.*

CHAPTER FIFTEEN

Lily looked at Charlie's fob-watch, which he had left behind at the side of his bed. It was twenty past eight in the morning, two days since he had left again for another secret mission. He had said it would be local, the Irish Sea, Liverpool Bay, maybe along the Lancashire coast to Fleetwood. He hadn't been sure, as this time there was supposed to be a lot of top brass involved from the navy and the operation was 'hush hush'.

Lily was thoughtful, as she pushed Isabel along in the perambulator to her parent's villa, the latter warmly dressed in a homemade white knitted dress and cardigan. Was it worth all her husband's anxiety, just so they could find enough money to buy their own house? She had seen him change from a confident man, dressed smartly in the modern striped suits he liked to wear and walking along with a bit of a strut, as befitted a chap who worked in an important industry, to someone who had become rather edgy. He'd lost weight, more than he should, as his frame was thin to begin with and he'd jump at any sudden sound. He had gone back to sitting near the landing stage recently, lost in his thoughts as he stared into space across the Mersey. The biggest thing and in Lily's mind, the most important thing, was his inability to maintain an erection when she allowed him to make love. She had hoped they would have another baby in the future, now that Isabel was a lot easier to look after and didn't cry so much,

"So when do you think you'll be getting your new place, Lily?" asked Mannion, once she had settled Isabel on a pillow by Hannah. They sat at the side of her mother's bed, which had now been moved to the front room downstairs. "I had a walk along there at the weekend and it looks as if they'll be snapped up if you don't get a move on. Three have been sold already."

"Yes, I know, Father. I walk that way when I'm taking Isabel for her constitutional, but Charlie is worried about losing his job and doesn't want to tie himself down if we have to rely on his savings in the future."

"Pooh! That shipyard has enough work on to keep your husband going until he retires. Talk about a job for life, especially if there's another war."

"Another war?"

"Yes Lily, there are rumblings. You only have to read the papers, there's a lot of speculation about them Austro-Hungarians looking for an excuse to attack the Serbians."

"Stop frightening her, Father, what's our country got to do with any of that lot?" Hannah passed her grandchild over, not to Mannion, who wasn't adept at changing napkins. "Here Lily, take Isabel, she needs her soil cloth replacing."

Another day dawned, another day when Lily wondered why Charlie hadn't returned from his secret mission. If he was only going to Liverpool Bay, or a little further up the coastline, where had he got to this time? Perhaps she should push the pram as far as the shipyard and inquire of that nice Mr O' Neill, who Charlie had said was an approachable fellow and ask if he had any notion of when her husband would be back.

"It's the *Bravery*," said the man guarding the gate, when Lily eventually got to the shipyard, as Isabel had been sick and she'd had to change her clothes. It seemed that every time the child had things made from milk, it would set her off again. "The friends and family are over there."

He pointed to a small crowd that had gathered at the side of a row of office buildings. A man was waving his arms about, as if in a bit of a rage.

"What's the *Bravery*?" Lily ventured, not sure whether to ask the gate man if she could enter the dock to speak to Charlie's superior instead, as he seemed to be a bit agitated over something.

"*HMS Bravery*, it's one of these new things called a submersible. They're out in Liverpool Bay on sea trials. They say there's twenty of 'em, if you don't count the crew."

"Sea trials?" said Lily faintly, only just becoming aware that this might be something to do with her husband's secret mission. "What has happened? My husband said he was going on a sea trial the other day."

"Then 'e'll be aboard the *Bravery*. They say it's stuck... got a man down there in a divin' bell... 'e says they've a load of mud down there and the propeller got stuck. Do yer want ter go through, join the others? Oh dear, shall I get yer a chair?"

Lily did indeed need a chair, as her legs had buckled and there seemed to be a buzzing noise around her forehead and ears.

"I'll get yer the company nurse."

An ambulance cart, drawn by four black stamping horses, came along aside the gates just then and Lily was forgotten, whilst the driver, a doctor and his nurse were granted access into the dockyard. She sat there watching, as the cart drew up alongside the buildings, where a woman dressed in a long blue dress, short white cloak and a frilly ribbon tied hat, came out to join them. They seemed to be waiting. Waiting for what, Lily wondered?

More kerfuffle. A shiny black car, the occupants dressed in business suits sat inside looking grim faced, as the driver hooted his horn for access.

"They've had word that the lieutenant commander 'as got it shifted," the gate man announced to Lily, when he came back from saluting stiffly at the dignitaries. "Poor buggers, begging my French, madam, but if it weren't fer 'im, they'd be goners. 'E'll get a medal for this, I'll be bound."

"Can *I* go in?" asked Lily in a voice she heard herself using, but wondering at the calm way she spoke when inside she was quivering like a jelly. "I'll have to take the baby, but I'm sure she'll stay asleep."

"Aye, get yerself in there and let's thank our lucky stars we've got people like the lieutenant commander."

Or God, thought Lily, who had been sending up silent prayers and making all sorts of deals with her divine maker if He would only send her Charlie back again. There'd be no more talk of buying houses and she wouldn't resent him being master in his own home. She was just in time to see a tug boat berthing further up the high stone wharf and, behind it, with a crowd of people standing on the deck, was a dull grey, cylindrical vessel, that looked to Lily like a picture of a beached whale she'd once seen.

It was three days before Charlie was allowed to leave the Borough hospital and in that time he had decided that even if Lily was to take Isabel and return to her mother, there was no way he was ever going to set foot on anything that floated ever again. It had nearly finished him when the announcement had come over the speaker that the propeller had got stuck in very deep mud on the sea bed and, that all personnel should be aware that there was only a certain amount of oxygen in the vessel. They must restrict their breath, which contained carbon dioxide and could be fatal to all in the crowded conditions of the small vessel. That announcement had been enough to cause Charlie to have a panic attack and he was led away to his bunk by a member of the crew, who had been ordered to remove any stupid cretin who might jeopardise the other men's sanity.

It wasn't only me, he had thought irrationally, whilst the heavy dullness in his chest and the heaving of his lungs led him to think that it was only a matter of time and everyone would be fighting for air just like he was. He had seen the wildness in the eyes of the others, especially young Jimmy Baines, who looked about to make a dash towards the hatch to try and open it. He had heard the thrusters reversing and whirring and the indicator buoy being released. His last thoughts before he had, mercifully for him, fainted, was if they never floated up again, how could Lily be expected to visit his watery grave?

Back home, after the doctor had advised him to blow into a paper bag next time he had a panic attack, Lily made a fuss of him by cooking his favourite meal of steak and kidney pie with a rich gravy, garden peas and boiled potatoes, in an effort to lift his spirits. Charlie sat morose, wishing day on day that he had never left his Scottish paradise. One thing was certain, though: he was finished dicing with death in an underwater coffin and had said that much to Lily, who had nodded her head but didn't seem to have much to say on the subject.

He spent his waking hours reading, down at the landing stage if it wasn't raining, or walking along to The Grapes, where for the first few evenings locals treated Charlie as if he was a returning hero. The grog helped dispel those gruesome nightmares, when Charlie's chest felt as if he was being crushed by a great wall of water as the vessel split in two from the weight of an ocean on its hull. The whisky helped him sleep, even if his snoring did keep his beloved awake and it was then that Lily became a nag. She didn't act like his beloved anymore and had withdrawn all his marital entitlements, because he was spending all their money on drink.

After two long weeks of seeing her husband drunk as a mop and pushing frantically against the front door each night if he couldn't see to put his key in the lock, Lily had told him that she was going to get a job. "This can't go on, Charlie. If you're not willing to find another job, then I will." She had stood there ashen faced, bewildered that the man she'd put her trust in was a sot and not only that, was drinking their precious savings away. Yes, she knew all his excuses, knew he had been troubled with nightmares and who wouldn't be after the trauma he'd been through, but there were others in the household who were dependent on him. "I'll have to get a job, Charlie. We can't afford to live whilst you're swilling all the housekeeping down your throat. Bertha said that she will look after Isabel and Mabel could do with a hand in the floristry shop."

"No wife of mine is going to work for a living... you're just a bloody nag, Lily."

Charlie huffed and puffed and said the same thing to Ernie Morris, when the next night, propping up the bar in a stupor once again, he bemoaned the fact to his drinking mate.

"Aye, not like yer other wife, Mary Casson," Ernie had said, his eyes all bloodshot and his face all puffy, having been a heavy drinker over the years. "She were a worker, though mostly on her back."

"Eh?"

"I said, the other one, Mary Casson."

"I don't get your meaning."

"She was a prozzy – yer know, 'ave any man fer a shillin'? Told me once she was goin' ter give it up 'cause she'd found a decent fella, but once yer'd gone missin' she was back on the game again."

After the cramped conditions in a limited space when Charlie had worked on the submarine, it seemed wise for him to look for work in the open air. He could have had his old job back in the development office, Mr O'Neill having said he could when Lily went there to pick up his final wages, but somehow the very thought of going near a shipyard again made Charlie shudder.

It came as a bit of surprise to Lily, when he came back from The Grapes one Saturday evening, having cut his visits down to a couple per week and announced that a cousin of one of the chaps he drank with was thinking of giving up his market garden. All he would be asking for his enterprise was twenty-six pounds, which included the price of the stock, goodwill and the table he had at the local market. He didn't own the house that was on the land though and that was seven and sixpence in weekly rent. The other problem was that the property was out in Wallasey, which meant Lily would have to leave her family behind.

Twenty-six pounds was about all that Charlie had left in his savings account. Without a job there would be endless months of make-do and mend and perhaps even having to borrow, perish the thought, from his now not so wealthy father-in-law. He had decided to give in and allow Lily to help her sister, by making funeral wreaths in the evenings when Isabel was asleep, though it didn't make him much of a man if he couldn't earn their keep.

CHAPTER SIXTEEN

It was in April 1909 when Lily, Charlie and Isabel sat on the front bench of a removal wagon, which would take them and their possessions to a place called Pear Tree Cottage, just off the Poulton Bridge Road in Wallasey. It was the second trip that day for the horse and driver, as they had gone ahead with the first load of possessions, which had consisted of the sofa and two armchairs, kitchen table and chairs, Lily's display cabinet, a mahogany dining set and a black piano. The previous owner of the place, pleased that he could put his feet up for a week or two because twenty-six pounds was more than he had ever earned, had volunteered to keep an eye on things between visits. Lily, unhappy with the whole situation, but not having much choice in the matter since she had made her bed and must lie on it, thought it was more ideal to have a husband working for a living than hanging around doing nothing most of the day.

Mannion had not been pleased when he had heard that his son-in-law, he who had been a local hero for the part he had played in bringing the *HMS Bravery* back up to the surface (according to one of the local papers), was walking away from the job for life at Cammel Lairds and taking away his little princess to a different town. Not Lily now, but Isabel, who at three years old had replaced her mother in Mannion's affections. He tended to be scathing in his attitude towards Charlie's dreams of resurrecting his former enterprise, if it involved taking his grandchild away. Though what could his daughter do? She'd been a fool to marry for the second time, when she could have stayed in her parents' home, sheltered from the problems that this husband had brought upon her.

Charlie had walked from Rock Ferry to Wallasey a few weeks

before, to check out that the man wasn't selling up for any other reason than becoming tired with his thriving business. He then met with the landlord that owned the house, who demanded the first week of the rent in advance. He had not told Lily that the house they would live in was so archaic that it didn't even have an inside bathroom. He had set his heart on the place after first setting his eyes upon it as he walked up the brew, situated as it was on a hilly incline overlooking the Penny Bridge. There was a large greenhouse filled with tomato plants on the land, a smaller one complete with a flourishing grapevine, a tool shed filled with all the implements he would ever need, and an orchard, the trees awash with blossom that heralded an excellent harvest. It even had a sheltered area behind a wall nearer the cottage, which was stocked with row upon row of regimented dahlias. For the first time in many months he had felt happy, especially as he had spotted an imposing looking stone church with diagonal buttresses up on the nearby hill, that he and his family might worship in.

Lily's spirits, however, had plummeted even further when she saw that the docks at Wallasey Pool were only a few minutes walk away. Furthermore, when she saw the cottage, squatting as it did on the corner of a main road, which might possibly get choked with carts, cars and omnibuses for carrying the workers to the dockyard, became even more of the opinion that they should load their furniture back onto the wagon and retreat back home to Rock Ferry.

It wasn't until Charlie had sat Lily down on a wooden bench in a paved, lavender hedged area in the garden, whilst blonde haired Isabel toddled around looking into buckets and wheelbarrows, to gently explain to her that there was no going back, as their savings were all gone and they had to make a go of it, did it hit her that she had got herself in a same situation as she had before. This time not in a tumbledown manor house in the middle of the country, with a husband that had an upper class hyphenated surname and no money to speak of, but in a tumbledown cottage on the edge of the docks, with a husband who could well be committing them to a life of poverty.

She felt trapped and even more so when she walked into the kitchen. It was dark and sparse, the gas mantles were chipped and grubby and the tiles were cracked, both on the dirty looking flagstone floor and the mildewed walls. A door opened onto a shabby scullery, which held a stained slop-stone sink and a battered copper for doing the washing in. There was a smell of gas coming from a stove in the corner and one of the shelves that had probably held more than its weight could carry had come away from the wall. There was another door that she couldn't bring herself to open fully, as it housed some steps that would probably lead to an even smellier cellar.

It was all too much for Lily and she fled outside and hid in the orchard, where she could let her tears flow out of view. Charlie, aware that he'd been high handed by making this life changing decision without even consulting her, was unrepentant. She'd have to make some sacrifices, knuckle down, or back to her parents she'd have to go. In the five years that he and Lily had been a couple, there had been small, underlying changes in Lily that Charlie had not been fully aware of. She'd grown up; gone was the petted daughter whose only thoughts were of her appearance to her family and outside world, gone were the romantic dreams of a wonderful marriage to a man of wealth and substance and, recently, gone were her thoughts of betterment, a brand new house in an affluent suburb, rubbing shoulders with the wives of men in commerce and solicitors. Her time at Brookvale had served her well.

After weeks of scrubbing, cleaning and making the four bedroom cottage habitable with a good Axminster carpet laid in the best room, with the help of Bertha and occasionally Ellen, who would travel over on the omnibus that stopped along the dock road, Lily felt able to spend a little time looking around. Charlie – now seemingly in his element tending to his vegetable patches, greenhouses, a new herb garden and the abundant perennials in his flower beds – was planning to put a table out at the front of the cottage, where workers from the dockyards could purchase fresh produce on their way home. He had dismissed the opportunity of selling from the stall at Leasowe Market, as the idea of a table would be so much easier and better for his health than rising at the crack of dawn and pushing a laden cart up a rather steep hill. He had stopped short for the moment at providing egg sandwiches, now that he had also built a hen run and bought a few good layers, as a small shop that sold sandwiches and bakery goods existed nearby and he wouldn't like to get on the wrong side of the owners. Lily, happy to assist if required one morning, but seeing that Charlie was making a good fist of displaying his produce without her, made her escape, holding Isabel tightly by the hand as the little girl was apt to wander.

Across the road was a big old house with the date 1621 etched into a stone mantle over the front door. Lily, fascinated by the fact that the wide, diamond-paned windows, with stone mullions in between, reminded her of Brookvale, had been waiting for the moment when she could introduce herself to their neighbour, who she hadn't seen since they'd arrived. There was silence, after she had knocked on the old oak door, then peeped through one of the front windows to see if there was any sign of life within. She could hear a shuffling, someone violently coughing, so she waited with Isabel for the person to answer the door.

The man who stood in the hallway looked familiar, though she couldn't say why, because she didn't know anyone who lived in the vicinity. He was small in stature, had a short white beard and an old lined face, his fair hair was sparse, but he had kept it short, not straggly. He was dressed in a blue velvet dressing gown that had seen better days and he wore black leather down at heel slippers on his feet.

"How do you do? My name is Mrs Lily Wilson. My husband and I have recently moved into Pear Tree Cottage, I thought I would come across and introduce myself. This is my daughter, Isabel."

The man, who from the look of him was possibly almost blind, as his faded blue eyes seemed milky, smiled down at Isabel, then patted her on the head. "Wilson you say? That's a bit of a coincidence. My name's Wilson too. James Wilson."

"We must be related," Lily joked. "Well, I've just come to say hello and if there's anything you need Mr Wilson, let us know, as we do try to be good neighbours."

"Aye that I will, but me sister Emily and our Jo pop in a couple of times a week. They do a bit of cleaning and cooking for me, since me dear wife passed away."

He turned and coughed violently into his handkerchief, after Lily and Isabel had said goodbye and walked down the path.

It wasn't until Charlie came in for his meal around midday that Lily mentioned the coincidence of having a neighbour with the name Wilson. As Charlie had always kept to the story of his father's demise and had no interest in seeking out a would-be relative (he had enough with Lily's lot without adding more), he had shrugged his shoulders and had gone to wash his hands in the scullery.

Now that Charlie was at peace in his small corner of the world, marital relations were resumed, though it was Lily who initiated it. She had forgotten all the trauma of having a colicky little daughter and now that Isabel was nearly old enough to attend a nearby convent school, seeing as Mannion had offered to pay something towards his granddaughter's education, she thought it would be pleasant if they were to have a son to keep Charlie company; not that the child would be much of a help for at least ten years, but more help than a daughter would.

Charlie, living as he did in the fresh sea air and producing baskets of flavoursome Wallasey tomatoes that disappeared from his stall out front as soon as he put them there, had no problem in doing his duty. In fact, he found that Lily was more amenable in their lovemaking and was quite happy to do the deed now without extinguishing the light as she used to. It would be only a matter of time before she announced that there would soon be another little Wilson on the way.

Lily had settled now, enjoying her large kitchen with its cooking range and chunky, wooden table. Charlie had whitewashed the solid stone walls and had built her a couple of cupboards where she could put her pots and every day crockery. Her saucepans hung from ceiling hooks and the scullery with its gas stove, stone slop sink and an old fashioned copper for washing clothes overlooked the privy, housed in a narrow brick building by her washing line.

There were two best rooms either side of the front door: one where she kept her grand-mama's piano and could be used as a dining room on Sunday; the other, with the ebony cabinet full of her best English bone china, decorated with rosebuds and gilt and small family mementoes that she had gathered over the years, would be called the parlour. The pear tree that had given the cottage its name and had been trained to grow up the left wall had grown above the cottage roofline, where its branches overhung the high stone perimeter wall and the fruit was a magnet to passing children.

The house had probably been built in the early part of the 19th century, as Lily had discovered, when on the morning after their arrival she had found that there were two sets of stairs. One set lead from an upper back room down to the kitchen, perhaps for the use of a servant; the other on the landing ran down into what Lily called her sitting room. Charlie had checked out the cellar and found it housed the coal, the gas pipes, spider webs and a few mouse holes. Of course, the place lacked a bathroom, something which Lily had grown used to both at Rosemount and then at Mersey Mount, so once more she'd had to get used to doing without one. She made do with an all over wash in the scullery with a flannel, as she had also had to do at Brookvale.

The small shop sited just a few hundred yards up from the cottage had a large display window and emitted a lovely smell of baking through the open front door every morning, except Sunday. The owners, Arthur and Daisy Thomas, where originally from North Wales and usually went back on Sundays in their van, to collect seasonal fruit from the abundant orchard on Arthur's brother's farm. Rosy red apples, yellow pears, Victoria plums, golden yolk eggs and salted Welsh butter were often on sale on the premises and Arthur also sold his products from a stall on Leasowe Market, along with some of the confectionary that Daisy produced.

It had to be said that when Charlie took over the market garden, he was in direct competition with the Thomas's for the dock workers' custom, though his wares were minimal and not such a threat, if he only supplied produce from his vegetable garden. However, as time went by, money grew tight. Even by selling bunches of flowers to passing trade, they still were having problems with making ends meet, so Charlie suggested that they too should sell their produce as his mother had before from a market stall. Lily suggested they take in a lodger, as what did they need four bedrooms for?

Her idea had at first met with Charlie's disapproval. He didn't want a lodger, didn't want his peaceful haven disturbed, but he had to admit that extra money would come in useful now that winter was on its way once more and he didn't fancy puffing up the road to Leasowe with his produce. Even with Mannion's contribution of a hundred weight of coal, dropped off once per fortnight, the house was damp and the only source of heating that they could afford was keeping in the embers in the kitchen range. A lodger would pay for some extra heating and they could light some bedroom fires.

Charlie was now faced with the winter of 1909, when the fog swirled in from the dock lands, a bitter wind that seemed to attack every bone in his body. He succumbed to any coughs and colds that were doing the rounds, which restricted his breathing. The thought of having a lodger brought a certain relief to all these worries, once he had grown used to the idea, though it couldn't be permanent. Once the buds were on the trees again, he wouldn't want a lodger.

Lily had to man the stall when Charlie couldn't manage it, all dressed up in many layers of winter clothing and one of her husband's caps, whilst Charlie sat with Isabel helping her to read and count, so that she'd be a bit ahead when she started at the convent school. One afternoon, when Lily had decided enough was enough and there was only a couple of bunches left in the pail, a tall young man requested some flowers for his lady love.

"Tis' cold for yer, missis, standing out in all weathers. I've seen yer these last few days and said ter meself, I'll get my Kathleen some flowers on pay day. She lives over there, her dadda's the man who lives in the tollhouse. We're to be wed next summer, if we ever get a place that is."

"Is it difficult to get a place then?" Lily didn't know and hadn't yet got around to placing a card advertising for a lodger in the post office window at Liscard.

"It is, missis. I managed to get digs with a chap who works alongside me, but it isn't ideal workin' together, then sharing a place as well *and* it's over on the other side of Birkenhead Park."

"I see," said Lily, her spirits soaring as she thought that this nice young man might fit in very nicely in their household. He was working, looked clean, presentable and if his fiancée lived across the bridge, he wouldn't be spending a lot of time in their company. "I have a room to rent and I could do you a bit of breakfast too."

So Lily and Charlie welcomed their new lodger, whose name was Jack. He was given the third bedroom, Charlie still insisting that the smaller fourth room would be a bathroom one day, which had a view over the orchard and hedges of lavender.

It was coming up to Christmas and Lily, well versed now in the making of floral wreaths, did a roaring trade from her stall. The trend to display a seasonal wreath of holly entwined with red ribbons and a few heads of white chrysanthemums on the front door of a person's home had begun to catch on with the workers from the docks. Not that it was just dockyard workers that passed their stall to and from the dock lands. Chemical industries, such as the one that Jack worked for, oil and gas companies with their storage containers and sundry offices; all had businesses growing down there.

One crisp morning, when Lily had just finished selling the last of the sprouts that Charlie had grown in abundance that year, she noticed a funeral carriage, its two black stallions stamping impatiently with their nostrils billowing in the chill of the air, as a coffin was loaded upon it by two black suited men. The carriage was outside the home of Mr Wilson and, sensing that the poor old bloke had gone to his maker, Lily hurriedly whipped her apron off and, leaving the stall unattended, she sped across the road to pay her last respects.

A woman, short in height and a little rotund, with salt and pepper hair and wearing a black armband around the left sleeve of her shabby blue coat, waited on the pavement for the carriage to move off with the coffin.

"I hope you don't mind," Lily said, puffing a little, as the house was on a bit of an incline. "My name is Lily Wilson and I live across the road at Pear Tree Cottage. You must be Mr Wilson's daughter? I called across to introduce myself to your father one day and he didn't seem to be very well."

"No, it got him in the end, poor Dad. Been sufferin' for years with a weak chest and this last month he's been coughin' up blood. A merciful release though. We think he must have caught somethin' on 'is travels."

"Travels?"

"Yeah, 'e was a mariner, went all over. One time when we were kids we didn't see 'im fer years. Mam used ter joke that 'e were a typical sailor, a woman in every port. Anyways, I'll be off, got ter meet the others at the cemetery. Isn't it strange 'avin two Wilson's livin' opposite each other, I wonder if we're related?"

CHAPTER SEVENTEEN

It was July 1911 before Lily was certain that another little Wilson would make his appearance and, according to Bertha's calculations, the birth would be early in the New Year. The two sisters had grown quite close to one another as the years began to quickly pass them by; more so now, with their mother, Hannah, having gone to her rest in heaven, probably due to the enormous pressure of her weight on her heart. Mannion, cut to the quick by the demise of his adored wife and housebound because of painful gout, became dependent on some of his many daughters to keep him going in his final years. Frederick, unmarried and now a foreign diplomat, was only seen spasmodically.

Bertha, in charge of it all, as she lived the closest to her parent's modest home and had more time on her hands now that the Patterson aunties had passed away, became the provider of Mannion's daily meals. Some of them were cooked from the seasonal offerings of fruit, eggs and vegetables, courtesy of Pear Tree Cottage, taken across to the house in Carlton Road by a driver who now rented the old Wilson house across the Poulton Bridge Road. The man made his living delivering any goods that were up for transportation, parking his horse-drawn truck at the side of the stable that was built on land nearby. Ellen, once again, was called upon to keep her father's house in good, clean order, even though she was now mother to a pair of snotty nosed rascals. Mabel, who had become the manageress of the florist shop on Borough Road, was there in the evening to keep her father company. Lily, when she wasn't required to man the stall outside the house and once Isabel had started at the convent school, would walk across the Penny Bridge, sometimes trekking through the narrow streets near

Birkenhead Park until she reached her father's home. Mostly, and especially when she found she was expecting again, she caught the omnibus from the Laird Street depot.

It was a warm day in July when Lily, holding Isabel by the hand, stood outside Mannion's house, waiting for Bertha to answer the door. The convent school was on vacation and both Lily and Isabel were wearing chiffon summer dresses: Isabel's knee length and white, Lily's calf length and violet; Isabel wearing a straw boater trimmed with a matching ribbon and Lily wearing a larger version of her daughter's. They had been there for some time and were just about to leave and catch the bus to the market, as Isabel had requested the visit there as a treat (to a six year old the market was a really exciting place), when Bertha, wiping tears away from her face with a large, white handkerchief, answered the door.

Alarmed that her father might be at death's door and concerned that perhaps this would be her last chance to say goodbye to him, Lily left her daughter standing on the doorstep and sped to the kitchen-cum-living room. But Mannion, still as large as ever, was sitting in his armchair in front of the fire, staring gloomily at the newspaper that he had open in front of him.

"I knew something like this was going to happen," he said mournfully, not taking in the fact that a different daughter was standing over him with a face full of concern. "That Hollweg fellow, that new German Chancellor... it says here that he wants Britain to reduce our naval armaments and the Germans will sign some bit of paper and do the same. I wouldn't trust that lot as far as I could throw them and if Lawrence knew what's good for him he'd get a shore job and pack in the sea."

"Surely it's just a lot of posturing, 'cause he's a new to the position? That's what Charlie would say it was." Lily beckoned to her daughter, who had been standing anxiously in the hallway listening to her grandfather, who didn't seem to be his usual jovial self.

When her heart had stopped beating madly, Lily sank thankfully on the sofa with a bewildered Isabel. Bertha put the kettle on for a soothing cup of tea to calm all their nerves, over the initial shock of listening to her father warning that German submarines would one day pounce upon the merchant ships that sailed the Atlantic between Liverpool and America, which brought food and other products to a growing population.

"I heard Charlie talking to one of the dockyard workers the other day and he said that he'd heard from one of the German sailors that there's a lot of civil unrest back there. A war with France and Russia would prove popular, but it would be fought on land not the sea. The sailor had said that Germany had no cause to fight a war with Britain."

"Humph, well we'll see. I'll write to Frederick and find out what he's got to say." Mannion decided not to continue the discussion with those whom he felt were his unworldly daughters, after having succeeded in frightening poor Bertha, whose sea going husband he reckoned would be in the thick of it. From the reports he'd been reading recently, it seemed that the German military commanders were spoiling for a fight.

A similar discussion was going on between Charlie and his new pal Frank Pollitt, the delivery driver who rented the old house across the road. They had become firm friends, after Frank, seeing an opportunity to sell fruit and vegetables from his horse drawn cart, had approached Charlie and asked if he would be willing to supply the produce for his new enterprise. Of course, Charlie leapt at the chance of expanding and had even taken on a lad to do the heavy digging, leaving him with the pleasure of picking the produce and the occasional hoeing and weeding.

"I can't see why Britain would want to go to war with Germany," Charlie was saying. "Why would we, when even our monarchy is related to them? According to what I've been reading, if there was a war it would be the Austro-Hungarian Empire fighting the poor little Serbians – they've been itching for a fight with them for years."

"So they say." Frank, a large, heavily bearded man, an ex-docker, who due to an injury at work walked with a limp and was married to a nurse who worked at Victoria hospital, sounded dubious. "But me eldest boy, who as you know has just finished his army training, was saying that word 'as it some sort of treaty was signed years ago with Belgium."

"Well, what's Belgium got to do with anything?" Charlie was at a loss to understand why a piece of paper signed with Belgium could draw Britain into any impending war.

"France, mate. We're allies of France and if Belgium was invaded, France would be as well."

"But what has France or Belgium got to do with Serbia?"

"Don't know Charlie, I'm at a loss meself."

Life in the Wilson household was now a lot more comfortable financially. Once Frank had got his delivery up and running around the leafy lanes of Oxton, where wealthy merchants and the nouveau riche had built houses suitable for their grand lifestyles, they didn't need to take in a lodger. Besides profiting from the growing demand for his produce – principally still from the passing dock land trade but also from the flour mill that had been built further along the busy road – Charlie was able to take things a little easier. Danny, his young labourer, had proved to be worth his weight in gold in all things appertaining to the production of fruit and vegetables. Furthermore, the Thomas's had sold their shop to a woman who preferred to run the place as a bakery and sandwich bar, and was happy to order all the free range eggs that Charlie could supply.

Jack, their lodger, after a pleasant wedding held at nearby St. Hilary's to which the Wilson's had been invited and after a weekend in New Brighton for the honeymoon, had moved into the tollhouse with Kathleen and her father, but still called in now and again just to say hello. It was of his opinion too that war couldn't be far away. Look how there'd been the possibility of one over the Second Moroccan Crisis and the prevention of expansion of the Balkan War into broader conflict. Not that he or Charlie understood the motives of these politicians with their posh sounding lordship names, who were in charge of all things to do with foreign affairs, but they liked to sound knowledgeable. It was a man thing to keep an eye on what the government of the day was up to – that's why those women suffragettes, who were causing a lot of mayhem all around, were proving to be such a pain.

"You'd be as well trying to get back into the shipyard, Charlie," Jack said, whilst sipping a glass of homemade parsnip wine, which Charlie had recently found he was proficient at producing.

"You might think it'll be the younger men that'll be called up first and that could be true, but you're only – what, thirty-nine? – and already experienced in one of them submarines the navy'll start using. My boss was saying only the other day that people in reserved occupation wouldn't have to go to war."

"With my luck, they'd have me down in one of them again." Charlie felt a shudder at the thought of it and hoped he wouldn't get his nightmares back. His life was perfect just as it was. A thriving business, a good wife, a pretty daughter and another longed for baby on the way.

Lily felt worried as she listened to the men 'chewing the fat', as Charlie was apt to call his discussions with any male that had the time to listen when they stopped at the Wilson's stall. As the months flew by and her body had grown bigger with pregnancy, she yearned for the quiet life she had known back in Greasby. The only talk of war then was when Roland had spoken of faraway lands, where despots, rajah's and tyrants stood in the way of the mighty British Empire, who were intent on civilizing the world, whether the world liked it or not. A war in Europe, even if it was to be fought in a little known place called Serbia, seemed too close to home to the protective instinct in Lily, especially when she saw the increased shipping that came into the Wallasey docks.

Three things that winter caused Charlie to revisit his refusal to consider returning to the shipyard: his fruit trees got blight, probably, he thought, due to the import of foreign apples, any diseases being spread by the rats who continued to leap across the short distance from a ship to his orchard; his vegetables, mostly cabbages and sprouts, were ruined overnight by a sudden dip in temperature, causing a kind of frostbite that burrowed into their core and Frank, having nothing much to sell now on his delivery round, took an inside job at the flour mill. Finally, Charlie's lungs, exposed to the bitter wind chill as he haplessly examined each round heart or head for some sign that the vegetable was sellable, began to find that his breathing was becoming restricted yet again.

Lily, relieved on one hand that a desk job for Charlie would be more reliable than his market garden, and that if war was declared, though still unlikely if the newspapers were to be believed, he would be safe in an office instead of being sent to the front line, worried that she would be expected to look after the dwindling produce on the stall. After all, there were still the flowers, hot house grapes and a few fat marrows for sale and as her girth increased, with the birth of her baby due in February, she didn't feel like standing there in the freezing cold.

It was Danny who came up trumps, on being told that there might not be a job for him if his employer got work at the shipyard. A couple of hours tuition on how to add the shillings and pennies and what change he'd have to give to a customer, saw him taking the place of Lily more than once on the stall.

Mr O'Neill, still in charge of the office where Charlie used to work before his panic attack on the *H.M.S Bravery*, was a little put out, to say the least, when his ex-employee turned up looking for his old job, expecting it still to be there even though he had been absent from his desk for over three years. If it hadn't been for the fact that the navy had ordered enough warships and submarines to make one think that the government was planning to defend its nation against a major invasion, O'Neill would have kindly said, to this ingenuous little man who stood before him, that his position was no longer there. However, no one knew the date, the hour, or whether Britain would be caught with its pants down, so being a man who liked to meet his obligations ahead of the rest, he decided that it wouldn't do the shipyard any harm to have an extra man, even if that man *had* declined to go on sea trials!

Lily, worried to death that the new baby might be born into a hand-to-mouth existence, could finally plan ahead for a decent spread at Christmas and kill a chicken for their festive meal, instead of needing it alive for its eggs.

Six year old Isabel, educated as she was by the nuns at the local convent school, soon came home with a smattering of French, had a knowledge of arithmetic and was adept at reading anything that had the written word. She had settled in well and enjoyed the strict regime of learning that the kindly teachers imposed upon their small charges and although neither Charlie and Lily were of the Roman Catholic faith, they accepted that though she took no part in the prayers, their daughter was still treated as a member of God's family.

On fine days the pupils went out to play in a lovely garden just behind the church. There was a huge lawn there, where the weeping willow trees made a graceful shelter for the black-robed sisters to sit and work at their beautiful embroidery. Those of the sisters who were not on duty would tuck up their skirts and play games with the children along the gravel paths. There were statues of the Virgin Mary and all the saints placed into little alcoves that were cut into the hedges around the garden. There were archways too and one day Isabel took the opportunity to have a look beyond the area that was forbidden to the youngsters. Just a look; no one would notice if she took a peek into what she saw was a kitchen garden. A garden smaller than her Papa's, but with a dozen white hens scratching and clucking and a nun hoeing the soil with all the energy she possessed.

Lily gave birth to her second baby as the snow began to fall in the third week of February. The local midwife, Miss Margaret Shaw, was in attendance when the doctor on examining Lily had decided that, considering Isabel had been a fairly easy labour, Lily could give birth at home and not in the nearby hospital, though with her tiny frame there might have been a possibility of a breech birth. The couple were a little disappointed, after ten hours of Lily's exertion, that the baby whom they later decided to call Irene wasn't a boy, but were grateful that their offspring had the required number of fingers and toes on her hands and feet. It also seemed that their market garden now would be just an extra source of income, as Charlie had settled back into his office job and Danny, until he got his call up papers, was keeping an eye on things.

CHAPTER EIGHTEEN

By 1914, the German chancellor, Theodore von Bethmann-Hollweg, who had worked so hard in the past to convince Britain that there should be a reduction, not an increase of military armaments, found that he had come up against the wishes of his naval commander, Admiral Alfred von Tirpitz, who along with Kaiser Wilhelm was itching to start a war. Not having a good enough reason to attack Serbia, because it would bring about the might of Russia, who was a friend of the small country, the pair waited for a valid excuse, building up their military weapons and even picking the name for their hostilities of the 'Great War'.

Most people in Britain were unaware of the whirling pool of discontent that was happening so faraway in Europe. They didn't consider themselves Europeans and unless someone threatened their own existence, why should they be concerned? Many in the second decade of the 20th century hadn't even been out of their villages and couldn't point on a map to where these foreign sounding names like Serbia were. Enjoying the warmth of an English summer, they didn't really care.

Lily, Charlie and their two young daughters – Isabel, a slim seven year old with long fair hair, and Irene, chestnut haired and toddling – took their first holiday together at the end of June, at a small bed and breakfast in Morecambe, travelling by train from Liverpool. Morecambe was not so brash as the nearby Blackpool, or so Charlie had heard from his office colleagues, where the mill owners of Lancashire put on special trains to transport their workers on Wakes Week; a time when the mill would shut down and everyone, even the bosses, took a week's holiday. The B&Bs would be full, the arcades, the theatres and the Blackpool Tower would be packed and the landladies would be working flat out to cater for their lodgers needs.

In Morecambe, staying in the large bedroom of a Victorian built, three-storied, terraced house in a quiet street near Happy Mount Park, the family enjoyed the luxury of electric lighting, with Irene being in trouble for constantly pulling on the light switch. There was also a bathroom and an inside toilet and, although they had to pay for the privilege, each were able to have a soak in the ceramic bath. It was a happy time for all of them, with Charlie contentedly paddling with his daughters in the shallow end of the lido or in the chill waters of Morecambe Bay. Lily enjoyed the music played each day in the bandstand and both agreed that the floral display in the gardens gave food for thought, should Charlie ever want to landscape his acre instead of working the land. They took a ride on the tram to Blackpool, eyeing in awe the giant Ferris wheel that people queued for hours to take a ride on, walked to the top of the enormous tower that was modeled on the one that they had in Paris (Charlie didn't, he sat on a bench watching the tide come in on Blackpool sands) then thankfully, finding the crowds too much to cope with along the busy streets, piers and esplanade, they caught the tram back to their lodgings.

It was as Charlie put the key in the lock of Pear Tree Cottage, after puffing up the incline from the Penny Bridge holding Irene with one hand and the family's cardboard suitcase in the other, that he had a sudden pang of remorse for the way he had taken Lily from the comfort of their marital home on Mersey Mount, before that Rosemount Terrace, and plonked her in this shabby, damp smelling dwelling, with no bath or inside toilet. He looked with dismay at the flagged floor in the kitchen, the dim lamps, the old fashioned range, walls that could do with another coat of distemper and the Persian rug, which badly needed replacing as it was all scuffed with ingrained dirt. He remembered how she had been so proud of it.

He watched, as the mother of his two darling daughters went straight to the range to put a light to the fire that had been left in tidy readiness, took the suitcase from him and placed it in the scullery ready for the washing of the contents next day. She filled the kettle, gave Isabel her housekeeping purse and told her to fetch a plate meat pie from the bakery, then proceeded to peel some potatoes, all the while keeping an eye on Irene, who was sitting on the floor talking animatedly to her little rag doll.

This matronly looking woman was his Lily, he thought sorrowfully. The girl he had called his beloved, whom he had dreamt about and wrote little poems to. What had he done to her? Eleven years on, they were living in a wreck of a house, with no modern trappings of his success, when she should have been living in a beautiful house on a leafy avenue somewhere. She was a saint to have put up with the ups and downs of their marriage, though he couldn't help thinking she had let herself go somewhat.

Her figure, once held together by corset-like undergarments, bulged discreetly around the waist of her skirt. Her peplum jacket now strained across her ample bosom and her hair had more grey than chestnut, which she wore in a bun at the nape of her neck. She looked aged beyond her thirty-eight years and recently he had been feeling a wave of discontent, because now she wasn't the girl he had fallen in love with and he felt short changed somehow.

Lily looked over in exasperation at Charlie, who was still standing where she had left him by the back door, looking a little lost and as if he needed someone to give him orders. She couldn't help smiling to herself wryly, when she thought of how she had changed from a frivolous young miss to this bustling body who had become such a good organiser. Bertha would have been very pleased with her all those years ago, if she had shown one iota of the energy that she put in to keep the body and soul of this small household going. And Grand-mama, Grand-mama who despaired that Lily had no talent other than arranging flowers, would be gratified to see the woman that Lily had become. *Not with a wealthy husband though*, a voice inside her head mocked. *No splendid house and servants, no nursery maid to see to your daughters' needs. Just married to a glorified gardener, who had a mother that sold flowers at the cemetery gate.*

"Hadn't you better have a look around the greenhouse?" she asked Charlie suddenly, with a sharp tone in her voice. She wondered why, after such a good family holiday, when the pair of them had got on so well despite having to keep their lovemaking to the early hours of the morning when they were sure their children were asleep, she was suddenly feeling dissatisfied.

"Did you leave the window open in the greenhouse, Charlie? The tomatoes might have been affected by a draught."

"There's no need to worry, Danny would have checked and he was keeping an eye on the place as you know."

"Well, don't just stand there, then, find something to do. Perhaps you could go as far as putting the water into the teapot."

Charlie shrugged and did as he was told – at the look on her face, he wasn't going to argue.

Now that Charlie had a good job paying top wages again, it had been decided that it would be he who would pay for Isabel's education, seeing as she could read any book put in front of her, write very well and speak French fairly fluently. Irene also had her name down at the convent and would begin her education when she was four.

Mannion, still a creaking door but a danger to himself now he gone a little senile, had been given a bedroom in the home on Temple Road, as Mabel (a member of the suffragette movement now, especially so, since Emily Davidson had been killed under the legs of a horse in her pursuit of a vote for women), had decided when asked if she would give up work and look after her father instead, that she would rather walk on hot coals Instead she chose to share the rent of a two bedroom flat in a house on Shrewsbury Road, with a woman she had met on one of the rallies in Liverpool.

There seemed to be so many changes now, in Charlie's opinion. People like Mabel, for instance, who didn't need or want the protection of a man, be it father or husband, was quite happy earning a wage with only herself to think of. Another of Lily's sisters, Caroline, an older one that Charlie had only met at weddings and funerals, was at this moment sailing across the many seas in an emigrant ship bound for a place called Perth in Australia. She was to start a new life with a husband and three almost grownup boys, looking for a better place, a peaceful place, to live in.

And there would be thousands more like Caroline, Charlie thought, with war almost on the horizon, now that someone called Archduke Franz Ferdinand, heir to the Austro-Hungarian throne, had been assassinated. This had given a much needed excuse for the Germans to take a strike at Serbia, even though the emperor of that country, who had never been close to Franz, wasn't really bothered.

Charlie, up to his neck now in helping to launch battleships, submarines and all sort of smaller vessels that the navy had decided were necessary if suddenly Britain was called upon to help an ally, read his daily newspaper avidly, trying to make sense of it all. Germany, who seemed to have been spoiling for a fight for quite a while, offered what became known as a 'blank cheque' to Austria-Hungary, which meant unconditional support on whatever action the country decided upon. Germany, however, was more agreeable to war with France or Russia, who were supporters of Serbia, but according to the newspaper hoped to avoid a war with Britain. Much encouraged by this show of support from Germany, it was decided by Austria-Hungary to revoke Serbia's national sovereignty, when really all they had to do was to ask for Ferdinand's murderers to be handed over.

So on 4th August 1914, Charlie and his colleagues in the office heard that British Foreign Secretary Sir Edward Grey had announced that Britain was to fight to defend Belgium neutrality, as German troops were to occupy the country whilst en route to France.

"What the hell has Belgium got to do with us?" Charlie said, no doubt voicing all the opinions of the men who were listening to their manager's announcement after he had read out the telegram.

Many volunteers rushed to join the armed forces later, as there was a widespread misunderstanding of what this war would be like.

Most thought they were doing their bit to help crush the brutal aggression of the German Empire, encouraged by the government of the day who had control over what was written in the newspapers. It was only in the following year when casualties were mounting fast, the numbers enlisting dropped off and conscription was brought in for all unmarried men, known as the 'call up.'

CHAPTER NINETEEN

When the hostilities ended over four long years later, the armistice signed and millions of men having died in a futile war that should have been over by Christmas, many families were left traumatised after losing their main breadwinner and fatherless children were brought up in even worse poverty than they were before. But the kaiser had been given a bloody nose as far as many people were concerned, although he probably didn't feel the effect personally in his retirement in the village of Appledorn, Holland.

Charlie, amongst others who hadn't lost their lives and were in a reserved occupation, found themselves trudging the streets looking for work. The shipyard, its navy contracts fulfilled and no more orders in the pipeline, had shed its workers, leaving only a skeleton workforce behind.

When Charlie and his colleagues were vital to the war effort they had been presented to King George V and Queen Mary, but now they had to present themselves to the unemployment office, where a means test decided if they would have enough to eat.

Not that it was the case in the Wilson household, as Lily, used to frugal living and make-do and mend, had been very canny during the war years, banking Charlie's wages and assisting Danny in the market garden, until he had enlisted in the Liverpool Pals and had marched off to die in the fields of glory. She had provided as much as she was able from their land and their laying hens, with the table outside the cottage proving popular with the passing dock land trade.

The country was certainly no fit place for heros to return to. Those who were lucky enough to survive found themselves coming back to broken homes and unbearable poverty. To top it all was the spread of Spanish influenza, which visited on a population whose bodies, weakened by the deprivations of good food due to the German U-boat campaign of sinking the ships that carried the food that Britain imported, hadn't got the ability to shrug the infection off. Lily, once again, had a husband who was morose and melancholy and even the dock lands were idle after four years of noisy intrusion into the Wilson family's ears. *What was the point of working in the garden again, with no passing trade?* Charlie had said to himself.

It was a harrowing time for the couple, after Isabel went down with scarlet fever, contracted no doubt from her fellow students at the local school she now had to attend along with Irene, who had been most put out at having to leave her beloved teachers at the convent. Charlie was not able to pay the fee for their private tuition anymore and Lily wanted to hold onto her precious savings. Isabel was sent away by the family doctor to a hospital on Vyner Road in Bidston, which was earmarked for its isolation on the outskirts of the town. Irene also fell ill, though not so acutely as her sister, and Lily spent most of her time nursing her small patient. A wet, white sheet was suspended from the lintel of the bedroom door and the child tossed and turned as the fever took hold. It was inevitable that Charlie took to drink once more, finding solace in the company of other poor souls, with their recent tales of blood and gore to tell at the local tavern.

While the children were ill and Lily was confined to the cottage – except for cutting a few flowers from the garden and placing them outside the gate in a bucket, with hope in her heart that someone would have a few coppers to spare for a bunch, as Charlie was drinking their hard earned savings away – she met up with a shady little man called Kenny. At that time, betting wasn't a legal form of recreation, but there was usually someone of Kenny's calibre hanging around a pub or a street corner that knew all the ropes involved in the sport.

Lily met Kenny one morning, when he knocked at her door to tell her he was taking two of her bunches. One for his mother and one for his sweetheart, who he was hoping to make an honest woman of one day. Whilst he was handing her the money, he asked would she be interested in doing a bit of business? There was a horse, a dead cert, who was running in the Grand National at Aintree that day. With a bet each way, especially with his insider knowledge that the horse didn't have a wooden leg, Lily would be rewarded with instant riches for her bet. Lily smiled to herself, as she gave back the money that he had just handed over and watched as he drew wads of paper and money out of his long overcoat pockets, licking the end of his pencil, then writing down her name. She thought herself a mug, but why not dream of riches for a while? She was tickled pink when the following Monday she saw Kenny hanging around the front gate, the collar of his coat pulled up against a chilly wind, a trilby pulled low on his forehead, looking every inch a spiv from a gangland movie. She was fifteen shillings richer and it was the first time in her life she had ever placed a bet.

It was eight weeks before Isabel made a full recovery – a long time to be away from her family, who weren't allowed to visit the hospital for fear of spreading germs. Irene had caught a lighter dose of the disease and although she had tossed and turned and gone through the same delirium, the doctor was pleased with her progress after the fever broke and she was on the mend. Lily, however, was whacked.

Eliza, one of Lily's older sisters, who had been in her teens when Lily was born, earned her living as a dressmaker and now that her children had flown the nest and her husband was dead from influenza, she turned her front room into an alteration shop, over the Penny Bridge in nearby Claughton. Trade was good, now that no one had much money to spend on new clothing and she was in need of a girl who was handy with a sewing needle.

At a family conference, something that the sisters had started after the war, when on a Sunday afternoon they would all turn up to visit Mannion and share light refreshments together, it was decided that as Isabel was only a few months away from her fourteenth birthday, she would fit the bill. She had not been to school since she was ill and was fully conversant with hems, stitching, pattern cutting and sewing buttons, which she was taught at both the convent and the local school. Lily, fully aware that there was no way Charlie could pay for more education for their daughters, though of course she wouldn't say so to her sisters, jumped at the chance of having one less mouth to feed. Eliza had said it could be a live in position, and so she gave her permission there and then.

Irene, the baby of the family and coming up to eight, was a quiet little girl, with imaginary friends, Louloubell and Jonny, who lived in the undergrowth in the orchard. She spent a lot of her time reading, as from an early age she had learnt to keep out of the way when Lily started her nagging and everyone got an earful if they happened to be in the way. Her favourite place was in the bough of one of the gnarled old pear trees, where she could keep an eye on the back of the house, in case a parent might be out and about. Not that she had any qualms about her father, she was his pretty pussycat and they got on very well, but she did blame him for her lack of education. Now that there was not much money coming in, she had been taken out of the convent school that she had started at four years old, where she had quickly picked up the rudiments of reading and a little French. For the moment, she didn't attend a school at all. It seemed it was money, 'the root of all evil' according to Charlie, which caused all the rows and the bitter words she heard between her parents.

By March 1920, Charlie had given up looking for any kind of work. At forty-eight, he couldn't see how trailing around getting 'knock backs' from companies who, if they had any precious work, were looking for a younger man, was doing anyone, including his shoe leather, any good. Occasionally, if the weather wasn't too wet or the wind too bitter, he would dress warmly in his once-best overcoat, his battered bowler hat and the fingerless gloves that Lily had knitted him and spent an hour hoeing a drill, cutting back the overgrown branches of his fruit trees, or cleaning out the hen house. Lily, bless her heart, still had a little bet on the horses and gave him a shilling from her winnings to spend at the local tavern now and again. It was there one night that Charlie met a man named Tony.

Tony O'Reilly was one of the few survivors of a German attack, after signing on the *R.M.S Lusitania* as a steward before the liner had been sunk near Kinsale in Ireland. He retired on medical grounds when he found a sympathetic doctor who agreed he was unfit to enlist in any of the British forces, then found he could make a good living as an entrepreneur. There was always a willing crewman who had dropped anchor in the Port of Liverpool, then had made his way to one of the many pubs that stood on every corner in the dock land area, who could supply Tony with most things from his travels, providing it would fit in his kit bag. At the time he met Charlie, who in his opinion looked an honest man, he was heavily into contraband. Cigarettes, tobacco, spirits or wine from Bordeaux, he wasn't bothered, providing he made a buck, which was an expression he was fond of using.

Bert, the man who stood behind the bar at The Coach and Horses, had pointed Charlie out as someone who might be interested in renting out his garden shed, after hearing Charlie bemoaning the fact that the tools in his shed were getting rusty with disuse. Tony, desperate to find storage for the many boxes arriving on an incoming ship from Rotterdam, due in for repairs at the Birkenhead Pool the very next evening, jumped at the chance of a new place to hide the merchandise, as Plod had been sniffing around his gaffe again.

"I hear yer might be interested in a bit of business?" Tony, a tall, lean man in his early forties, with yellow teeth as he smoked a lot, said affably, coming over from where he'd been standing at the bar with another man. "It's Charlie, isn't it? It's you that has the land on the corner of Poulton Bridge Road."

"That's true," said Charlie, puffing up a little with pride, when he heard that someone was addressing him with a bit of respect. "Had it as a market garden before the war, but it's too much for me now. Needs a younger man to work it."

"Well, I'm sure I could find someone to take it on fer yer, if yer wanted, Charlie. I've lots of contacts and there must be plenty out there that would work for reasonable wages. I'll keep me ear out. Meanwhile, I'm lookin' for somewhere I can store a few boxes. A lockup really and there'd only be me that would have the key. I hear you might have a shed or suchlike that I could rent?"

"For the right price." *Lily would go mad if there were people traipsing through the yard into the gardens,* Charlie thought.

"I was thinkin' two quid a week and a bottle of whisky." That would get him; Bert had said that Charlie liked a drop of whisky now and again.

"You're on. There's a separate entrance on the dock road, save you coming through the front gate. The shed is at the back of the orchard. Hang on, though, it's nothing illegal, is it? The missis'll go mad if it is."

"No, pal, rest assured the boxes are kosher." *It's the contents that aren't,* he thought to himself.

Lily, fed up again with make-do and mend, had started buying *The Woman's Weekly* magazine. It was more to scan the fashions than anything else; she was feeling dowdy and nothing like the young miss who liked to wear whatever was in vogue all those long years ago, so had decided to treat herself to a pattern and a length of material. It would be just enough to make a calf length summer dress, with cap sleeves and a button bodice. If truth was told, however, it was Irene who was in more need of a summer dress to wear. The hand-me-downs from Isabel or any older cousins were long gone, especially so from her sister, as Isabel had been as thin as a willow and Irene was a little more plump.

Lily had rid herself of the wide brimmed hat that she had alternately trimmed with feathers or flowers of felt after the war was over. She now sported a cloche, a type of bell-shaped close fitting hat, that flattened her hair and made her face look a little more rounded. But it was fashion and she and Isabel, on one of the rare weekends that her daughter came to visit, had a lot of fun together as they tried to cut one out of a piece of thick blue felt that the girl had brought along. One weekend, much to Irene's surprise and gratitude, Isabel brought her a calf length, peach, cotton dress, with a drop waist, buttoned bodice, Peter Pan collar and little puffed sleeves. She had sown it herself with the help of her Aunt Eliza in the dark winter evenings.

It now seemed that Isabel had a beau – not that she had discussed the matter with her mother, but she had decided to take her younger sister into her confidence as she knew that Irene, who would probably listen to Isabel's tale with some astonishment, wouldn't tell. In 1920 Isabel was only just fifteen, but it seemed she had attracted the attention of a young man, some three years older than herself, who worked at the butchers along the road. She had turned into an attractive young lady, anxious to follow the latest fashions seen in her aunt's woman magazines, or when window shopping at the new department store, Saltbury's, that had just opened in Grange Road. The two girls were sitting on Irene's bed, out of earshot of their parents, when Isabel, not having a confidante of her own age, decided to tell all to her sister.

"He's ever so nice, Irene. He has black curly eyelashes and lovely brown eyes. He really is my heart's desire." Isabel had sighed, unwittingly parroting her mother's thoughts when she had thought that she was in love with her cousin, Lawrence, all those years ago. "His name is Duggie, Douglas really, but he prefers Duggie. He works in the butcher shop, just along the row from Aunt Eliza's and I met him when he came in one day to have his trousers shortened. He's asked me if I would like to go to the Argyle Theatre with him."

"Did he ask you in front of Aunt Eliza?"

"No silly, he knows I'm too young to start walking out with someone and I had to tell him that I wasn't allowed out of the house once the shop was closed for the day. So, he's asked me to meet him outside the park gates next Sunday. I can pretend that I've come over here for a visit, Aunt Eliza doesn't check that I've been here."

"She wouldn't because she trusts you." Irene still only a child at that time, was astute enough to know that what Isabel was planning to do was a very naughty thing.

"Well, I'm going to meet him anyway and you'd better keep your mouth shut, or they'll be no more pretty dresses for you."

Irene treasured that dress and couldn't bear to part with it, until inevitably one day the generous seams of the bodice couldn't stretch anymore and even Lily couldn't fix them. Financially, things hadn't got any easier, with Lily scratching a frantic living from her efforts in the garden. Charlie, hampered now by a winter cough, had taken himself off to bed, where he read his precious newspapers and back copies of the *Lloyds Register*, which he still kept in his father's sea chest that had been liberated from Jessica Parsons. Not that his ill health had stopped him from shuffling in his worn out slippers along to the Coach and Horses once a week, where an envelope was left behind the bar with his name on it. He told Lily that it was something from the benefits, when he handed her twenty shillings to pay for food and the 'bloody rent', which seemed to be rising every year.

It was in the garden on a chilly afternoon, after Irene had been instructed to look for eggs in the undergrowth, as two of the hens had seemed to have stopped laying but might have been hiding them away, that she had a sighting of Tony O'Reilly. She was talking to her imaginary friends, Louloubell and Jonny, who were always there when she had something to tell them, and had stood near the open door of the shed after she had heard noises of things being pushed about, bottles rattling and a couple of grunts came to her ears as she waited. It wasn't polite to enter a place without permission from a grown-up and from the back of this person, who she had seen using a key to remove the padlock, he was a grown-up.

He nearly dropped the box he was carrying when he saw the sweet little girl, her chestnut hair all done up in ringlets and wearing a patched cotton dress that was far too short, a much-plucked shabby green cardigan and scuffed black boots that looked too big for her.

"For the love of Mary and all the saints!" he spluttered, nearly dropping the box in his agitation. "Where did you spring from, Alanna?"

"My name is Irene, not Alanna, sir. I live in the house at the top of the orchard. Papa didn't say we had someone living in our shed."

"Just moved in yesterday, so I did. Back in Ireland, where I come from, little girls are to be seen and not heard, and Alanna in Irish means little child, so it does."

"Oh."

"Well, run along now and don't yer come back agin, or I'll tell yer pa yer've bin disturbin' me."

"Yes, sir, I'm sorry sir."

With that, poor Irene fled, much chastened by this funny speaking stranger. Though being a child with a secretive nature, it felt nice to have a knowledge she didn't have to share.

CHAPTER TWENTY

By the summer of 1921, Lily found she couldn't carry on with the way things were for much longer. She was waking up with a headache, her first thoughts being to what they were going to eat that day and to what she was going to put on Irene's sandwiches, as the child was now attending the local Church of England school in Liscard, a mile away. She was going to have to take her engagement ring to the pawn shop, otherwise how was she going to find the money for a pair of new shoes for Irene? The walk there and back again was wearing out the soles. Next it would be Grand-mama's ebony display cabinet and the black piano going as well, if the fortunes didn't change for the Wilson family soon.

She found it hard to look at herself in her mirror during those days, dismayed as she saw the weather beaten face, lined with worry, staring back at her, with crows feet nestled under her dull eyes and a mouth that had lost the habit of smiling. There was no money to be spared even for a small tub of face cream, a necessity for a woman who had reached forty-five. The last time she'd had her hair trimmed was courtesy of Eliza's scissors, at one of their sisterly get-togethers.

It seemed that the benefits, which Charlie collected every Friday morning from the office on Victoria Road, before popping into the Coach and Horses for a weekly bevvy, had been withdrawn; something to do with Charlie being quite capable of continuing his business as a market gardener and if heavy digging was a problem, he could always take on an unemployed local lad to help. Of course, Charlie wasn't telling lies when he related all this to Lily, as the benefits department had said all this to Charlie many months before. He had jumped at the chance of O'Reilly's offer, seeing it as a way of making money without slogging his guts out in all kinds of weather, trying to grow vegetables on his weedy land.

Lily had appeared to be coping well in his eyes, tending the grapevine, picking the ripe tomatoes and gathering the tubers for the next glut of flowers. She always had something on the table when she called him from upstairs for his evening meal, so why pay for a labourer? Lily was quite capable of keeping things going for them all. It was a crying shame when O'Reilly – not a man, it seemed, who stayed in one place for very long – decided to move his operations back over the water to Liverpool.

He was a bit dismayed, to say the least, when Lily announced that she was going to look out for another lodger. The landlord had been around wanting to put up the rent, something he seemed to be doing annually. When queried this time by an irritated Lily, who asked what extra facilities would be provided if they were to pay the extra, putting up as she did with a dilapidated house with no mod cons, still with an outside toilet, he'd backed off for the moment, saying that he'd have to have a think. She didn't have to stay there if she wasn't happy with the property and there were a lot of families around about who would love to live where she did. Her tongue, increasingly sharp when she found she couldn't even afford to put a bet on with Kenny nowadays, made Charlie spend more time at the Coach and Horses whilst Irene, a timid child, dawdled home from school.

The old house across the road, tenanted before the war by Mr Wilson then by Frank, who had left the area when his wife, a nurse, was transferred to a bigger hospital during hostilities, had been up for sale by the owner and had been on the market for some time. There had been the occasional interest, a chap called Mr Rea who had a coal round and rented the stable that went with the place, but no one seemed to want to buy the big old building, circa 1621, which must have been the oldest house in Wallasey.

Then one day, after Lily had idly spoken to Bertha about the big house across the road during one of her visits, saying how it was such a shame that the place had lain empty for such a long time, a family arrived. Not a local family, Irene decided, when she heard the children whooping and calling as they charged around the garden that lay behind the perimeter wall. They didn't have the Mersey twang, more a language of their own that she didn't understand, which was Welsh, or so she learnt later from Bertha. It appeared that the new family were distantly related to them via the Patterson's and had travelled all the way from a place called Swansea in Wales. Tom Patterson was taking up a post as a lecturer in the recently completed building at the Liverpool School of Tropical Medicine. Having an avid interest in historical architecture, he had been delighted to hear of the old place on Poulton Bridge Road, after he had written to Lawrence, his cousin, for information on the area, especially with Wallasey being only a short train ride under the River Mersey to Liverpool.

There was an older boy, Richard, who had just turned fourteen; Evan, who looked to be around Irene's age; and a little girl, Myfanwy, who was aged seven. Bronwen Patterson, their mother, was small, dark and a bit nervy, looking as if a puff of wind would knock her over, but extremely pleased to meet Lily, hoping that she might have made a new friend.

"Students," Lily had said to Charlie, in a voice that brooked no argument when she had come back from across the road to introduce herself, looking well satisfied after a long time spent chatting over a cup of tea with Bronwen. "That's who we'll be having to stay. Tom, who's got a plum job at the Liverpool School of Tropical Medicine, said there'll be a lack of accommodation over there for students and as they'll mostly be from middle class families, who are able to afford to send their children to universities and colleges, they'll be able to pay a little more."

It wasn't long before their first student moved in, a young lady by the name of Dorothy Kershaw, a blue stocking if ever there was one. She reminded Lily a bit of her sister, though her personality was not hidden under a bushel like Mabel's, more the opposite; she was a bluff and hearty girl like Henrietta used to be and was dismayed to find that the cottage was devoid of a bathroom or inside toilet. She managed to put up with the woeful facilities for a month. To the family's fascination – especially Charlie's, who expected members of his household to wear feminine apparel – Dorothy would don a pair of breeches on her return each evening from the college, studied for hours burning more oil than Lily would have liked and went to play a game of hockey in Crosby on Saturday mornings.

Dorothy was closely followed by Mostyn, a sensitive young man from an upper class background who liked to spend his evenings with Charlie, discussing the research being done on a black fly at a laboratory in Sierra Leone. It was thought to be the cause of river blindness, or the link with mosquitoes as the cause of malaria. He described the lecture rooms where the students listened in fascination to information gained by pioneers in their field; he spoke at length about the research laboratories, the museum and an insectary that had been built on the new building's roof in Pembroke Place, praising the founder, Sir Alfred Jones, a visionary of the future. He in turn was fascinated with Charlie's sea trial tales and didn't mind sitting in the outside toilet, providing he had an oil lamp of course.

At the weekends, he would sit Charlie on a garden bench and set to with the hoe or a pair of secateurs, regaling Charlie with tales of his father's team of gardeners at his manorial home. The family fell in love with the easygoing student – especially Irene, who hung on his every word. They were deeply upset when at the beginning of 1922, after returning to his home in Berkshire for Christmas, he wrote to say that he had been offered a graduate post at a research lab in London.

It was during the time of Mostyn's stay that Isabel, a bit of a stranger really, preferring to help her aunt make the Sunday dinner for Eliza's married offspring and grandchildren, sent a letter that came one morning to say that she was intending to visit and would be bringing a surprise for them. Mostyn, on hearing that there was to be a visitor and having met Isabel on an earlier occasion, had said that he had been invited out for luncheon that day. This had dashed Lily's hopes of matchmaking, as her lodger, usually a very polite young man, had tended to ignore her elder daughter,

So, there was only the family waiting, whilst carrots nearly boiled dry in the saucepan, and the potatoes and roast lamb frazzled in the oven tin, when Isabel arrived. She was dressed in a fashionable, cream, knee length flapper dress and matching cloche hat with red T-bar shoes, full of apologies as there had been an accident with a dray cart, which had hampered their walk across the Penny Bridge. 'Their' walk left the three of them puzzled, until Isabel drew a lanky, ginger haired young man through the front door and proudly introduced him as Duggie.

"This is Duggie, Papa, Mama. Duggie works down the road from me in the butcher's shop and we've come across together today to tell you that Duggie has asked me to marry him."

To say that her parents were stunned was an understatement, although Irene, tickled pink that she might have the chance of being her sister's bridesmaid and get a new frock out of it, was grinning ear to ear.

"Oh Isabel," she said, rushing to her sister and throwing her arms about the now anxious-looking girl's waist, stopping suddenly to wonder why her parents had scowls upon their faces. Well, her mother did; her father looked a bit dismayed, but he was holding his hand out politely.

"How do you do, young man?"

"I'm all right, Mr Wilson. Isabel's told me a lot about yer, says yer were one of the first to trial them subs." He blushed with embarrassment as he spoke and couldn't bring his eyes to look into Charlie's.

"Well, you'd better come in, you're lucky that there's still some dinner worth having."

Lily, rather rudely, refused to shake the young man's hand. "Take your guest into the parlour Isabel, and Irene, you can help me in here.

If that doesn't take the biscuit," she muttered angrily, as she set

Irene to making the sauce from the bunch of mint leaves she had gathered earlier from her kitchen garden. "A girl with Isabel's education wanting to marry a butcher's boy, turning her nose up at the son of a lordship. To think I could have had Mostyn as my son-in-law! When I think of the things we've gone without, just so she'd have the same advantages as I had and now she's going to throw it all in my face by marrying a butcher's boy. Well, she can wait until she's twenty-one, because there's no way I'll give my permission for her to marry him."

"Does Duggie cut up little animals at the butcher shop? Is that why you're cross?" asked Irene, licking the spoon, as she loved the taste of mint once it had been added to a little vinegar. She knew the answer because she had seen the many carcasses hanging down from hooks in a Liscard butcher's window, but the thought of their visitor doing just that made her think that she should dislike him too.

"Well, they're already dead when they come to the shop," said Lily, looking for a moment with distaste at the piece of meat she was about to carve into. "But that isn't why I'm cross, Irene, it's because I wanted somebody better for Isabel, because of the good education that she's had. Anyway, stop licking that spoon and put those potatoes into the tureen. After you've done, go and set the kitchen table. I'm not going to serve dinner in my best room for that one."

"So after dinner, is that when I invite you into the study and offer you a cigar, then you ask can you have my daughter's hand in marriage?" Charlie asked jokingly from his armchair near the fireplace. You cut could the tension in the parlour with a knife; Duggie was sitting alone on the sofa, while Isabel was pacing, her thin face wearing a worried look.

"Ha, funny, Papa. No one does that anymore."

"Your mother will expect it. I had to ask permission from your grandfather."

"That was years ago. We're living in the 1920's now and women are allowed to vote."

"Some have got the vote if they're over thirty, but don't forget that you're still a minor and if you're mother says you can't get married, then you've had it."

"And you wouldn't go against my mother?"

"When have I ever?" Again Charlie tried to joke, but he knew that if Lily were against the marriage, he would back her.

"Then I don't know why we're even sitting here, if that's going to be the answer. Come on, Duggie, let's go; I'm sure your mother will feed us if we go there now."

"Isabel, your mother might…"

"Come on everyone, dinner's out on the kitchen table." Irene stood at the door.

"We'll eat here then, seeing she's gone to the trouble of cooking it, but after that we're going back home."

Irene made her escape as soon as the meal was over, running across the road to the Patterson's house. Confronted at the door by her new cousin, Evan, she promptly burst into tears. They sat in the branches of an old cherry tree, watching the two black horses in the stable nearby while Irene poured out her tale. They agreed that grownups were the strangest of folk, especially parents, who didn't often smile.

Charlie, unusually for him, helped Lily clear the table and stack the plates and tureens on the scullery draining board ready for washing. On a nearby shelf, an apple pie sat on a plate next to a jug of cream, waiting to be served by Lily. She had bought the cream especially from the dairy when she had received Isabel's letter, Charlie thought sadly, wondering if it had been intentional on her part not to serve it.

"Cup of tea?" Lily said briskly, after adding a dash of soda to the water in the sink and swirling it around vigorously. "I'll just put this lot into soak, then I'll make it."

"I'll put the kettle back on," Charlie said, beginning to feel his chest tightening at the thought of her confrontation, which was bound to happen in a minute or two. "I thought I'd take a look at those strawberries that Mostyn planted in the pots. They should be ready for selling in a week or so."

"Not so fast, Charlie. It's your daughter, too, that we'll be discussing – you can look at the strawberries later."

"I can't see anything for us to talk about, Lily. You've made your mind up that you'll not allow her to wed the poor blighter, so I can't see the point."

"Yes, but I want you to know why I don't want us to give our permission, otherwise it will look as if I'm being stubborn."

"You've made it clear that you don't like the lad, why harp on it?"

"Don't you see? We'd be throwing away all that good money that we paid out for her education, just for her to marry someone of his ilk, when she should be marrying at least a doctor or even a solicitor!"

"Wasn't that the reason why you wouldn't marry me when we were younger, because your parents had paid for a good education and you thought me beneath you? From what you have told me, you weren't *that* happy with Roland De Crosland."

"That was totally different, I was expected to marry well. My father would never have allowed me to marry a shipyard worker and I was given no choice in the matter of whom I married."

"No, but I was good enough for you when you were back at your parents' house and you hadn't got a penny to your name."

"Shame on you, Charlie Wilson, dragging that up after all these years of happiness together." Lily had gone white and she began to dab at her eyes with her pinafore.

"Happiness?" Charlie flung the word back at her angrily, as he stamped out to the garden. "Well, if all these years have been happy ones, I'd have been better off being happy on my own."

Christmas came and went, with none of the usual family parties. Only Bertha turned up with a pretty dress for Irene, bought in New York by Lawrence, who still travelled the world in his fifties. A dour man now, with a full head of white hair, a moustache and a beard, he ruled his crew with a rod of iron, but had a soft spot for this niece who reminded him of a young Lily.

Ellen came too, bringing along a pot doll for Irene, with miniature clothing that she had spent a lot of hours stitching, her postman husband gone now as he had perished in the war. There was no word from Eliza, nor of course from Isabel, and the sisterly meetings that were once attended by all had been disbanded. Their father had left this mortal coil when, after suffering from a fatal bout of pneumonia earlier in the previous year, he had died, virtually a pauper after death duties had been paid.

Irene was ten now and, not fully understanding why this particular Christmas felt so different from the ones she had known before, she spent more of her time with the Patterson's, where at least the children's parents didn't bicker. There was also a big dog now, a Welsh border collie to play with called Nuts.

CHAPTER TWENTY-ONE

It was just after Irene's birthday in February, a non-event really, except that she was allowed to have Evan and Mfanwy around for a birthday tea, when Lily provided jam sandwiches and a sponge cake. Evan and Mfanwy had brought her a book as a birthday present – *The Little Princess* by Frances Hodgson Burnett, a copy of which had been bought in Liverpool by Uncle Tom. From her mother and father, desperate for money now they had lost their lodger and were waiting for another, there was the promise of a treat at Easter.

It was a Monday when Lily, having seen her daughter off to school holding hands with young Mfanwy and with Evan skipping along the road ahead, saw the postman hovering by the gateway.

"Mornin' Mrs Wilson," Dickie said, peering at an envelope that he was carrying. "Looks official, it's not from one of your family I'll be bound."

"Thank you, Dickie." Lily snatched the envelope from the postman's hand. "If it's anything you should know about, I'll be the first to tell you."

"Oh, thank yer very much," he replied, missing her sarcasm. "I've time fer a cup o' tea, if yer've got the kettle on. Me bag's not so heavy today."

"Got to go, Dickie. Charlie's not up yet and I've still to make his breakfast."

"I don't mind waitin', Mrs… "

Lily had already gone. The envelope, partially blurred by the ink of a franking machine, could only be the answer to a dream that she had half forgotten. Six months earlier she had seen a delivery boy, posting a newspaper through the front letterbox. She had frowned when she had picked it up from the red stone tiled floor, deciding to have a word with the shop in the village. Charlie always ambled up there if he wanted a newspaper and there was no money to spare for a daily one. To celebrate the launch of this national publication, the editor was proposing a competition for its new readers: buy a copy for the next six days, cut out the daily coupon, fill them out with name, address and add two reasons why you would buy the paper in the future then send it to the editor at the address shown in London.

It had been a bit of a bind to say the least, having to find a few coppers from their already limited income, to pay for the newspapers at the end of the week. Charlie felt disgruntled, because he liked to read the opinions of the more professional type of reporter, but agreed to Lily's plea of a more downmarket broadsheet just until she had collected all the coupons, if it would keep the peace. When the bank draft in the name of Mrs Lily Wilson fluttered to the floor and she read that she had won £365, one pound to spend on herself for everyday of the year, she nearly fainted. She'd forgotten about that, which was what had caught her attention when she had riffled through the paper to see if it had a fashion or cooking section. Those had been her two reasons, which had obviously caught the editor's eye. How *would* she have spent one pound a day for the next coming year? *Now I will find out*, she thought as she picked up the bank draft with trembling hands, and read that it had to be presented to the Liverpool Union Bank on Bold Street, Liverpool. She went into the kitchen to make a calming cup of tea.

It wasn't until a few minutes later that she emerged from a sort of utopian trance, where she had sorted all her problems out courtesy of this new cash flow. First she would put a deposit on a house – there was a row of semi's being built just off Leasowe Road, where the fresh air from the ocean, rather than the oily pool across the road at the dock lands, would do Charlie's chest good. Then she would pay for Charlie to see an eye specialist. He'd been complaining for some time that his vision was becoming a little murky and he couldn't focus as well as he once had. Irene seemed to be doing well at the local church school; she hadn't complained and could read and write as well as Lily had when *she* was a youngster, so she wouldn't pay out for another private school for her daughter, but buy her pretty frocks and fancy shoes instead.

Charlie of course, coming down the stairs a little later, wearing his old velvet dressing gown and wondering why there was no smell of fried egg cooking in the pan, was just as astonished as she had been. Lily, not really wanting to come clean just yet, because he would probably spoil her plans as he had been apt to do in the past, saw him sit down with a thump onto the kitchen chair after being told, asking her what she planned to do with it.

She was just about to share the plans that she'd been making up until he had interrupted them with his appearance, when suddenly a vision of Isabel came swimming before her eyes. Isabel, who she had not seen or heard from since the day she had come over for Sunday dinner with Duggie, in Lily's eyes a no hoper. Even at Christmas there had been no communication from the alteration shop, as Eliza, or so it had appeared, had taken Isabel's side.

Hadn't she always dreamt that one day her daughters would walk down the church aisle, dressed in frothy lace on her way to a marriage with the love of her life? Something half forgotten, when there was no possibility of such a thing happening. This was her chance to make things right.

"The first thing I'm going to do with the money is to make sure that Isabel has a decent wedding."

Charlie stared at her in amazement, as the first thing he was sure she would have wanted was a move to a better house.

"Isabel?"

"Yes, Isabel. It's time that girl got married. She'll be eighteen in a couple of weeks and I'm not having my sisters say I stood in the way of her happiness."

"Your sisters have been saying that?"

"Well, I don't know if they have or not, but it's all right for them as they don't have daughters."

"Henrietta does."

"Apart from her, anyway she doesn't count, I never see her."

"So how are you going to go about it? You'll have to eat humble pie and that's never agreed with you."

"Ha, ha, ever the joker. You can come with me."

They chose the following Sunday afternoon for their visit, after they had caught the ferry from Egremont on the previous Wednesday and travelled across the Mersey to the nominated bank. Irene had been invited across the road to one of the children's birthday tea. Worried about what reception she would receive when they got to Eliza's house, Lily was relieved that her youngest wasn't with them.

The couple walked across the Penny Bridge to Conway Street, wearing their Sunday best, albeit shabby, then through the park until they reached the row of shops where Eliza had her business. The window shutters, tattered and faded, were down, as one would have expected on the day of rest. Only a few leaves, whipped up by a sudden wind, lay on the pavement ahead of them and there was an eeriness about the row, as not everyone lived in the rooms above, using them mostly for storage.

Lily was now worked up like a spring, having gone over a hundred times in her mind what she was going to say when she first set her eyes on her daughter. She was put on the back foot when, after her continual knocking, the young man – the cause of all the problems with her and Isabel's relationship – came bounding down the stairs with a cautioning finger to his lips.

"Shhh," he said, not in the least surprised when he saw who was standing there, having peered through the window and then opened the shop door. "We've just got 'er off, had a bugger of a night with 'er crying."

'Er' seemed to be directed to a pram, which had been placed in a corner of the alteration shop.

"I beg your pardon, young man," Lily managed to gasp, not expecting to be greeted in that manner, nor even to be setting her eyes on him just then. "We've come to see Isabel. Kindly advise her that her parents are here."

"If she'll see yer."

"Don't take that tone with me, kindly."

"If we could just see Isabel please, Duggie, we'll try not to keep her too long." Charlie stepped in front of Lily; they'd be there forever, argy-bargying, if he hadn't.

"Okay, do yer wanna come up then, save waking Tilly Mint?"

Whoever Tilly Mint was neither Lily or Charlie asked or wanted to ask, as they followed the young man up the bare wooden stairs. She might have been one of Eliza's grandchildren or, perish the thought, their own grandchild. Why was Duggie talking so authoritatively about it? *They had only seen their daughter last November and now it was April...* Lily did a mental quick calculation, could Isabel have been expecting a baby then? Maybe that was why she had been so hoity-toity, seeing her chance of marriage to the baby's father disappear as soon as she had come up against her mother's snobby attitude. Lily supposed, put in that position, she would have felt the same.

The young woman who lay on the sofa in the upstairs living room, covered with a patchwork counterpane, stared at her parents with hostility in her eyes. There was silence for a moment, as each person, including Duggie, stood awkwardly around her, wondering what to say or do.

"Can I get yer a cup or tea, or something?" That was what Duggie's mother would have asked, if she had unexpected company.

"Nothing for me," Lily said sharply, not knowing how to approach this new situation.

"Yes, thank you, no sugar." Charlie's mouth had gone quite dry and he felt as if he was going to have a nosebleed.

"I suppose you saw her then?" Isabel's voice was confrontational.

"Well, we weren't introduced," said Charlie, looking around the sparse room, wondering if he might sit on a chair.

"Sit on the sofa by me," Isabel said softly, moving her legs and patting a place further down from her. "It's been a bit of a shock, Papa. I did want to tell you, but you were both dead set against having Duggie for a son-in-law. Did someone tell you that I gave birth last Saturday?"

"No," he said, looking over at Lily, who it seemed was still in shock. "Who would have? Your mother had something to tell *you,* so we took the chance you were in."

"Oh." Suddenly Isabel looked boldly at Lily. "What was that then?"

Lily looked confused for a moment. Did she want to spend her hard won money on a daughter who had flown in the face of all convention? She was not, it seemed, even bothered that she had not only given birth to an illegitimate child, but was also living with the father of the child in sin! Good gracious, what were her sisters going to say when she paid for a wedding and the child was there as well? And Eliza, where was Eliza? She must have been in on this secret kerfuffle; Isabel couldn't have faced this debacle on her own.

"Where's your Aunt Eliza?"

"Oh, she living with Duggie's mother for now, they seem to get on really well. She thought it only fair that Duggie and I should have some time on our own, to get used to little Sadie."

"She did, did she? Sadie, is it? Well, the reason your papa and I came over…" She paused while Duggie handed over a cup of tea on a saucer to Charlie and then made as if he was going to leave them alone with their daughter.

"No, Duggie, you can listen to what I've got to say. The reason we came over is to offer to pay for you to have a nice wedding, Isabel. Believe it or not, I was young once and I always had a dream that you two girls would have the most splendid weddings that I could afford. As you know, with your father being of ill health and not able to work as well as he used to, money has been tight, but I've come into a little money now. Anyway, as you've put the cart before the horse, perhaps it won't be the kind of wedding that I wanted for you."

"That's very kind of yer, Mrs Wilson, Mr Wilson."

"Are there strings, Mother? Are you expecting me to come back home, stay until my wedding day and pretend I'm going down the church aisle as an innocent virgin?"

"Certainly not, Isabel and don't speak so disrespectfully!" Lily took in a gulp of air after her daughter's coarse language, at the same time listening to Charlie, who had also begun to object.

"You can remain here with your heart's desire and your little offspring, while I make the necessary arrangements down at the town hall. I'll be in touch!"

Suddenly, Lily couldn't get out of the room quick enough; she was so stunned at her daughter's behaviour.

"You were a bit harsh on her," said Charlie, as he linked Lily's arm. After being shown out of the front door by Isabel's boyfriend, he could feel her body trembling through her heavy winter coat. "And that was our granddaughter that you dragged me away from when I was trying to have a peep."

"She's our granddaughter when Isabel's legally wed. First thing on Monday I'll be down to the office in Hamilton Square to get the formalities started. Don't tell our Irene about it just yet, or she'll be pestering forever for a frock."

The marriage of Douglas Deeley and Isabel Wilson took place four weeks later on a rainy Wednesday morning, in a civil ceremony conducted at the town hall. On the same day, the birth of Sadie Louise Deeley was registered by her father and became the official grandchild of Charlie and Lily, whilst ten year old Irene became an aunty to the little dote. No one, except close family, were invited, as discretion was the order of the day.

CHAPTER TWENTY-TWO

"So I gave fifty pounds to Isabel, it cost me two pounds, twelve and sixpence for the ceremony and the meal at the cafe, your new suit, mine and Irene's dresses and those silly shoes she insisted on having. When is she going to wear ballet slippers for heaven's sake? That lot came to nearly sixty pounds out of the money I won, so we've still got a lot to go at. I was thinking of a good deposit on one of those new houses off Leasowe Road." Lily sounded pleased as she related her accounting skill to her husband.

"And where will we get our income from once we've left here, your winnings spent and with no money coming in? No one will give me a job at my age and once the small-holding's gone, we won't be able to earn any money."

"I knew you'd say that. This is probably my last chance of being able to afford a decent house with an inside toilet, electric lights and a plumbed in bathroom. You always have to have the last word, don't you Charlie?" Lily's pleasure was lost and her spirits plummeted as she saw the austere years ahead.

"Well, go ahead then, do as you want, but don't come crying to me when you've spent the money. I suggest you put it in my bank and we'll use it for housekeeping."

This discussion had taken place a few days after Isabel's wedding and the couple had been sitting at the kitchen table, where Lily, having hidden the crisp five pound notes in the secret drawer of Charlie's father's sea chest (not that there was ever anything of value ever hidden in it before), was lovingly handling a few of the notes and discussing their future use.

"Can we at least go and look at one of them?"

"You can, but I can't see the point. What's the use of looking around something you'll never be able to have?"

"I could get a job."

"You've got a job, looking after me and Irene. Now the weather's getting better, I'll be able to work on the garden again. Duggie said he might come and help me."

"Duggie has got enough to do, now they've decided to rent that terrace house on Tollemache Road. She'll be having him up and down Grange Road looking at furniture for it and do you know something, they'll be having an inside bathroom and lavatory?"

"Oh for pity's sake, Lily, don't you think that I would like a brand new house with an inside bathroom and lavatory? I'd like to be indoors in the middle of winter, when the wind is rattling the privy door and it's so cold in there, it freezes your... well, I won't say what it freezes, but if all the money is spent in one go, what are we going to live on?"

"Fresh air," said Lily rudely and got up from the table and walked away. *I should have stayed at home and looked after my parents,* she thought, not for the first time, as she walked up the path to the hen house with angry tears welling in her eyes, shooing away the birds as they pecked around her bare legs, squawking; a lot less irritating than being married to a man who was usually right when you sat down and examined why he had said what he did. Mabel had the right idea, though, beholden to no man and working now for a female politician who had her eye on a constituency in Cheshire, sharing a rather nice house in the city of Chester with a colleague.

Lily felt trapped, not for the first time: duty bound to Charlie and Irene, when here she was, the possessor of a small fortune but unable to spend it her way. She'd treated herself to a posh dress for Isabel's wedding day, but that was all she'd have of note hanging in the battered old wardrobe, amongst the knitted jumpers and handmade skirts she had stitched for herself over the years. Her guipure dress, which had fitted her well until her babies had made their appearance, had long gone, given to a niece who had needed an elegant dress for some event or other. It was never returned and why would Lily have wanted it back anyway?

By mutual assent, the new house off Leasowe Road was never mentioned again. Lily hid her disappointment and accompanied Charlie to an eye specialist at Liverpool Hospital, where the man said that without an operation for the cataracts on both his eyes, Charlie would be walking with a white stick within the year. Of course, his eyes had to be the priority and if Lily resented that a lot of her money was to be spent on her husband's operation, she never said. It seemed that she had accepted her lot in life and had to make the best of it. She was nearly fifty, a grandma now and had spent the best years of her life living on the borderline of poverty, so who was she to change the cards she had been dealt?

It was 1925 and it had been a harrowing year for the couple, as Charlie, a guinea pig, really, in the days when surgeons hadn't a great deal of experience in removing cataracts, found that after the operations his vision was worse than before. There was nothing for it but to accept his lot in life and make the best of it. He could still potter in the garden, though not able to do more than snip a few flowers, feel if the fruit in the orchard or tomatoes on the vine were ready for picking, or stagger to the Coach and Horses in the evening time, where he could find a few cronies to chew the fat with. Now, with an increased rent (the landlord having insisted on it), the specialist's receipt sitting in her handbag, day-to-day living and a growing Irene who needed to be clothed and fed, Lily's money from her stroke of good fortune began to dwindle fast.

It was in the October of that year that Bertha had passed away, to the horror of her three sons. They were now in their twenties, but were reliant on their mother as they still called Temple Road 'home'. Bertha had gone the way of her mother and had piled the weight on, which in its turn had brought on problems with her heart and Lawrence had been away on the Atlantic run when his wife had been found by her daily woman. The funeral had been delayed until his ship docked in Liverpool.

Meanwhile, of all Bertha's sisters it was Lily who offered her three nephews a temporary home, since she lived in a house with four bedrooms. Eliza, with whom she was now on speaking terms, had taken in a lodger so had no room to spare and Ellen, who had remarried and moved out to Bromborough, lived in a two-up two-down.

Suddenly, Irene was surrounded by three strapping fellows, who broke the silence of the melancholy house and gave Lily something to think about besides her woeful self. Of course, their presence caused untold pressure on the amount of money left in Lily's purse, especially Matthew, who could eat his way through a saucepan of porridge or a cottage loaf without a second thought! Irene was intrigued by their presence and rather nervous, if the truth was known.

Matthew, at aged twenty-nine, had been about to sign on to an ocean liner from Liverpool to New York before his mother's death, but had decided to defer the trip. His job as an assistant purser required one hundred percent concentration, which he wasn't able give as he mourned his mother dearly. Mark, a trainee solicitor at twenty-seven, was engaged to be married, but preferred to stay with his brothers for propriety sake. That left Luke, who at twenty-five was one of a team of river pilots on the River Mersey, but had been given compassionate leave.

Lily, still attending to her stall outside the cottage, found she had to rely more and more on her thirteen year old daughter, with Charlie rising late as daylight meant nothing to him anymore. Gone were Irene's dreams of working hard at school, passing her matriculation, maybe going to a training college and becoming a teacher, as Lily, unable to cope with all the new demands on her time and money, whilst grieving for her sister at the same time, insisted that the child left school, even though Irene wouldn't be fourteen until the following February.

Evan, already fourteen and with another four years of education before going off to university felt alarmed that such a clever girl, usually near the top of the class for most subjects, was duty bound to give up school at such a tender age. He had walked with home with Irene from school each afternoon and the two cousins had become good friends, being usually seen chasing through the common land by St. Hilary's church, sitting on a bollard on the quayside or hiding in one of the orchard's trees. Sometimes they played on the carts or one of the lorries that Mr Rea used for his distribution, though not often as they grew older, as they usually got covered in coal dust.

One afternoon, Irene was up to her ears in baking pies and scones for the funeral spread, which were to be carried across by the family the next morning to Temple Road; all the sisters were taking a contribution. Evan, fresh home from school, called to ask if Irene would like to see a show at the Argyle Theatre.

"I've heard that Tommy Tiptree, the comedian, is on and Father said he would treat me to a couple of tickets for passing this year's exam." Evan was full of excitement, this being his chance to cheer poor Irene up.

"How are you, Irene? Frannie Baker and Emily Roper said to give you their regards when I saw you next."

"Oh, I didn't know they cared." Irene was feeling down in the dumps, as she knew that certain members of her school year couldn't wait to leave school and only wanted shop jobs until they married, which was a crying shame to her.

"Of course they did, it was because you were so shy that you didn't get to know them."

"I didn't have chance to get to know them, living all this way from Liscard. Anyway, who wants to be friends with someone who has an unemployed gardener for a father?"

"Oh Irene, I do," Evan said, when he saw the tears of frustration forming in his cousin's eyes. "That's why I've come to ask if you would like to come to the Argylle with me."

"I'll have to ask my mother. I'm not sure she'll let me. As you know Aunt Bertha is being buried tomorrow and it's been pandemonium here, helping Mother look after my other cousins until Uncle Lawrence got home. Anyway, I'll have to go now; I'll get it in the neck if I've not finished the baking."

"I'll leave you to it then, come over and see me anytime."

The front room in the Temple Road house was full to bursting with the mourners who had come to support Lawrence and his family. Lily and Bronwen, who was to be representative of the Welsh side of the family, Irene, and Isabel, who by now had another child to care for, dashed around the kitchen, filling cups with tea, making extra sandwiches and slicing up the many cakes that had been baked by some of the kindly wives who had come along. Irene's pies and rolls had gone in a flash and the family marveled at the many people who had arrived to pay their respects for Bertha, both there and at Flaybrick Cemetery.

Ellen, on duty in the living room, walked around with drinks on a silver salver, whilst a grieving Lawrence and his three sons stood chatting in small clusters to family and friends. Eliza, on babysitting duty caring for Sadie and the new baby – a little boy, this time – sat in a corner by a cheerful fire. Henrietta, up to her neck in children in a rectory south of Harrogate, and Frederick, having risen to dizzy heights in the Atlee government, had sent their commiseration by telegram.

Lawrence tapped his glass with a spoon, asked for silence and began to make a speech, welcoming them all on such a sad occasion and thanking them all for their much-needed support. He announced that he had recently been considering retirement and now that his wife had gone to her reward in heaven, he would be relinquishing his captaincy. It was time to get his land legs back and become a landlubber for a change. He raised his glass and asked them all to drink a toast to Bertha.

Lily, who was listening with Bronwen at the kitchen door, said a silent prayer, wiping away the ready tears of grief for the death of her sister whom she had grown close to over the years. Then her thoughts went to Charlie, housebound now, unless he was pottering around in the garden, which he knew like the back of his hand. He had mourned the departure of her nephews, after Lawrence had announced that he was going to employ a live in cook and bottle washer to see to the males of the family, who would still be residing in the Temple Road home. Charlie was going to miss their lively presence, their discussions on the current state of politics and their willingness to read his daily newspaper to him, which lately had been reporting on the growth and strength of the T.U.C.

A little later, most of the mourners had disappeared and Bronwen and Irene were putting the leftovers into the scullery. Lily was putting the finishing touches to an already tidy kitchen when Lawrence, looking as drunk as a mop and his breath smelling strongly of brandy, stood in the kitchen doorway staring intently at Lily as she took off her apron and tidied her hair.

"I don't suppose you'd take on the job of looking after me and the young fellas, would yer, Lily? Seeing as you were wanting to be my helpmate all those years ago? I'm not asking you to take the place of Bertha, but I seem to remember you thought of me as your heart's desire back then."

Lily stood there, letting the years stretch back until she reached the day of her humiliation, when a young Lawrence, strikingly handsome in his captain's uniform, held out his hand and she was thrilled at the prospect of marrying him. Then Charlie, dapper little Charlie, who had always worshipped the ground that she walked on, despite the hardships, the deprivations and the austere life they had endured together, came springing to her mind.

"That was then and this is now," she said briskly, trying to imagine the once handsome man, whom she had long ago thought she was in love with, comparing him, now bloated and fat, with her own still slim husband. "And if I had to live my life all over, it would be Charlie who I would choose as my heart's desire."

What else could I say, she thought later, as she sat on the side of Charlie's bed. No point in mourning all those years, when they were gone forever. He had made his choice to marry her sister and she'd only been trying to get back at him.

"I'd bury you under the pear tree," Lily said lightly, after telling her husband who had been at the funeral and their reactions to it, not liking to tell him that she had been paying the Co-operative an amount each week for his own death policy. "Anyway, Charlie, you'll live to be a hundred. This happens every winter, you taking a chill and being confined to bed."

"I don't want to live until I'm one hundred," he answered miserably. "What's the point of living now that I can't even see to read a newspaper? I may as well be dead."

"Shush now, Charlie, don't speak like that. How would Irene and little Sadie feel if they heard you talking like that?"

"But not you eh, Lily? You'd be off like a rocket with your winnings, buying a new house for yourself and probably finding another man to replace me. I know you've got some of that money stashed away; I've still got feeling in my fingers and if you want to hide your money you need a better place than the old sea chest. I wouldn't blame you neither, who'd want to live in this hovel of a house?"

"We do, Charlie, it's our home and the land around it has given us a living all these years. I'll tell you what, you get better and we'll go to Morecambe for a week next summer. We'll take Irene and ask if Sadie can come with us, too. You'd like that, you can paddle again in the sea and get a bit of the sun on your face."

"Perhaps, we'll see what happens. I'm tired now, Lily, I want to go to sleep."

At the beginning of 1928, to add to Lily's worries that hadn't receded over the years, Isabel arrived on the doorstep accompanied by Sadie, baby Stephen and a suitcase containing the family's clothes. According to her daughter, Duggie, finding that married life and two small children were clipping his wings somewhat and he couldn't even spare a few coppers to have a pint each night at The Claughton, had found himself a fancy piece and gone back to live with his Mum. Isabel had nowhere else to go, not being able to afford to pay the rent or stay with Aunt Eliza, who had moved back into the upstairs flat herself and there was no room for the children.

Of course, Lily was not one to shirk her duty took the family in, on the proviso that Isabel did her share of the housework and didn't expect her to babysit. Irene was delighted and took to her role as live-in aunty, playing little games with the children and taking them for evening strolls. Charlie loved to sit and listen to their high-spirited chattering.

Irene by now was working as a junior at Saltbury's department store in Grange Road. She disliked it intensely, seeing as she was the 'go for' and was paid a paltry sum for her efforts. All her dreams of going to teaching college or being able to speak a foreign language fluently had disappeared, after Charlie had no longer been able to pay for a private school. She felt bitter when she remembered her formative years at the convent, where she was taught to speak a little French by the kindly nuns.

Now she was marking time until she met and married a decent man, not one like Duggie, according to Lily, and certainly not her distant cousin Evan, who after asking Irene to go to the Argylle Theatre had, when Lily refused to give her permission, taken a girl from Victoria Road instead. She had ignored him then if she saw him walking to his gateway and felt relieved when her mother told her that the family were moving to a house in Crosby.

Irene had grown into a pleasant young lady with a gentle nature, who cared very much for her father but only felt a certain duty-bound respect for her mother. She found Lily hard to get along with, given that her mother could be snappy, intolerant and expected everyone to jump to her tune. There were quite a few ding dongs between Lily and Isabel, as obviously two women never really get on whilst sharing a kitchen, so Irene could often be found reading in the orchard or taking the children on long walks along the esplanade at Leasowe. Of boyfriends there were none, although plenty of young men from the warehouse at Saltbury's had often asked her out on a date.

One day, Irene came in from work feeling tired and a bit frazzled, as the floor walker at the department store had laboured the point of a bit of dust that had settled on top of her display counter, which was unbeknown to her. She was asked by her father if she could spare a few minutes to talk to him. Feeling intrigued, she sat at his side on the sofa, while sounds of the children whooping around the garden and Lily shouting after them, came to her ears.

It appeared that one of her great aunts on the Patterson side, who lived in a small village called Irby, had recently lost her husband and, feeling lonely, had written to Lily and asked if Irene would like to stay for a while? It seemed that Great Aunt Miriam was living in a brand new bungalow on the outskirts of the village and with it being a new development, there were no streetlights as yet and it faced a vast tract of farmland that stretched down to the sea. Now that she was a widow, Miriam was feeling a little vulnerable.

What Charlie didn't say was that Isabel, on the pretext of having a weekly visit to a friend, had met up with a man called Robert and was hoping to get a divorce. Lily thought it best that Irene, being a young and innocent girl, wasn't there to get caught up in the unpleasantness. It suited Irene. Although she had only seen her great aunt once or twice at family gatherings, she had seemed a pleasant old soul.

CHAPTER TWENTY-THREE

With Irene settled at her great aunt's and catching the bus to work each day from Irby to Birkenhead, Lily and Charlie turned their attention to the problem in hand. Suffice to say, Robert was a better catch than Duggie, according to Lily's way of thinking. Although working in a bar as a tenant manager for a local brewery, he *had* served his time as an officer in the last world war. He was older than Isabel, more mature and had taken to being Sadie and Stephen's 'uncle' very well.

Lily had been furious when Isabel let it slip that she had met Robert in a less than salubrious public house over the bridge in Conway Street, but with Charlie's warning ringing in her ears that she would lose her daughter and grandchildren if she started her usual creating, Robert was invited around for Sunday tea and given the once over. The fact that his father had lost his fortune in a dodgy financial transaction abroad and that Robert had a medal for valour in the line of duty with a limp to prove it caused Lily to agree that perhaps Isabel had made the right choice in her beau this time. She agreed to take her share in the care of the children whilst Isabel did a spot of courting and waited for her divorce from Duggie to come through. It was a drain on Lily's purse again, not helped by Duggie, who was mean with the money that he sometimes bestowed on his wife. Isabel, a dab hand at alterations, trained as she had been by her Aunt Eliza, put a sign in the cottage window to help out with the finances.

One Saturday afternoon, about two years after Irene had moved in with Great Aunt Miriam, Lily called into the department store where Irene worked to tell her that Isabel and Robert, now newly married courtesy of Duggie furnishing details of his adultery, had found a place to rent in Southport and to ask if she would like to come home again. Of course, Lily didn't say that Irene's wage would come in handy once the happy couple had gone.

Irene had her own news to impart to her mother. It appeared that she had been seeing a well-to-do young man who was the elder son of the owner of a large building company and he had recently asked her to marry him. Lily insisted that Irene brought her fiancé to meet the family just as soon as she could.

Isabel answered the door to the couple next day, looking as if she was expecting her new baby at any moment. Her divorce from Duggie had come through opportunely, enabling her to marry Robert in the registry office a few weeks before. There were no new pretty dresses this time and no money for a wedding breakfast in a local café. Isabel had worn a big coat to cover her bump on the day.

"Irene!" Isabel was all smiles as she looked beyond her sister and saw a handsome, dark haired man, slender and of medium height, dressed in a grey two-piece, double breasted suit and wearing black shiny shoes, standing behind her.

"Is this your fiancé? We wondered when we were going to meet him, after Mother spoke to you yesterday. You are naughty keeping us in the dark about him."

"Eddie, this is my sister Isabel. I only told Mother yesterday that I was engaged and she said I was to bring you over. I bet she didn't think I'd bring you over so soon."

"Who is it, Isabel?" asked a feeble voice from within, while the sound of noisy children greeted their ears from one of the bedrooms above.

"It's Irene, Dad. She's brought her fiancé over to meet us. I'll just go and put the kettle on the hob and make us all a cup of tea."

"Hello Papa," said Irene, walking into the rather sparsely furnished room, where her father, dressed in faded brown, corduroy trousers; an old, white, collarless shirt and a thin, plucked, fawn cardigan, lay on a sagging, blue, moquette covered sofa. "I've brought Eddie, my intended, to meet you. This is Eddie; Eddie, meet my father, Charles Wilson."

Eddie nodded politely and put out his arm to grasp the man's bony hand in his, whilst feeling sorry for the poor old bugger.

"Is Mother about, or is she in the garden? That's where I would expect her to be."

"She's out there with Isabel's husband, bringing in the new potatoes. This is the first time they've had the opportunity, what with it lashing with rain yesterday."

"Poor Papa. Is there nothing more that they can do for your eyesight? Can it not get better? What did the doctor say?"

"Stop your worrying Irene, what will be will be. Eddie, come over and sit by me, I've still a little sight left to take a good look at my future son-in-law."

"Pleased to meet you, sir," said Eddie, sitting down beside the man and staring into the pale, worn face. "I believe you used to be a sparky, working on the submarines?"

"Yes, that was so, Eddie, I think that's how I began to lose my eyesight. Being underground for long periods makes your body think you're a mole."

Eddie and Irene laughed politely at his little joke, but they both felt compassion for the man.

"So Eddie, are you an old fashioned man? Have you come to ask for permission to marry my daughter?"

"Of course sir, that's why I'm here today: to ask for Irene's hand in marriage."

"I'm sure whoever our Irene has fallen in love with will make her happy. She's a practical girl with a good head on her shoulders; she won't have chosen the first man who came along. Come here both of you and let me give you my blessing." He took both their hands in his and gave them a wry smile.

The couple looked upon him sadly. Though Eddie had never seen the man before, he could see that he was wasting away. He'd heard from Irene that her father had never been robust since spending a long time underwater, marooned in a submarine when the propeller had got stuck in a sand bank out in Liverpool Bay. It was a wonder the man was still living, because as Eddie watched Charlie took in big gulps of air and turned his head fretfully towards the open window. Though the day was fairly mild, the room was chilly, not helped at all by the miserable fire in the grate.

"Can I get you a blanket, Papa?" asked Irene, perturbed by the racking coughing spell that had followed and the thinning of her father's features since she had seen him the last a few weeks before. He hadn't been able to make Isabel's wedding and so a buffet for friends and family had been laid on later at home.

"If you would, Irene. I don't seem to be able to get warm nowadays."

"Sit down, Irene, I'll get him one," said Isabel, who had just brought in a tray. "You and Eddie drink the tea that I've made you, there's a blanket in the lobby I can fetch him."

A noise from the back kitchen made Eddie and Irene prick up their ears.

"It's your mother coming in with Robert," gasped Charlie. "Don't tell her that I've had a coughing fit or she'll have me taken to hospital. I had to sleep down here last night, because I was keeping her awake with my breathing."

"We won't say anything Papa," Irene promised sadly. "But maybe you should be in hospital after all."

Lily came stomping through the kitchen into the parlour, wearing an old pair of men's socks and a grubby, blue mackintosh over her navy ankle length dress. She wore a floppy, knitted hat over her tangled, grey hair and looked askance when she saw that she had visitors.

"Irene," she said in annoyance. "Why didn't you tell me you were coming today? I only saw you yesterday, you could have told me then."

"We only just made our minds up to come over today, Mother. This is Eddie, Eddie Dockerty, my intended."

"Caught me on the hop, haven't you? It would have been far

better if you had given me warning and then I could have got something in."

"We've got a seed cake that I baked yesterday, Mother, and a batch of scones I made this morning."

"Yes, Isabel, I know that," Lily snapped. "But I am sure Irene's fiancé is used to something a little grander, with him coming from a better class of family. I know of the Dockerty's; I once attended a fundraising event of theirs, in another life."

"Mother!" said Irene, feeling uncomfortable with her mother's attitude towards Eddie, though understanding why, as Lily herself had been born into a well to do family.

"I'm sure I didn't come here to be fed on the fat of the land, Mrs Wilson," said Eddie, smiling congenially and ignoring her brusque tone. "I came to meet my future family and I love to eat seed cake, it's one of my favourites."

"Hmm," said Lily, though she was beginning to feel mollified, seeing as he was a handsome chap without any airs and graces. His presence was taking her back to her own youth when she had set her heart on Cousin Lawrence. "I'll go and get Robert, he's in the garden. I want to get the potatoes in while there's still a bit of sun around."

"I'm here, Lily," shouted Robert from the kitchen. "I'm just taking my boots off, then I'll bring us in a couple of teas."

"No time for that, Robert. Get in here and meet Irene's fiancé, then we'll get back to it."

Robert came into the room. A big, strong man, whilst Isabel was little and normally dainty. He had to duck under the lintel before he greeted Eddie with a ready smile. "Slave driver, your mother," he said to Irene. "Has me working from dawn to sunset, all day and every day."

"Rubbish," Lily snorted. "I was up at six this morning, manning the stall while you were turning over in your nice comfy bed."

"Can I see your ring, Irene?" Isabel asked excitedly, looking forward to seeing at least a diamond on Irene's ring finger. She knew that she'd be bound to feel jealous, not having an engagement ring of her own. Her sister was wearing white frilly gloves with her floral organza summer dress and so she couldn't see it.

"Ah, no ring I'm afraid," said Eddie, blushing slightly. "A bit of a hitch, I'm sure Irene will tell you about it."

"Mother, before you go back to the garden, could I ask you and Papa something?"

"Yes?" Lily asked, one eyebrow raised in question. "What is it? You're not in the family way, are you?"

"Lily," tutted Charlie reproachfully, "there's no need to take that tone, she's always been a good daughter."

"I'm only asking because she wouldn't be the first daughter who hadn't told me she was expecting." She looked meaningfully at Isabel, who was expecting her third child, conceived out of wedlock again.

"I wanted to ask if Eddie could move in here with you? He's had a falling out with his father and wants to find some work locally. It will only be temporary, until his father apologises for breaking a promise to him. I thought he could have my old room, especially with Isabel and her family moving."

"Mmm, what kind of work would he be doing locally? There's only the docks and he doesn't look the type to be a stevedore." Lily pretended to consider the situation, but another wage coming in and another pair of hands in the garden would be just the ticket.

"I'm a skilled tradesman, Mrs Wilson. It won't be too difficult to find a job." If the old mother said no, Eddie supposed he could always go to Caitlin, his married sister. That would put the cat amongst the pigeons, as she lived in the bungalow down the lane from the family home.

"So can Eddie stay then?"

"As long as you continue to stay at Aunt Miriam's. I don't want people pointing fingers at us and saying we're running a bawdy house. Now then Robert, I think we've just time for you to work on another couple of trenches and Isabel, tell those children of yours to stop their racket upstairs."

"Oh, thank you Mother!" Irene sounded relieved. She didn't

hug her stony-faced parent, as Lily had never welcomed physical contact from her daughters and probably never would.

Eddie seemed a pleasant enough young man, Lily mused a few days later, after her new lodger had helped her by chopping down one of the plum trees that had caught the blight. The wood would come in handy to help keep the fires going in the winter and she planned to ask him if he could repair one of the panes in the greenhouse, now that the crop of tomatoes had finished and she had picked the grapes on the vines.

For the first few nights Eddie had made himself comfortable on the sofa, but today had been the day of Isabel's removal and, after helping the family into a taxi cab with their scant possessions, he had moved himself into one of the spare bedrooms. Not Irene's; Lily was hoping for her daughter's early return, when Eddie became the prodigal son and went back to live at his parents' home.

"So, what did the foreman say?" Lily asked, as she prepared a tray in readiness for Charlie's supper, seeing as he couldn't even make it to the lavvy that day and had to use the chamber pot under his bed.

"I have to get a bloomin' union card from somewhere before he'll take me on. Dad never agreed with his men being in a union, so we never had one. I wouldn't mind, but I would only be laying drains before the footings go in – the chap was saying it'll be another warehouse. I'm thinking I might go over to Neston tomorrow, as my uncle, who inherited the Sheldon Property Company instead of my granddad, might be in a position to help me out."

"Oh, the Sheldon Property Company? That sounds grand." Lily was agog at what she was hearing. So the young man *was* from a well-heeled family.

"I don't know much about it, except that a great aunt founded it way back in the 1860's. She started out as an immigrant fleeing the Irish famine and ended up a millionaire!"

"Well I never, so it could be that you and Irene will be inviting most of the great and good of the county to a lavish wedding! As soon as you name the day, Eddie, I'll go to Saltbury's and buy myself a hat and a smart frock."

That'll be never, thought Eddie, not daring to tell Lily that his father would never give his permission to wed a Protestant, as Irene was, when the Dockerty's were from a long line of Catholics dating back to 1803. He would have to wait until he was twenty-one before being able to marry Irene in the registry office.

"I'll have to get Irene to start looking out for a wedding dress pattern, then Isabel can make a gown that befits the occasion. She is very good with a sewing needle and it will be something for Mr Wilson to look forward to, especially if it is held on a warm day. Not that he will be capable of walking Irene down the aisle, so we would have to ask her Uncle Lawrence to carry out that honour." How strange would that feel, to see Lawrence giving her daughter away?

Eddie was out at work on the day that Charlie went to meet his maker. A coughing fit that morning, just as the sun had come out of the clouds and promised to take the chill from the autumnal air, caused Lily to run down the hilly street to get help from the man at the tollhouse. Charlie was blue by the time the man had run to the nearby telephone box, as Lily was shaking so much that she would never have been able to dial the numbers. He was dead by the time the ambulance had come at a frenetic pace from Victoria Hospital, a few miles away.

Lily was inconsolable and babbled inconsequentially to Irene, who had been called from work to the hospital, that she had never loved Charlie, hadn't really wanted to marry him as she was still in love with someone else and now he had gone and she had never got around to telling him that he had always been so dear to her. Irene put it down to the grief that her mother was feeling, after watching her terrified husband trying to get air into his lungs. She brought Lily back in a taxi, which neither of them could afford.

Eddie was waiting for them on their return, neatly scrubbed

from his recent ablutions in the water butt outside. He had known something was wrong because he had seen Lily's note on the kitchen table when he had got in from work. Not that he could read it, because his father had preferred to have his daughters educated whereas he raised his boys as working men, but he recognised the word 'Irene' at the beginning and 'Mother' at the end. He made the two sobbing women a comforting cup of tea then set about frying eggs and bacon for their supper. Irene and Lily said they couldn't eat, but Eddie insisted that they ate something as they would need their strength.

Later, worn out with the day's events and feeling every inch her age as she lay next to the empty space where Charlie had slept for all those years, Lily couldn't help but worry for her future years. She would have to move from Pear Tree Cottage; there was no way she could stay. She was down to her last ten shillings and a widow's pension, if they gave her one, would only pay the rent. Of course, there was Irene; she might be persuaded to move back in and her wage would keep the wolf from the door.

A sudden movement caught her eye as she dozed intermittently, fretting upon who she should tell about Charlie passing over and whether his policy was paid up to date. It was dawn outside and the weak sun of the morning told her that night had turned into day.

"Charlie, is that you?" she cried, groggy and still in a state of disbelief that the man who had been her husband had gone, after all those years.

The apparition sat on the end of her bed was a great deal younger and handsomer than Lily remembered and wore clothes from a bygone era, which made him look dapper and well-groomed. They weren't the ragged garments that Charlie had recently worn.

"I'm here Lily. Not gone just yet, it's not my time and I can choose to be an Earth bound spirit for the moment. I thought that this bloomin' chest of mine would do for me in the end."

There was a sense of peace as she gazed upon him, but then a great feeling of sadness when she looked away for a moment and he was gone. Undeterred, she walked down the stairs in her dressing gown to set about her usual tasks of riddling the embers in the kitchen range and putting the kettle on.

Had she dreamt it, had her grieving heart conjured up an image of Charlie so that she could convince herself he was happy and had gone to a better place? Happier than she had made him, with her nagging tongue and her waspish ways; she had never once told him in all those years that he was the man she loved. Had she been living a lie, pretending to the world that all had been well, when deep inside she longed for her youth and her heart's desire back in her life again?